BLIND INSTINCT

MICHAEL W. SHERER

Blind Rage
"Tremendous book. Flat out loved it." —Ken Bruen, Shamus, Macavity and Barry Award-winning author of *Green Hell*

Blind Instinct
"Amazing thriller very well written!!! Highly recommend!" —Cathy Fleming, Amazon review

"Gripping and intense—bring on #3!" —Brenda Telford, Goodreads review

Mistaken Identity
"Sherer keeps the live wires of his complex plot sparking and distinct. Jenny is a ticked-off but highly capable heroine, whose family of cops adds depth and texture so that motivation and revelation keep coming to the very end. This is a sharp and satisfying thriller." —*Publishers Weekly starred review*

"*Mistaken Identity* revs up as characters are introduced and then goes all out in a high stakes Indy race of a novel. You come to know the characters. You know who you're rooting for, but the plot turns fast. It's fingers crossed until the last turn and the redemptive end."
—Kirk Russell, author of *No Hesitation* and *Gone Dark*

"Sherer is a master at creating unforgettable characters. Take Jenny Roberts. She's smart, complex, a little bit broken and totally kick-ass. *Mistaken Identity* starts your adrenaline flowing and ramps to a frenzy. A thriller that's impossible to put down."
—Chris Goff, author of *Red Sky*

Stolen Identity
"...high-octane, compulsively readable thriller from Thriller Award finalist Sherer...is a first-rate hijacking of any thriller reader's attention." – *Publisher's Weekly*

"This book is terrific. Well plotted, all the elements of a classic thriller with a fresh take on the characters, especially the hero. It paid off every promise and more." —S.G. Redling, bestselling

5

author of *Flowertown* and *Trigger*

"Love it!" —Timothy Hallinan, author of *Street Music*

Night Drop
"Looking for an adrenaline rush? You'll find that and more in *Night Drop*. Blake Sanders is back, and that means the action is nonstop!"
—Alan Russell, author of *Multiple Wounds* and *Burning Man*

"I LOVED this story. *Night Drop* is a fast-paced, tension-filled thriller that will grab you by the throat until the very last page. Blake Sanders is one of the most intriguing characters I've read in years. This is definitely Sherer at his best."
—KT Bryan, author of *Team EDGE*

Night Tide
"A great, great read! Even better than *Night Blind*, and that's not easy." —Timothy Hallinan, author of *The Fame Thief*

"A cracking good story and a first-rate thriller."
—J. Carson Black, *New York Times* and *USA Today* bestselling author of *The Survivors Club*

"A tight, well-constructed story and characters that leap from the page. I'll definitely be back for more."
—Robert Gregory Browne, author of *Trial Junkies 2: Negligence*

Night Blind
"An appealing, empathetic lead."
—*Publisher's Weekly*

"This is an exciting, well-crafted thriller and most certainly a satisfying one."
—*Mysterious Reviews*

"Thriller writer Sherer renders a sympathetic lead character and an engaging . . . story line in his latest."
—Allison Block, *Booklist*

"Loved every page of it."
—Brett Battles

"A tightly paced page-turner that's impossible to put down. Terrific!"
—Allison Brennan

"Pay attention. You won't want to miss a word."
—J.T. Ellison

"Rich, complex, and deeply satisfying."
—Bill Cameron

Also by Michael W. Sherer

Tess Barrett Thrillers

Blind Instinct
Blind Rage

Identity Series

Mistaken Identity
Stolen Identity

Blake Sanders Series

Night Strike
Night Drop
Night Tide
Night Blind

Emerson Ward Mysteries

Death on a Budget
Death Is No Bargain
A Forever Death
Death Came Dressed in White
Little Use for Death
An Option on Death

Suspense

Island Life

BLIND INSTINCT

BLIND INSTINCT

by

Michael W. Sherer

*To the too few gentlemen
in the world who understand
how to treat a lady.
Girls rock.*

BLIND INSTINCT

BLIND INSTINCT

Prologue

Washington, D.C., a few weeks earlier.

Austin Dunn sat across the table from his father and drew patterns on the linen tablecloth with his finger. He stifled a yawn. Quickly looking away so his father wouldn't see how mind-numbingly bored he was, he pretended to take in the trappings of the formal dining room and the people at the other tables. As usual, his father had picked one of the stuffy, high-end restaurants in town not far from his office. He'd sent a car to pick up Austin from the private school Austin attended near home. Well, the house where they lived, if you could call it that. More like a museum. Huge, ostentatious, filled with someone else's old crap, er, antiques. Nothing like the modern suburban home they'd left behind four years earlier. He still hadn't forgiven his parents—his father—for that brilliant move.

Only snippets of the conversation at the table registered as Austin's gaze bounced from the couple at a booth in the back leaning over the table murmuring in low tones to the maitre d' at the front desk greeting a fearsome foursome from the Hill, dressed in expensive suits, silk shirts with French cuffs and Italian leather shoes. Austin knew the drill, knew that the men, now following a hostess into the atrium dining area, paid for clothes like that either with taxpayers' money or the money they got under the table from lobbyists and the companies those lobbyists represented. Nothing got done in Washington without a little grease, and grease in this town was green, not that nasty black stuff smeared all over a mechanic's coveralls at a service garage.

Two athletically built men, also dressed in suits, took the table closest to the front. Their suits, however, were more utilitarian lightweight wool, and these two held themselves with military bearing. Whereas the powerbrokers disappearing into the atrium had polished nails and carefully styled hair, the pair at the table had short haircuts and no hint of having been anywhere near a salon of any kind. One faced Austin, but his eyes scanned the room and the hallway back to the kitchen. The other had his back turned, head swiveling from the front door toward the atrium, and Austin saw the coiled wire leading from his ear under the back of his collar. Secret Service agents. Austin knew the detail included at least two more agents, one in the driver's seat of an SUV parked across the street from the restaurant, and another somewhere on the street, probably in the alley behind the restaurant.

Austin caught the eye of the operative facing him, waved and gave him a goofy grin. The man's steely expression didn't change. Austin's smile turned to a frown and he shook his head. Jerks couldn't take a joke. He shifted in his seat and turned his attention back to his own table.

"...can't tell you how much I appreciate your support, Josiah," his father's guest was saying. "Senator Latham's been pretty tough about meeting deadlines."

"He has to be," said Austin's father. "Chairman of the subcommittee on defense spending can't be seen showing favoritism."

"Of course not," the guest said hastily. "Just as I wouldn't expect you to when you win the election in November."

"Thanks for the vote of confidence, Travis," Dunn said, "but I'll be able to give you even less support if I'm elected than I can now. You know that."

The guest nodded. "What I meant was that everyone knows defense projects get delayed all the time. No one blinks an eye. Senator Latham's really holding our feet to the fire on this one."

"Then I guess you better not disappoint him," Dunn said. He glanced at Austin and went on. "Look, I appreciate your support, too, Travis. Your campaign contributions have been more than generous. But there's really nothing I can do or say that would change Jeremy Latham's mind about anything, let alone your project. And even mentioning it could compromise my impartiality and reflect negatively on my character."

"I'd never ask you to do that, sir," Travis said. "I just wanted you to know where we stand."

"Noted." Mr. Dunn looked at Austin again. "Have you decided what you'd like to eat?"

Austin glanced at the menu in front of him and nodded. As fancy as it was, at least the restaurant had a hamburger—for eighteen freaking dollars—and fries made from weird kinds of potatoes, even a blue one. Austin ordered the burger and a side of mac-and-cheese, in which they put a few drops of truffle oil so they could charge twelve bucks.

"So," Austin's father said when they'd ordered, "would you like to tell Mr. Barrett what you've been up to at school?"

Austin shrugged and flipped his fork over on the table. "Not much."

The guest gave him a smile that looked genuine. "Can't be that much fun getting dragged to one of your dad's business lunches."

Austin shrugged again. The guy couldn't be a total geek. After all, he wasn't that old, and his dad had said he'd taken over the top job at MondoHard when his brother had been killed in an accident. MondoHard, which made some of the coolest video games in the world.

"Tell you what," Barrett said. "Do you have a smart phone?"

No, duh. "Um, sure." Austin whipped his phone out of his pocket.

Barrett took out a pen and a notepad from his inner suit coat pocket and jotted something down. He tore off the slip of paper and handed it to Austin.

"Check out this website. There's a game app on the site you can download with the promo code I wrote down. It's still in beta testing, but I think you'll like it. One of our young developers wrote it. I've had my eye on him for a while."

Austin reached out as if the slip of paper might bite and slowly took it. "Cool. Thanks."

"Sure. No problem."

"I'm sorry that Austin's being a bother," his father said.

What a shame. He'd disappointed his father again. The words quickly faded from hearing as Austin typed the URL Barrett had written down into the browser on his smart phone. In less than two minutes he'd downloaded the game app and pulled it up on his phone. The title scrolled up along with some sick graphics. *Never Bitten.* He toggled some virtual buttons to get a feel for the game. On screen, two hands came into view, one holding a mallet the other a wooden stake. He toggled the button again and the hands disappeared. He moved right and saw a nighttime street scene. He toggled the other way and saw the street in the other direction. He toggled up to see a full moon. With a swipe of his finger his screen character started walking down the street. All of a sudden a werewolf jumped out of a doorway ahead of him.

Never Bitten, huh? This game app had possibilities.

1

Total darkness forced Tess to rely on her other senses. She practically had to feel her way around, but fortunately she was in familiar territory. She scrabbled toward a better position on silent feet, straining to hear the slightest sounds, to feel and smell changes in the air around her.

She turned and stood her ground, panting from exertion. He'd stalked her for the past fifteen minutes, circling, assessing her weaknesses, slowly running her to ground. She knew what he was capable of, the violence he could wreak with a few small moves. He could easily kill her if she let him. She would not, despite the heart that banged her ribs like a prisoner rattling the bars of a jail cell, the tremor that threatened to knock her knees together. Despite the fear that ran in a cold rivulet down her spine, she wouldn't let him take that from her.

Openness surrounded her. Level ground buttressed her stance. He'd tried to back her into a corner, but she'd been too smart for that. Now he had nowhere to hide, no way to disguise his approach. She ignored the thumping in her chest and rasp of her breath, and focused instead on the sound of *his* breathing, *his* beating heart. The hitch in his breath, the sudden increase in his heart rate gave her a second's warning as he coiled to spring. The air in front of him moved as he did, and she felt it whisper past her cheek. The pop of an ankle joint, the rustle of fabric, the change in his breathing all told her the direction, speed and angle of his attack.

It came with a fierceness even she hadn't anticipated, but she was ready. A foot and leg whistled toward her side. She whirled, turning her hip into the blow, and leaned away from it. When it landed, she snaked her arm around his leg, wrapped her palm on top of his kneecap and pressed down hard as she continued to spin away. He grunted in pain, and rolled with her throw to lessen the pressure on his knee. His momentum took him over her leg and onto the ground beyond with a thud and the smack of his palms as he broke his fall.

She whirled toward him and settled into a low, wide stance, waiting for his next move. He gathered himself in a crouch and sprang at her, snarling. She felt his hands close around her throat, smelled the ginger and garlic on his breath. Before his fingers locked, she thrust both hands up between his arms, breaking his grip. Wrapping one arm around his neck, she turned her hip into his body and grabbed her wrist with her other hand, securing him in a headlock. The move likely would not have worked on a larger man, but she'd judged his size correctly, not much bigger than her. But then she was tall for a girl.

As she continued to spin into him, his feet left the ground and she flipped him over her hip. She held on tight, squeezing his neck in the crook of her elbow and fell back with him, landing on his chest as he went down, her weight forcing the air out of his lungs. She heard him try to suck in a breath behind her and quickly straddled him, pressing her knees onto his arms to keep him from striking. Crossing her arms, she slid her hands up alongside his neck, fingers grasping the collar of his shirt. She gripped the fabric tightly and pulled her elbows apart, the leverage squeezing the back of her wrists against his carotid arteries, cutting off the flow of blood to his brain. If she kept up the pressure she would render him unconscious in about fifteen seconds, now ten, nine, eight...

For a moment he bucked wildly under her, and she strained to hold on. His movement grew weak, and he tapped her lightly on the shoulder. She let go, and jumped to her feet, gently rubbing the sore spot on her neck where his fingers had dug into her flesh. She extended her other hand. Her foe clasped it and pulled himself to his feet beside her.

"Better, missy," he said. "I not kill you or kidnap you this time."

"What's the matter, Yoshi?" she said. "Can't admit you got beat by a girl?"

Despite her sarcasm, Tess glowed inside from the rare praise and the knowledge that she'd done it. She'd finally bested her jiu-jitsu teacher. And it hadn't really been a fair match. Yoshi was a black belt; Tess Barrett was blind. Her gratification was short-lived.

"Yes, you beat old Yoshi," he said. "After you die five times before that."

"Come on, Yoshi," she cried. "Give me a break. At least I got you this last time."

"Sure, sure, I give you a break. But bad men no give you break. You beat them or they kill you. Simple truth. Now we go again."

"Again? No way! I'm exhausted. Can't we just quit for the day?"

"Again. Now." His voice was stern.

Every muscle in Tess's body ached. They'd been at it for more than two hours, twice as long as her normal afternoon practice, and Yoshi had been relentless. She didn't know what had gotten into him, but he'd been especially rough today, less forgiving of her mistakes. Before she could even assume *jigohontai*—defensive stance—Yoshi grabbed the lapels of her *gi*, the traditional martial arts uniform, and easily threw her over his hip. She landed hard and gasped for breath, blinking back tears of pain and frustration.

"Again," Yoshi commanded.

Warily, she got to her feet and quickly adjusted her stance. Once more Yoshi attacked before she was ready, grabbing her arm and pulling her into a shoulder throw. She smacked the mat with her hands as she landed, absorbing some of the force then rolled away, ending up in a crouch. She heard Yoshi's footsteps cross the mat toward her. Instead of rising to her feet, she leapfrogged on a diagonal, planted herself as Yoshi changed direction, and tripped him up with a leg sweep. She was on him in a flash, and as he rolled underneath her she blocked a flailing hand, quickly grasped it in a wristlock and applied pressure. Slowly twisting his arm, she rolled him onto his stomach and bent one knee into his kidney, putting her weight on it.

When she heard him slap the mat twice, signaling surrender, she let go and settled back on her haunches to catch her breath.

"Better," he said.

He put a hand on her shoulder. She shrugged it off, stood up, and stepped away from him, eyes burning and legs trembling, not only from fatigue, but the anger that seethed through her.

"Okay, we finish for today," he said.

Tess didn't reply. She wanted to bolt from the room, but she forced herself to stand still, arms at her sides, her face a bland mask. She waited for the words a sensei formally used to end class.

"*Gokurosan rei*," Yoshi said finally.

"*Doitashimaste*," she replied, bowing.

He stepped in front of her, and when she grasped his sleeve he led her out of the gym. When he stopped in the hall outside, she let her arm drop to her side.

She bowed again and said, "*Domo arigato gozaimasu, sensei,*" putting a little emphasis on the last word.

Yoshi sighed.

She'd made her point, but she didn't feel any better.

2

Travis cursed under his breath as the razor nicked his skin. He snatched a tissue from the box on the bathroom counter and daubed at the spot of blood welling from the tiny wound. He didn't have time for this. When he pulled the tissue away, blood continued to ooze. Quickly putting the tissue back on the cut, he pressed harder and continued to shave with his other hand. Not the most ideal way to get it done, but he was running late. By the time he finished scraping off the day-old growth of beard his face had stopped bleeding. He rinsed off the remaining shaving cream and patted his face dry then hurried into the bedroom and dressed.

The coat and tie he normally would have had to wear when he had an office meeting scheduled stayed in the closet. They were part of a uniform, just like the one he'd worn as a captain in the Army Special Forces. But the army uniform had fit him better, and he'd found it far more agreeable. During most of the time he'd spent in Afghanistan in SICC—Strategic Intelligence Collection and Containment, a secret army intelligence unit—he'd worn native dress, baggy pants, a long coat called a *shalwar kameez*, and a different type of Pashtun hat, *topi* or *pakol*, depending on what part of the country he was in.

Now he threw on some khakis, a short-sleeved polo shirt and a pair of deck shoes. Just as his tribal costume in Afghanistan had helped him blend in, these clothes would help him look like half the people at MondoHard, the company his brother James had started. The other half of the company's employees dressed even more casually—jeans and T-shirts, mostly. At least what he had on was more comfortable than a coat and tie. He frowned at the thought of James. Travis was pretty sure James hadn't planned on him ever running the business let alone taking over now that it had grown to a multi-billion-dollar-a-year venture. He wasn't thrilled about the direction his life had taken, but he didn't have much of an alternative. Somebody had to step up, and Travis had been the logical choice.

He grabbed a sweater from a shelf in the closet on his way out. At least his assistant didn't have him down for any dog-and-pony shows today. The endless meetings he suffered through most days made him feel like a circus animal, performing on command, an elephant that could do headstands. It was mildly amusing, but really, what was the point? In most cases, all he did in those meetings was smile and assure investors their money was safe and growing, or assure board members that the company was pursuing the right strategy, or assure employees they weren't screwing up.

James had been so much better at all of that. Travis was a soldier, a man accustomed to action and to making unilateral decisions in the field. Sure, Travis had taken orders from his superior officers in Afghanistan, but typically they'd given him a target and the leeway to take it out in whatever way he saw fit. They'd been smart enough to recognize that he worked best autonomously, free from the bureaucracy that ran the rest of the army. He and the other members of SICC had taken out several terrorist cells in "the 'Stans," mostly in the mountains north and east of Kabul. The enemy he'd been fighting since his return to the U.S. a year earlier was just as deadly and even harder to find.

Before heading downstairs, he double-checked the calendar on his smart phone to make sure Robyn hadn't scheduled something for him. The only notation that popped up consisted of four letters, "JTam." It was his own code for "Jack Turnbull, a.m." His meeting with General Jack Turnbull wasn't even officially on his calendar because he didn't want anyone to know he and Jack were getting together. Anyone with half a brain could probably figure out what the notation meant given enough time, but they'd have to hack his phone first.

Skipping down the stairs two at a time, he nearly ran into Tess at the bottom.

"Whoa," he said, sidestepping to avoid her. "Good morning."

Her face was flushed, and the smile on her face said she was happy about something. She grasped the banister and pulled herself up the stairs two at a time.

"Hold on a second," Travis called after her. "Where are you going?"

She stopped and turned. "Oh, good morning, Uncle Travis. I have to get ready for school."

"Where's the fire?"

Her face turned a deeper shade of scarlet. "They announce the theme for spring tolo today. I'm so excited."

"What's a 'tolo'?"

"A school dance. It's where the girls invite the guys. I can't believe you never heard of tolo before."

"Deprived childhood, I guess. Just like yours is going to be. You're not going."

"What?" she shrieked. "You're kidding!"

Her disappointment pierced his heart the same as if she'd plunged a KA-BAR in his chest.

"Come on, Tess. You know I can't let you go. Have you already forgotten that a week ago people were trying to kill you?"

"But you stopped them." Her voice faltered. "I ... I thought you took care of them."

"Yes, we took care of *those* men," Travis said softly. "That doesn't mean whoever was behind it won't send more."

"It's not fair! You're letting me go to school. What, classes are safe, but a dance at school isn't? You can't do this to me!"

"We just have to take extra precautions," Travis said. "Until I figure out how to keep it from happening again."

"No!" Tess stamped her foot. "You can't stop me from going. I didn't get to go to prom last year, and this is the first chance this year I've had to go to a dance. I'm going."

"Tess, please. I'd never forgive myself if anything happened to you. This is my job now, to keep you safe."

"Yeah, well, you're *not* my parent, and I *don't* have to listen to you!"

The pain in his chest felt as if she'd just twisted the knife. "No, I'm not your parent."

The longing those words stirred deep inside surprised him. It wasn't simply a wish for her respect, to get along better, or a desire to have her do what he said without question. He really did want her to think of him as more than "Uncle Travis," more than the stranger who'd shown up in her life a year ago just before it had all gone to hell. He couldn't change what had happened, as much as he would have liked.

"But I *am* your guardian," he went on. "I'm responsible for your safety and well-being until you turn eighteen. And until that happens, parent or not, I'm in charge, and you'll do as I say."

She glared at him, her bright blue eyes homing in on him like laser beams, nearly convincing him that she must have miraculously regained her sight in the past few seconds.

"I *hate* you!" she seethed.

Before Travis could think of a reply, any reply, that wouldn't make things worse, she turned and bolted up the stairs and disappeared down the hall. Travis started up the steps after her, but hesitated when he realized he didn't know what he'd say even if he caught up to her.

"Don't be late for school!" he yelled up to the empty hallway.

Trudging back downstairs with heavy steps, he glanced at his watch and remembered how late it was. He grabbed a windbreaker from a coatroom off the foyer, and practically jogged to the kitchen to find Alice and tell her he was on his way out.

"Did you eat?" she said as he brushed past heading for the garage.

"I'll grab something later at the office," he said over his shoulder. He paused at the door to the garage and smiled at her. "Don't worry, Alice. I won't starve."

He took the Range Rover from the first of the six bays in the garage. He tried not to look at the almost identical vehicle in the farthest bay, or what was left of it. The SUV was a total wreck, the result of tumbling down a mountainside in an avalanche. An avalanche that he and his security team had caused. Tess had been blinded in the accident. Her parents, who had been in the vehicle, too, were gone. He tried not to think about it.

He backed out and threw it into gear. Tires squealed as he raced up the drive. He pushed the remote to open the gate, and as he neared the main road, he glanced right to check for traffic. Seeing none, he spun the wheel to the left and pulled out, nearly running into a BMW. Travis stood on his brakes, but the BMW had already slowed and swerved as it turned into the drive. *Oliver.* The car had belonged to Tess's mom Sally, Travis's sister-in-law. Oliver, Tess's new assistant, had been given use of the car to get Tess to school and wherever else she needed to go.

Travis gave Oliver a quick wave and pulled out onto the main road. The asphalt was slick with a light but steady drizzle that was a hallmark of northwest weather. Travis tromped on the accelerator, and the powerful SUV leaped ahead, big tires gripping the wet road. He drove with confidence, feeling the vehicle's four-wheel drive propel him through the curves. Though he knew he was pushing it, he didn't let up. His lateness and the argument with Tess had thrown him off-kilter, and he took his aggression out on the gas pedal. He was used to being in control. Even in the field where conditions and situations changed in an instant he'd always had a contingency plan, and back-ups to those as well. Life with his niece seemed to involve constant improvisation.

His cell phone rang, jerking him out of his reverie. He thumbed the Bluetooth switch on the steering wheel that allowed him to answer.

"Barrett," he snapped.

A disembodied voice filled the car. "Where are you?"

"General!" Travis nearly saluted. "'I'm on my way, sir. I got caught up in some business at home."

"Tess?"

Travis felt his face grow warm. "How did you know?"

Turnbull chuckled. "I had two daughters of my own, Travis. I know what you're going through."

"I wish I did." Travis rounded a curve and immediately slowed at the sight of a vehicle straddling the road.

"Uh-oh," he murmured. "Could be trouble."

"What's the problem?" the general asked.

"Looks like an accident up ahead. I'll call you back."

"All right. But don't be long."

Travis clicked off without a reply, eyes scanning the road ahead. Off to the left, an SUV had gone off the road into a ditch. Several dozen yards beyond, a passenger van sat in his lane, angled toward him, its front wheels just off the edge of the road. The scene was eerily quiet, and Travis quickly put his thumb on it—there were no people. As if whoever had been in the accident had simply walked away. Or it had just happened and drivers of both vehicles were injured or unconscious.

He pulled onto the shoulder thirty feet from the passenger van and stepped out of the Range Rover into the drizzle. The tinted windows reflected the gray sky and nearly colorless trees, and didn't allow a view of whoever might be inside. Travis glanced over his shoulder at the SUV now behind him. No sign of life. He approached the van slowly, rusty instincts squeaking at him, telling him something wasn't right. He straightened his shoulders and picked up his pace. He wasn't in Afghanistan anymore, and his suburban neighbors weren't likely to plant roadside IEDs. The people inside the van could be seriously hurt. He was within steps now. As he stretched out a hand to open the passenger door, the rear door slid open and a man with a ski mask pulled over his face jumped out.

Travis whirled to face him, settling into fighting stance, and then saw the personal defense weapon—a submachine pistol—in the man's hands. It was pointed at his stomach. Another masked figure rounded the back of the van and hurried toward Travis. He, too, carried one of the small machine guns.

"Stay where you are!" the second man barked.

Travis looked around wildly, looking for an avenue of escape. Behind him, the doors of the SUV in the ditch opened and two men stepped out aiming guns at him.

"Don't even think about it," the second man said as he walked up to Travis, "They would cut you down before you got ten feet."

Before Travis could reply, the man yanked a cloth bag over his head and grabbed him in a bear hug. Instinctively, Travis struggled to break free, but someone grabbed his ankles and snatched his feet out from under him. Something sharp stabbed his shoulder like a bee sting. The men carrying him flipped him over and unceremoniously dumped him on his face on the floor of the van. His hands were yanked violently behind his back, nearly wrenching his left shoulder out of its socket, and they bound his wrists together with plastic cuffs.

The world softened and slid, the men's voices becoming more indistinct as doors slammed and engines revved. Travis rolled into something hard as the van lurched forward and swung around in a tight turn. He tried to keep track of direction, but within seconds the world faded away as whatever sedative they'd given him sucked him under.

3

I have one of the world's most interesting jobs. I'm a seeing-eye dog. Well, seeing-eye guy, actually. A professional student until I learned the trust fund that had paid for a college degree, a master's and most of a doctorate had been raided and virtually emptied by my paternal grandparents, I went out looking for my first real full-time job at the age of almost 21. The part-time jobs I'd held through school since I was about 11 didn't count, and, yes, I'm very young for a PhD. candidate. I answered an ad for a personal assistant, and it turned out the person needing assistance was blind, a girl, and still in high school.

I hadn't been too sure about the high school part. My high school experience had been enigmatic at best, but then I hadn't experienced that much of it. I was in and out so fast, graduating at 15, and so focused on my studies that not much else had registered. And I'd approached the girl part with some trepidation, too, not because I don't like girls, but again because I hadn't had much experience with them. And the blind part? Well, that had taken a little getting used to also. I mean the girl, Tess, relied on me to be her eyes, to keep her from running into walls or tripping over curbs or falling down stairs (all of which I nearly let her do more than once my first day), and to help her with schoolwork.

Though I'd been in the job less than two weeks, already my apartment had been ransacked and I'd been shot at, beat up, and nearly killed several times. And I'd come to the realization that I wouldn't trade this job for the world, despite the fact that the job itself—waiting on a spoiled, pissy teenager—was a pain in the butt. Okay, so I'm exaggerating a bit. Considering she's a gagillionaire she's not *too* spoiled, and if I was blind I might be a little pissy, too. Turns out we're even when it comes to parents—neither of us has any. Hers died in the car accident that blinded her; mine, well, my mother died when I was an infant, and my father ran out on me.

The job definitely had its perks. Tess's house, large enough to have its own Zip Code, was a pretty nice place to hang out. Some meals were included—I had a standing invitation to breakfast since they needed me there early enough to take Tess to school; at school I bought lunch on Tess's account; and sometimes I stayed for dinner if Tess needed homework help. Rosa, the cook who'd worked there when I first started, made awesome Mexican food, but she turned out to be a psycho killer and industrial spy sent to steal something from Tess that Tess didn't know she had. (Sounds complicated, I know, but try to keep up.) Alice, the family's majordomo—house manager, I guess you'd call her—was a pretty good cook herself and had taken over after Rosa went berserk and disappeared. Alice had assigned me a BMW 6 Series convertible in which to chauffeur Tess around, and it was an exceptionally sweet car. And, they actually paid me to hang out with Tess, which made my landlord and creditors extremely happy—not that I was hanging out with her, but that I was earning enough to pay them.

On my way to pick up Tess for school a week or so into the gig, I ran a few minutes late. As I turned in the drive, a black Range Rover sped toward me through the gate. I hit the brakes and yanked the wheel in time to see Travis Barrett throw me a curt wave as he flashed by and barreled down the road behind me. I shrugged while talking my heart back into the confines of my chest. I hadn't made up my mind if Travis was a good guy or not, but since he was ex-Special Forces and Tess's guardian, I didn't want to get on his bad side. And I'm sure he had more important things on his mind than whether his inattentive driving ticked me off or not. After all, the guy had a multi-billion-dollar software company to run.

Since Travis had thoughtfully opened the gate for me, I continued on down the drive without stopping to swipe my security card at the magstripe reader on a post near the gate. A few weeks earlier if someone had told me I'd need high-level security clearance to get to work, let alone collect a high school kid from her home, I'd have looked around for the hidden cameras and asked which reality show I was on. Now I was glad for the extra precautions, another of which was quickly evident as I drove down the hill toward the house. A man the size of an NFL nose tackle stepped out from behind some trees and regarded my passage with a keen eye and impassive expression. Close-cropped hair and beard wreathed his ruddy face in flaming orange. I nodded somberly on the way past.

Red was one of a half dozen ex-military types Travis had selected as his security team to roam the property and keep an eye on Tess. A little older than the others on the team, he also was the only one who had exhibited any signs of friendliness toward me, or Tess. The others weren't particularly unfriendly, just intent on doing their job. And they performed with a level of intensity I'd seen only on professional athletes. Maybe. Not surprising given they were dealing with matters of life and death. They were a man short, in fact, because one of their team members, Kenny, had been killed the week before. The question was whether he'd died protecting Tess or because he was trying to kill her.

Using the remote to open one of the garage bay doors, I parked inside and hurried into the house. The side door led through a small mudroom into the kitchen, which is where I expected to find Tess. I guessed wrong. Alice stood at the sink, her back to me, washing dishes and muttering.

"Where's Tess?" I said.

Alice whirled around, a rubber-gloved hand going to her chest. She quickly dropped it to her side, but a wet handprint remained on her blouse.

"Oliver! You startled me." She brushed a strand of hair off her forehead with the back of a gloved hand. "She's upstairs in her room. She ate earlier."

I hesitated. "I guess I'll wait."

Alice pulled the cuff of one glove away from her wrist and looked at her watch. "No, you better go up and get her. Otherwise you'll be late."

I nodded and headed for the hallway.

"Oliver," she called after me, "she and Travis had a fight this morning. Just so you know."

I paused. "Thanks. I think." I continued down the hall with a little less certainty in my step.

I remembered the way to Tess's room though I'd only been there once before. The house was large enough that new employees should have been issued a map or GPS device to find their way around. I didn't need either only because I have eidetic memory. It's kind of like photographic memory, but not limited to visual detail. It's tied more to experiences. If I recall an experience, or the feeling of it, I can usually remember the details—sights, sounds, smells, etc.

Tess's door was closed, so I knocked softly.

"Go away!" The door muffled Tess's voice, but not her distress.

"You're going to be late for school."

"I don't care."

"Yes, you do care. Come on, Tess. We can talk about it on the way to school."

"I don't want to talk about it. Especially not with you!"

Unconsciously, I rubbed my shoulder as if that's where the barb had sunk in. I didn't have a ready reply.

"Well, not *you*, exactly," she said after a moment. "It's because you're a guy. You're all alike."

"I resent that. I'm not like any other guy you've ever met."

"You know what I mean. What did Alice tell you anyway?"

"Nothing, really. All she said was you and Travis had a fight."

She didn't respond.

"This is silly, Tess. We're already talking. It'd be a lot easier without the door in the way."

I heard rustling. The door suddenly opened, and she nearly stepped right into me.

"Whoa." I backpedaled and caught my balance.

She marched past me, backpack with her books and homework securely slung over both shoulders. Reaching her side in a few hurried steps, I took her arm.

She shrugged me off. "I can find my way without your help."

Her face was puffy and her eyes red-rimmed from crying, but her face showed nothing except grim determination now. Keeping the wall close to her side, she lightly brushed her fingertips along its surface as she walked. Trailing a step behind, I watched with admiration as she easily navigated the way to the stairs and negotiated her way down without hesitation.

"Where's the car?" she asked when she reached the bottom.

"In the garage."

"I'll wait here while you bring it around." She lifted her chin, striking a regal pose.

I bit off a sarcastic reply, reminding myself that she was, after all, my boss.

"Usual spring weather," I said as I walked away. "You should grab a coat."

Rummaging through the coat closet by feel should keep her busy. She would have insisted on doing it herself anyway.

Two minutes later, I picked her up at the front door, and we headed off to school. She sat with her hands in her lap, silent.

"You okay?" I asked.

"Peachy."

I didn't have a lot of experience with these matters, but I figured I'd opened the door—twice—and it was up to her to walk through it. I kept my mouth shut and let her stew.

The high school was the usual zoo, different herds migrating through the corridors like animals on the savannah—geeks hunched over tablet computers or smart phones, belongings on their backs; popular girls with heads together twittering and chirruping as they eyed the other herds in passing, books in designer bags slung over one shoulder, thumbs busily keying screens of their smart phones; jocks in school colors bouncing off walls and one another with mile-wide grins, eyes glazed as they read the screens of their smart phones; "normal" kids moving at a good clip, eyes ahead, books in hand, zigzagging through traffic. A few of them even held phones up in front of their faces, keeping one eye on the screen, the other on where they were going.

In the whirlwind of classes that followed, I had no time to press Tess for details. For the moment, at least, her tiff with Travis seemed forgotten, whatever it had been about. I hoped that was a good sign.

4

"**M**iss Barrett? Care to join us?"

The voice barely registered on Tess's consciousness. A nudge on her arm brought her back to reality.

"Hello?" Oliver murmured. "Earth to Tess."

A snicker from one direction and a titter from another let her know the whole class was staring at her. Her face flushed with embarrassment. Oliver nudged her again.

She batted at his hand and addressed Mr. Johnson. "I'm sorry. Could you repeat the question?"

Mr. Johnson heaved a sigh. "If I must. We just finished listening to a passage of Ravel's Piano Concerto for Left Hand in D Major. I asked you to name another composer who wrote piano pieces for the left hand."

"Um, Chopin?"

"Good guess, Miss Barrett. Now, can you tell me for whom Ravel's piano concerto was written?"

Tess felt her face burn hotter. She'd been so angry with Travis all morning that she hadn't been able to focus on anything. Now she was paying for it, and was as angry with herself as with her uncle. She was a better student than this.

"Wittgenstein," Oliver hissed next to her ear.

"Wittgenstein?" she said loudly.

"Also a good guess," Mr. Johnson said, "thanks to Mr. Moncrief, I suspect. Do you know who Paul Wittgenstein was, Miss Barrett?"

Tess elbowed Oliver in the ribs before he could say anything. The grunt she heard told her she'd hit the bull's-eye.

"No, I'm sorry, sir," she said. "A piano player, I imagine."

"A pianist, yes," Mr. Johnson said. "A concert pianist. And why might Ravel have written this piece for Wittgenstein?"

"Um, he was left-handed?"

A ripple of laughter went through the classroom. Tess slumped in her seat, wishing she could sink into the floor and disappear.

"No, Miss Barrett. Wittgenstein, in fact, was right-handed, but lost his arm in World War I. It's not enough to simply appreciate music in this class, Miss Barrett. I want you to understand why we appreciate it. A little more time on your studies next time, please."

"Yes, sir."

Tess heard more sniggers that faded quickly as Mr. Johnson moved on. She turned her head and whispered, "Don't help me."

Oliver whispered back. "I was just trying to—"

"Stop," she said. "Shhhh."

Thankfully, the buzzer ended class a few minutes later. Oliver guided her out where the waterfall of sound from hundreds of students swirling through the hallways cascaded around her, buffeting her in torrents and nearly drowning out her other senses. She clutched his shoulder a little tighter from behind as bodies bumped and jostled her.

She leaned forward and said, "Why'd you do that?"

Oliver didn't answer.

"I would've been better off saying, 'I don't know,'" she said, louder now.

His voice floated back to her over the din. "You're right. It looks a lot better if you admit ignorance than if you give a teacher the right answer."

"The *truth* is better. I didn't *know* the answer."

"Sure you did. I told you who it was. That's okay. I get it. You're on your own from here."

She let it drop. Stupid men. They had their own twisted sense of logic, and there was no reasoning with them.

The commotion in the commons was as bad as that in the hallways, only here the sounds reverberated and echoed off the high ceilings and cavernous space. The decibel level was modestly lower than in the cramped halls, but the constant deluge made communication difficult even with the person next to you.

Oliver guided her to an empty seat, and she felt him lean in close. "What do you want to eat?" he said over the din.

Monday. Pasta day. Tess craved a bowl of pasta, with Alfredo sauce, and lots of Parmesan cheese, but knew that most of it would end up in her lap. Not to mention that it was the equivalent of a heart attack on a plate. The double-edged threat of guilt and potential embarrassment quickly changed her mind.

"Turkey sandwich on wheat. Lettuce, no tomato, no mayo."

"Got it. Something to drink?"

She shook her head. "I've got a water bottle in my bag."

Oliver left without a word, and Tess turned her focus to the other voices around the table.

"I don't know," a girl said. "It's so hard, you know?" Fear cloaked her voice like a hoodie.

"No, it's not, Julie," another said. Tess recognized this voice—Jordan Taylor. It bubbled like a frothy, pink tutu. "It's just cheer."

"It's not *just* cheer," a third girl snarled.

Tess knew this voice, too. It belonged to Adrienne Moss. Her girl, one-time best friend, and now... Now, Tess didn't know what Addie was to her. Not her enemy. At least she didn't think so, but not much of a friend, either.

"Don't you *dare* say it's just cheer," Addie went on, voice venomous enough to kill small rodents. "It's hard, hot, sweaty work. I didn't get where I am just because of some cute smile and a nice spray tan. I worked my ass off. Anyone who says we're just brainless T-and-A with pom-poms can kiss my ass. Julie, if you want to try out, you better work your butt off, too. But I think you're ready. You're one of the best on JV.

"I'll tell you who won't make it, though," she continued in a lower voice. "Brittany. Girl thinks she's all that, but she can't dance her way out of a paper bag, and she sure as heck can't stunt. She's in for a surprise. What about you, Tess?"

"What about me?" Tess said, startled that Addie considered them on speaking terms.

"Next week? Try-outs? You coming?"

Tess felt her cheeks grow warm as giggles erupted around the table. "You must be joking." Her mind worked furiously. Had her year off put her so out of practice she couldn't keep up with Addie, of all people?

"Not at all," Addie said. "We wouldn't want to be seen as discriminatory." Sarcasm dripped from the words like acid from a leaky battery.

Tess scooped some up to flavor her reply. "Sure, I'll be there. Right after I help girls' basketball win state."

Tess heard some snickers, fewer than the ones at her expense, but at least these were *with* her, not at her. Addie's silence confirmed her direct hit.

"Hey, dork-face," Addie said finally. "What do *you* think? Should Tess try out next week?"

Tess stiffened and was about to reply when she realized Addie was speaking to someone else, not her."

"Yo, Matt!" Addie barked. "Try not to be rude. I'm talking to you."

"Shut up!" Matt said. "I'm not bugging you, so why are you in *my* face?"

A chair scraped the floor next to Tess, and Oliver murmured in her ear, "What's going on?"

"I don't know," she whispered back.

"If you're going to sit with us, dweeb," Addie said, "at least you could *try* to be social."

"Leave me alone, biatch."

"What's he doing?" Tess whispered.

"Fooling around with his phone," Oliver said. "Looks like he's playing a game app. Probably *Angry Birds*."

"Don't you guys know anything?" Matt said peevishly. He sighed. "It's *Never Bitten*."

"What's that?" Tess said.

"The coolest video game ever," Matt said. "Just came out. Like *Angry Birds*, *Zombieville* and a couple others all rolled into one. Now can I eat lunch in peace?"

Tess perked her ears, no longer paying attention to Matt. A buzz spread through the commons behind her. She put her hand up, fingers searching for and quickly finding Oliver's arm, muscles bunching and rippling under the fabric of his shirt.

"Listen," she hissed at him. "Something's happening. I can feel it."

Someone put a hand on the back of her chair, and a presence loomed behind her. She turned her head slightly and caught a whiff of a familiar scent—Toby.

"Did you guys hear?" Toby's voice cracked on the last word.

"What now, Toby?" Addie said.

"A kid killed himself. Committed suicide."

"Who?" Tess blurted.

"Don't know. Sophomore, I heard."

"What happened?" Addie spoke up again.

"They're not sure. They're saying he was fine a few weeks ago, but got depressed about something recently and started acting all weird."

"That's terrible," Tess said. "Why didn't anyone do anything?"

"I'll bet it was that mental case with the big ears," Addie said. "You know who I mean. They call him Dumbo because of his ears."

"It's Gumbo," Matt said, disgusted. "And he's not mental."

"Gumbo?" Addie said. "What kind of name is that? Isn't that, like, soup?"

"It's short for Gumby and Dumbo," Matt said, "'cause he's tall and thin, *and* has big ears."

"I hope it's not him," Tess said. "You're all so mean."

"Well, whoever he was," Addie said, "he was a loser."

5

As he slowly rose toward consciousness, Travis felt rather than heard the steady drone of engines surrounding him. The sounds worked their way out of his dreams and became more real. Other sensations edged into his consciousness. A crick in his neck. The desert sand bunker in his mouth. Chafed skin around his wrist. Numbness in one hand that had gone to sleep.

Jet engines. Their distinctive whine was easy to identify now. He kept his eyes closed and maintained the steady breathing that had marked his sleep. His muscles felt like Jell-O, and he wasn't sure he could move even if he wanted to. Very slowly, he opened his eyes, only to be met with darkness except a small, dim spot near his right elbow. He let his head loll toward it and felt fabric rasp against the whiskers on his cheek. He saw a vision of a bright red spot growing and spreading, and remembered he'd cut himself shaving. The cloth touched his cheek once more, and he thought of the hood they'd pulled over his head.

More memories came back to him then. *The SUV in the ditch. The van straddling a rain-slicked road. Men emerging from the van.* His shoulder itched, and now he remembered the bee-sting puncture of the needle. He thought back. Details might be the only edge he'd have somewhere down the line. They hadn't killed him, which meant they wanted him alive. An airplane trip likely meant they wanted him out of the way, in hostile territory, or... Out of the way and not easy to find, he decided. The fact he still wore the hood meant they didn't want him to have any idea where they were taking him. He'd counted five men—no, four, but had there been a fifth in the van? A driver? His head was still fuzzy.

They'd thrown him in the van, and within a minute he remembered hallucinating and feeling like he was floating out of his body. He must have fallen into a K-hole. Ketamine. Special K. He'd never taken drugs, but had learned more than he cared to about many different substances in Afghanistan. Opium and heroine from the poppies the locals grew because they could make more money than they could growing food crops like wheat or corn. Marijuana that usually came in the form of much stronger hashish. Meth and coke that always seemed to find their way into every society through its soft underbelly. Drugs used and abused by the weak to escape their lives and by the strong to feel more powerful, only to end up destroying all of them.

Ketamine was an anesthetic that army medics still used in the field as an option to morphine. More commonly used by veterinarians, the military still used it because it could be administered easily by people who weren't trained in anesthesiology. A lot of soldiers in the 'Stans had gotten their hands on Special K and taken it as a recreational drug. Travis could never understand why people would want to alter their consciousness and mess up their heads with any drugs, even alcohol.

He'd heard enough stories to recognize the effects, but judging from how quickly he'd lost consciousness and how relaxed his muscles still were, he guessed that they'd mixed diazepam with the ketamine. That was typically how a medic or corpsman would administer ketamine in the field. The benzodiazepine would partially counteract the hallucinogenic properties of the ketamine and serve as a sedative, knocking him out. Depending on the dose, ketamine's effects lasted only about twenty to thirty minutes. Even with the sedative added, he couldn't have been out that long.

So, the plane had only been in the air for a little while. And while he didn't know where it was headed, he could guess which direction the plane flew. Now that his eyes had adjusted, he could sense the light through the fabric. The interior of the plane was bright with daylight. To get him onto a plane without going through airport security or attracting attention, his kidnappers must be using a private plane, a small jet with relatively shorter range than a commercial jet. So they weren't heading over the ocean. If they'd been flying north, direct morning sunlight coming through the windows would have warmed his right side. South, and the sun would warm his left side. *Definitely east.*

He worked the fingers of his right hand to improve his circulation and restore some feeling. The movement chafed his wrist more, and he realized his hands were cuffed to the armrests. They hadn't bound his feet, but he wasn't going anywhere. Even if he wasn't cuffed to the seat, where would he run? He couldn't just take a stroll out the door at twenty thousand feet.

He listened for other sounds, but the noise from the engines drowned out almost everything else. Occasionally, he sensed or felt someone passing by in the narrow aisle rather than heard.

And once or twice he thought he heard the low murmur of voices, but couldn't make out any words. With little to do but wait, he counted, trying to keep track of time. By his reckoning, they'd flown for about half an hour when the plane began its descent. The jet probably had a cruising speed upwards of 480 knots, but Travis dialed that back, figuring the pilot might have to abide by flight controller's instructions. So, with the time he'd been out, they'd probably reached Idaho, maybe even Montana by now.

His ears popped as the jet continued on its glide path back down to earth. The plane banked a couple of times as it followed a landing pattern around an airfield. Travis heard the whining sound of servos extending the flaps then a grinding noise and dull thud as the landing gear locked into place signaling they were on final approach. He shifted in his seat, preparing to brace himself for landing. A sound at his shoulder jerked his head up. Before he could open his mouth, someone jabbed a needle in his arm again. Within seconds the world started spinning and even the black fabric in front of his eyes faded into oblivion.

* * * * *

When he came to this time, two people dragged him by the arms over rough ground. His shoes bumped and scraped along the hard unyielding surface. Groggily, he tried to get his feet under him, but they wouldn't cooperate. Sensing he was now conscious, whoever gripped his arms tightened their grasp, making his feeble struggles all but useless. The hood still covered his face, but Travis wasn't sure it mattered. His head was so full of fuzz and the remnants of visions from the K-hole that he wouldn't trust his eyes if he could see.

A few moments later, their pace slowed and the creak of rusted metal echoed around him. His captors dragged him a few more steps and stopped. He supported most of his own weight on weak and wobbly knees. Someone yanked the hood off his head as the grip on his arms loosened. An intense beam of light stabbed him in the face, and he squeezed his eyes to slits against the glare. Someone put a hand in the middle of his back and shoved him hard. Travis stumbled forward into the darkness and fell, banging one knee hard on the ground and skinning the palm of one hand.

He turned to face his kidnapers, but they'd already started back the way they'd come. The light from a large, high-beam flashlight illuminated some sort of tunnel and silhouetted three hulking figures walking away from him. Metal creaked again and clanged as one of them shut and locked a gate blocking the tunnel. The trio disappeared around a bend, and the light and sound of their footsteps faded until Travis was left in total darkness with only his breathing and thudding heartbeat for company.

He shook his head trying to clear out the cobwebs, and took stock. They still hadn't killed him, which was a good sign. In fact, they'd taken pains to keep him from seeing where they'd taken him and to hide their own identities, which meant they might let him go when this was all over. Whatever *this* was. They'd said nothing in his presence. Even more perplexing, they hadn't seemed interested in whether or not he had anything to say. He'd expected an interrogation of some kind, the painful kind, actually. He knew what kind of techniques the spooks—his counterparts in the CIA—in Afghanistan had used. Sure, Congress had banned waterboarding and other forms of torture. That didn't mean the techniques weren't used. Interrogators just got better at keeping it quiet.

Travis had never resorted to torture. His job had been to establish himself as a local and blend in. Or at least befriend the locals and use them to best advantage. He'd preferred carrots to sticks, always looking for the positive incentive, the favor or reward that would motivate a local to help pinpoint the bad guys. That didn't mean that subjects hadn't been roughed up on occasion. But he hadn't needed torture.

Whatever these people wanted, torture or no, they weren't getting it.

6

"You don't seem very upset," I said over my shoulder.

If anything, Tess had seemed preoccupied since getting the news at lunch that a fellow student had taken his own life. That kind of news always messed with my head. I didn't understand it. If I'd learned anything from my years of education and relatively short life, it was that things could change in an instant (like my financial situation when I was informed my profligate grandparents had raided my education fund). When circumstances look their bleakest is usually just about the time they start to improve. Too many kids don't see that or haven't experienced it.

Tess came back from the side road her thoughts had taken her down. "Upset? About that suicide? Of course I'm upset. Why wouldn't I be? Why would you even think that?"

"Sorry. You just seem to be somewhere else, like the kid's death didn't register."

Her fingers gripped my shoulder, nails digging into my skin through the thin nylon of my windbreaker as we walked out to the car.

"I didn't *know* him, so it's not like I'm going to have a breakdown, or burst into tears. But I feel bad for his family. What I'm more upset about is Matt. Didn't you think he was acting weird?"

"Matt's a geek. He always acts weird. Curb in two. Step down. One, two."

"That's not nice." She stepped off the curb without missing a beat. We seemed to be getting the hang of this.

"I meant it in the kindest way," I said. "I like Matt."

"No, really. Didn't you see what was going on?"

"He was playing a game app on his phone. Pretty focused."

"That's what I mean. He was so into whatever that app is it was like he wasn't even there."

I slowed as we approached the car and pressed the key fob in my pocket to unlock it.

"Matt's pretty intense, Tess. He gets absorbed easily in tech stuff."

She shook her head. "Not like this. Did you hear how pissy he got?"

She heard me open the door and automatically put her hand out to find the roof of the car and position herself to get in. I reached out to help her, but she'd already taken her other hand off my shoulder and put it on the open door frame. She quickly eased herself into the passenger seat and waited expectantly. I closed her door, tossed her backpack in the trunk and got in behind the wheel. Glancing over to make sure Tess was belted in, I started up and backed out of the slot.

"Okay," I said when we'd safely navigated the obstacle course through the parking lot as students left for the day, "so maybe he could have been more civil."

"That's not it." She drummed the center console with her fingers then lifted one to her mouth and nibbled on her fingernail. "There's something wrong. I just feel it."

Light rain pattered the car, leaving hundreds of fish-eye lenses rolling down the windshield, distorting the outside world. I flicked a switch and the wipers smeared the droplets against the glass then wiped them away in the second pass.

"It's probably nothing," I said. "We all have bad days."

"It's not nothing. Didn't you hear what people were saying?"

"About Matt?" I glanced at her.

She pursed her lips in annoyance. "No, about Ben, the kid who killed himself. I heard lots of people say he left a note. It said he got bit."

"What the hell does that mean?"

"I don't know, but Matt said the game he was playing is called *Never Bitten*. Don't you find that odd?"

"You think Matt's behavior is connected to the kid's death? I find *that* odd."

"Why do you always have to pooh-pooh my ideas?"

"What? I don't always..." I took a deep breath and checked the mirrors before it was too late to focus on what mattered. "Say you're right..." I tried not to let my voice make a face. "You're saying the game app might have made the kid kill himself."

"All I'm saying is that Matt's acting weird, and it could be because he's spending so much time playing that freaking game instead of talking to his friends."

I wished I could take back my original comment. She was definitely upset, and now I got to bear the brunt.

"Fine. While you're doing homework, I'll see what I can find out."

"Thank you." She sat in stony silence the rest of the way to the house.

I pulled into the second bay of the five-car garage. The slot closest to the house was reserved for the Range Rover Tess's Uncle Travis drove. The two vehicles in the spots on the other side of me—an older model sedan and a pickup truck—belonged to Alice Pemberton, the Barretts' house manager, and Yoshi Kato, the groundskeeper. I know, it sounded fancy for a house with only two people living in it, but since the house rivals a lot of French chateaus in size, I understood why. At the far end sat another Range Rover identical to Travis's except squashed as if someone had stepped on it, damage done by an avalanche. The accident had killed Tess's parents and blinded her.

For good measure, the guesthouse across the courtyard from the main house also had a garage that presently housed two hulking, black SUVs used by the security team that guarded Tess and Travis. One of them slid into an open bay behind me; it had followed us from school.

I retrieved the backpack from the trunk and guided Tess into the house. Alice met us at the kitchen door. Her pensive expression made me pause.

"Ah, there you are," she said. "Tess, can I get you a snack before you start on homework?"

Tess moved away from me, comfortable in her own surroundings. She kept one hand out in front of her, but walked through the kitchen with confidence and stopped at the big refrigerator

"No, thanks, Alice. I think I'll just get started," she said as she took out a bottle of water. "You coming, Oliver?"

"Right behind you."

"Hang on a minute, both of you," Alice said.

Tess heard the look on Alice's face and froze. "What? What is it?"

"It's Travis. He's missing."

"What do you mean, missing?" Tess clutched the counter so tightly her knuckles whitened.

Alice sighed. "We're not sure what happened. His assistant Robyn called from work an hour after he'd left wondering where he was. I had Marcus send someone out to look for him. I..."

In the few weeks I'd worked as Tess's assistant, I'd never seen Alice show much emotion. The woman had coolly faced off against an assassin with a kitchen knife while two others came in the back door armed with submachine guns. Now worry creased her face, and her voice broke. She straightened and collected herself so quickly I almost thought maybe I'd imagined her discomfort.

"I'm sorry, Tess," she went on. "They found his Range Rover abandoned less than a mile up the street. He was nowhere in the vicinity, and he's not answering his cell phone. It looks like he may have been kidnapped, but we haven't received any calls or gotten any demands."

Tess paled, and her hand went to her mouth.

"Oh, my god. Is it the same people who came after me? Why would they take Travis?"

"We don't know, Tess. There's no sense worrying about it until we find out more."

"Do you think they took him to get back at me? Oh, god, Alice, what are we going to do?"

"We're going to do everything we can to try to find him. In the mean time, we have to be patient while Marcus and the team investigate."

"This is all my fault," Tess moaned.

"No, it's not." Alice's voice knifed through Tess's self-pity, bringing her head up sharply at the sound. "I don't want to hear you talk like that, Tess. There's nothing you could have done to prevent this. Travis is resourceful. He's a soldier, and he's been in worse spots. He'll be fine."

"You don't even know where he is! How can you say he'll be fine?"

"Because I know a little bit about what he did for six years in Afghanistan, young lady. Trust me, if there's anyone who can take care of himself that person is Travis. Now why don't you get started on homework, and I'll bring you a snack in a minute. Oliver, take Tess to the library and help her get settled, please."

"Yes, ma'am."

Tess shrugged off my attempt to gently guide her toward the library, stubbornly feeling her way out of the kitchen and down the long hallway. Her arms flailed as she walked, like bug antennae, or a child playing Blind Man's Buff. She strode with confidence until her steps took her angling into a wall. The impulse to help her shoved me forward, but I restrained my hand just in time. She stopped, reoriented herself and set off again, this time trailing a finger along the wall. When she touched the library door, she turned in and crossed the open space with hands outstretched until they felt the back of a chair at a long table. She slid into the seat.

The library contrasted starkly with the rest of the modern house. On three walls, traditional mahogany shelving climbed two stories high. A huge stone fireplace divided the shelves on one wall. The fourth wall, made entirely of French style windows, let in lots of light. The study table with four straight-backed chairs where Tess sat stood in the nearest third of the room, a green glass banker's lamp hanging over it. A couch and easy chairs faced the fireplace. A smaller seating area and a study carrel filled opposite corners. A spiral staircase led up to a mezzanine-level catwalk that accessed the higher shelves, and an entire section of shelving opened up into a secret safe room. Closed now, the room had served as Tess's father's home office. Of course, he wasn't around to use it anymore, and Travis had taken over a small den down the hall.

I walked to the other side of the table and set the backpack on the table. "What's wrong?"

"Nothing." She shook her head. "Everything." She sobbed once loudly, her blues eyes brimming with tears. I froze, glad she couldn't see that tears rendered me helpless. She swallowed hard and choked back another sob.

"First Matt, then Ben's suicide. Now this."

"It's going to be all right," I fibbed.

"You don't understand. This morning I told Uncle Travis I hate him. That's the last thing I said to him. What if I never see him again?" Her lip quivered.

"You will," I said quickly. "Come on, Tess. The guy's like Rambo."

A couple of weeks earlier, Travis and the security team had saved our butts from a squad of assassins bent on taking out Tess and anyone else who got in the way in a firefight up in the mountains. I was still sketchy on details because I'd been jumped and knocked out cold as we were trying to escape.

"You don't really hate him, do you?" I said quietly.

"No. Yes." She threw up her hands. "I don't know! He's just so infuriating. He smothers me, worse than my mother ever did."

"Not your dad?"

"God, no. Dad was always cool. I mean, he could be maddening, too, because he always backed up whatever Mom said. But when it was just the two of us, he pretty much let me do whatever I wanted. It wasn't until Travis showed up that Dad got really protective."

"Yeah, well, now you know why."

"It isn't fair." She sighed and sank into her chair. "Guess we better get started."

I slid the backpack closer, pulled out some books and consulted the notes I'd taken regarding her assignments.

"Not that much today," I said. "What do you want to do first?"

"Math, please."

She knocked off the math homework quickly, and she moved on to music. Twenty minutes later, Alice showed up with a tray loaded with mugs of cocoa, cookies and fruit. She set it down without a word and left as quietly as she'd come in. Tess raised her head, sniffed the air and took off the headphones she wore. I took her hand and wrapped her fingers around a warm mug.

She sniffed again. "Hot chocolate?"

"Cookies and fruit here, too."

She nodded and bent her head to the cup. I was about to take a big bite from an apple when Marcus strode into the room. Tess stiffened and cocked her head slightly, a frown tugging the corners of her mouth down. The size and build of an NFL wide receiver, Marcus Jackson headed up Travis's security team. One of four former Army Special Forces soldiers on the team including Travis, Marcus had gotten the job by virtue of his former rank more than any other qualification. At least it seemed that way to me. Luis, a former Marine, and Kenny, an Army Ranger before he'd come to work for Travis, were junior in rank, but had almost as much combat experience. Kenny, though, had been killed in the firefight. The other three members of the security team—Fred, Barney and Red, a Navy SEAL—also had more experience than Marcus, but didn't outrank him. Nor did any of them want the job as far as I could tell. Despite having been a lieutenant, Marcus didn't seem like an officer or a gentleman. Tess didn't like him.

"Good, you're both here," he said as he approached us. "I just spoke with Alice, so I know she told you about Travis."

"Have you found him?" Tess said.

"Not yet," Marcus said. "But here's the deal. Until we find him or find out what happened, I'm in command. Do you understand? You don't make a move, you don't breath unless I know about it.

Screw up one time, and I'll snap a home monitoring bracelet on both your ankles so fast you won't know I was there. Are we clear?"

"You're going to make me a prisoner in my own house?" Tess cried.

"Not if you do what I tell you," Marcus said.

"Fine." Her voice was grim. "Then you better find him." Her nose wrinkled.

Marcus turned to me, eyes boring a hole in my skull. "I'm not going to have any problems here, right?"

"Not with me," I said.

Marcus stared a moment longer. With a curt nod he turned and walked out of the room.

"Is he gone?" Tess said.

"I think so."

Her nose was scrunched up again. "Do you smell that? I don't know where Marcus has been, but he reeks."

I took a cautious sniff, then a bigger one and caught a faint odor that reminded me of the countryside around the small town where my grandparents raised me.

"Manure?"

"Yeah, gross. And something else, too. I can't quite put my finger on it. Where's *he* been?"

The question made me pause. If Marcus had been out looking for Travis, he'd been checking out some pretty odd places.

"I don't like him," Tess said. "I just don't trust him."

"Who, Marcus? Travis hand-picked him."

"You weren't there! You didn't see what happened!"

"You mean to Kenny?"

At least she had the decency to blush. "Well, you were there, but you know..."

I sighed. Yeah, I knew. I'd been out cold. If someone hadn't jumped me and cold-cocked me, I might have had a fighting chance. Or I suppose I could be dead, like Kenny.

"I'm telling you, Oliver," she whispered fiercely, "Marcus shot him in cold blood. Kenny was trying to protect me."

"Maybe so, but like it or not, Marcus is in charge. You have to keep your nose clean."

She pouted, but didn't say anything. In a moment, she put her headphones back on and went back to her music assignment.

Tess finished the rest of her homework quickly, and I went to find Alice to ask if I could go home. Angry voices belonging to

Marcus and Alice spilled out of the kitchen. Though difficult to make out, some words, like Tess's and my names, carried clearly enough. I briefly considered eavesdropping, but decided whatever I might learn wasn't worth the risk of getting caught. I needed the job, and I could guess the subject of the argument in the kitchen. I turned around and went the other way, out the front door.

The rain had let up, patches of blue sky visible in the banks of gray clouds. In the driveway in front of the guesthouse Red was taking advantage of the lull to wash the grime from one of the SUVs. He looked up and nodded as I headed for the garage. Without thinking I abruptly changed direction and stopped a few yards away from him. He squatted by a rear wheel with a bucket of sudsy water and a stiff-bristled brush cleaning the wheel covers. He scrubbed in a circular motion, waiting me out. Red had taken me home one night and had checked my apartment for bogeymen under the bed. Not that I think there are monsters hiding behind the dust-bunnies down there, but I had a sense I could trust Red.

"Marcus went out today?" I said finally, deciding how to play my cards.

Red nodded. "Trying to figure out what the hell happened to Barrett."

"You know where he went?"

Red started to answer, but hesitated before shaking his head.

"Anyone go with him?" I asked.

Red turned to look at me then, his face expressionless. He didn't answer, which was all the answer I needed.

"She's a good kid." I nudged a stray pebble with my toe. "A little spoiled, but she doesn't deserve to get caught in the middle of whatever crap is going on."

He stared at me a moment longer, gave me a short nod and turned back to his work. I lingered, thinking I should say something else, but nothing came to me.

7

Rose Dunn leaned across the seat of her Continental GT before Austin could react and planted a wet kiss on Austin's cheek. A wave of alcohol vapor followed her in, nauseating him. He jerked his head away and swiped at it with the back of his hand. It came away a horrid shade of pink his mother called "Incrediberry" or "Glam Slam." One of those stupid names cosmetic companies thought were cute. Austin wasn't much on fashion, but he knew the names—and the colors—were a scam to get older women like his mom to buy them thinking that a shade of lipstick would make them young again.

"What'd you do that for?" he said. "God, Mom, not here in front of everyone. How many times do I have to tell you?"

The vodka fumes dissipated somewhat as she straightened in her seat. She was starting in on the Bloody Marys and Screwdrivers earlier and earlier these days. Austin took note of the stylish tennis dress she wore with a pink designer tennis sweater draped over her shoulders. It was a wonder she could drive let alone play tennis, but then she probably didn't bother taking her racquet out once she got to the club. Austin was pretty sure the pro at the club was giving her lessons in something besides tennis.

"Oh, right, I forgot," she said, her sweet smile turning to the sarcastic sneer she normally wore. "I might embarrass you. Whatever."

Austin yanked on the door handle and climbed out, his face already burning. He turned and tried to smile.

"I'll see you later, Mom."

She waved cheerily. "Don't forget, I have an appointment this afternoon."

"I'll get a ride home, don't worry." Austin glanced around to see who might be looking and quickly closed the door.

Four cars back, a hulking black SUV with tinted windows waited at the curb with its wheels already turned into the through lane. As soon as Austin's mom drove away, the SUV pulled out and followed at a discreet distance. Austin turned his head and watched an identical SUV turn into an empty slot in the faculty parking lot. Two men in suits climbed out as Austin walked to the front door of the main school building. They cut across the grassy lawn on a path that would intersect his, and fell in several yards behind him.

Inside, the dim hallway was empty. His footsteps echoed hollowly as he made his way to his classroom. He'd already missed half of fifth period and wondered for the umpteenth time why he had to go home for lunch. It would be so much easier to eat at school, but his mother insisted for some reason. Half the time she wasn't home anyway, so it didn't matter. Maybe if he brought it up he could convince his father that lunch at home was a dumb idea.

The door behind him opened with a huff of air and closed with a soft thunk. The footsteps of the pair behind him echoed in syncopated rhythm with his own. He didn't know why the government bothered with assigning a Secret Service detail to him. They did little to protect him. All they did was attract attention to him. Austin was sure he caught a lot more flak because he had a detail than he would have if they weren't around.

Muted voices from around a corner brought his attention back to his surroundings. He frowned. No one was supposed to be out of class. His pulse raced. All he needed now was a confrontation with a teacher, or worse, the headmaster. There was nothing for it. Ahead lay his class; behind tromped the Secret Service. He lowered his head and rounded the corner. The voices stopped. He raised his eyes and saw his worst nightmare.

Doug Herlihy slouched against a locker, spinning a basketball in the palm of his hand. His two homies, Blaise and Donnie, faced him with eager grins. All three turned simultaneously when Austin turned the corner, and their smiles grew wider. Austin broke into a cold sweat. The week before the trio had shaken him down for his allowance and had taken his iPod, too. The only reason he hadn't lost his phone to them, too, was because he'd plugged it into its charger and forgotten it that day. Normally, he kept a wide berth when he sensed any of them around. His heart beat faster. He didn't want to give up his phone to these yahoos. Heck, he didn't want to give them anything, but three against one, odds weren't in his favor. Who was he fooling? One on one, he'd still be chicken.

That's when he lost it. Sort of. The goons behind him were no use despite the Sig Sauer P229 pistols they carried. They wouldn't step in unless he was threatened by terrorists with assault rifles, or suicide bombers. He was on his own. Suddenly, the game app on his phone popped into his head. His avatar, Wolfsbane, took no crap from anyone or anything the game threw at him, from werewolves to vampires to zombies. With every step he took, he felt the strength of his alter ego spread from the steady pounding of his heart into his limbs. And the closer he got, the more his foes took on the likeness of the creatures in *Never Bitten*.

"Well, well," Doug said, pushing away from the locker. "What do we have here?"

Doug's canine teeth grew into long, sharp fangs and his brows drew together in an ominous, dark line. A chunk of rotted skin fell off Donnie's cheek, revealing jawbone and teeth. Blaise suddenly looked like he hadn't shaved in week. Rage coursed through Austin's body, and his vision turned red.

"Look, it's Afterthought!" Blaise snickered.

"Shut up." Austin said.

"More like afterbirth," Donnie slobbered, his left eye rolling half out of its socket.

"Shut up!" Doug commanded. He took a step forward and held out his hand. "Gotta pay a toll if you want to pass."

Austin picked up his pace. Only a few more steps now.

When Austin didn't slow, Doug's brow furrowed. "I'm not screwing around here, punk. Give it up."

Austin planted his foot inside Doug's reach and threw a punch into his midsection with all his weight behind it.

"Fuck off," he snarled, and walked away.

Doug doubled over in pain, mouth working like a fish to suck in oxygen. His buddies gaped at Austin as he strode away.

Austin felt his avatar slowly leave his body as if leaking through a small drain somewhere. In its place, Austin's muscles weakened to Jell-O and his knees quaked. But he held his head high and kept on walking. He thought of the threesome behind him and smiled.

Damn, that felt good.

8

The sound of voices intruded on Tess's concentration, causing her to hit the rewind button for the reader app on her laptop. She listened to the sentence again, but the voices still disrupted her focus. As if homework hadn't been hard enough when worried thoughts of Travis kept sneaking up on her. What an incredibly awful day it had been. With a sigh, she closed out of the reader. Nearly finished with the passage for Comp/Gov class anyway, she could listen to the rest before she went to bed. For now, she turned her attention to the voices elsewhere in the house.

Her hearing was no more acute than it had been before the accident. She just noticed sounds more without the sensory input of sight to occupy her brain. The same was true for her sense of smell, though she'd trained with Yoshi to process and recognize smells in a way someone might learn to read with their eyes. She couldn't smell any better than Oliver or anyone else, but her enhanced ability to recognize and name scents had prompted her reaction to Marcus earlier. While Oliver may have noticed an odor immediately, and even noted its unpleasantness, she'd noticed its components, its unusual nature and had tried to identify it. When she'd pointed it out to Oliver, he'd identified at least a portion of it—manure. Not dog poop, though. Something with a grassy note. And then there had been the other, metallic scent, unrelated to the manure.

Tess shrugged it off. She'd think about it later. The voices closed in despite the speakers' attempts to converse in hushed tones. Two people approached from the direction of the front of the house. Alice's voice was easily recognizable. But Tess didn't know the man she was talking to. Someone Alice knew, apparently. It must be a tradesman from one of the many services Alice employed to maintain the house and grounds. Tess waited, expecting them to pass by on their way to Alice's office, but they paused outside the library door. She held her breath.

The door opened.

"Tess?" Alice sounded tentative. "You have a visitor."

Footsteps crossed the hardwood to the Oriental rug under her feet that Tess still remembered so vividly. She stood and turned, facing the man as he stopped.

"I'm pleased to meet you, Tess," he said. He spoke softly but his voice was a resonant baritone. "My name is Jack Turnbull."

Tess put out her hand. "Nice to meet you, Mr. Turnbull."

He chuckled and shook her hand firmly. "It's General, actually, but please call me Jack. I was a friend of your father's, and even closer to your Uncle Travis."

"I'm surprised we've never met if you were friends with my dad."

"I spend most of my time in Washington, D.C., so it was difficult to find time to visit. Now I'm sorry I never did. I would like to have known you growing up. You've turned into an extraordinary young woman."

Definitely not ordinary, Tess thought ruefully. She didn't know anyone her age who was blind. But she didn't feel extraordinary in any sense. It was just one of those compliments adults pay when they're trying to be nice.

"Why did you want to see me?" She didn't feel comfortable using his name yet.

"I have something important I need to discuss with you," he said. "Perhaps somewhere a little more private?"

Tess gripped the back of the chair to keep her hand from shaking as her pulse quickened. "Alice?"

"It's all right, Tess," Alice said. "You can trust him."

"Then why the long discussion on the way in here?"

"You heard that?" Alice said, her voice incredulous.

"I didn't have to hear the words to know how long it was, and how heated, I might add."

Turnbull laughed, startling her. "She's ready, Alice. I told you not to worry."

"Ready for what?" Tess demanded. "I'm always the last to know what's going on around here."

"You can use James's office," Alice told the general. "It's clean." There was a pause then Alice said, "Yoshi sweeps it every day. I don't trust anyone else."

"That will be fine," Turnbull said. "Tess? I assume you know where it is."

Tess was still digesting what Alice had said. Though he often had a broom in his hands, Yoshi didn't do indoor housework. Which meant that Alice was referring to bugs, the electronic kind.

Tess shook her head. She still couldn't get used to the fact that Alice and Yoshi were much more than they purported to be. Her whole life Tess had thought of them as an odd appendage to her family. She knew they were housekeeper and gardener, but they'd always felt more like eccentric relatives. Two weeks earlier, they'd fended off three armed attackers with their bare hands.

"Tess?" Alice's voice broke through her thoughts.

"Yes, of course I know," Tess said. "Follow me."

Tess turned ninety degrees and counted off the number of paces she knew would take her to the bookcases along the wall. She put her hands out and felt along the shelves, fingers nimbly taking in information and letting her know where she stood. They found the edge of a section, counted books in toward the center of the shelf and stopped. Tess tipped three books back on their spines and reached in over them until her fingers touched the small wood panel that slid aside, revealing a hidden keypad. She tapped in the remembered sequence and heard the familiar click. She righted the books, grasped the edge of the shelf with her fingertips and pulled. The entire section swung out on well-oiled hinges.

The general let out a low whistle. "I'll be damned. A panic room. Very clever."

"It's my dad's office," Tess corrected him.

"And a very nice one at that," he said, his voice moving past her into the room beyond. "James always did keep things close to the vest. Travis didn't keep many secrets from me, but James was a different story."

She followed him inside, burning with curiosity about his comments, and pulled the bookcase shut behind her. Inside her father's office, the door was simply a section of wood-paneled wall, but between the two sides the door contained both soundproofing and a sandwich of thick steel and Kevlar plates with sand as the filling. The door alone weighed several tons, more than the doors on most bank vaults. As she turned around, she caught the subtle scents of leather and something woodsy, comforting smells that made her think of the grandparents she never knew.

"I apologize for the intrusion," Turnbull said. "But I need your help."

"*My* help?"

He took her arm gently and steered her to a chair. "Let me explain and maybe you won't be so surprised. I've been a friend of your family for a long time. I knew your grandparents."

"But—"

"I know. They died before you were born."

Her father had never talked about it much, but Tess had been aware of having no grandparents like other kids when she was growing up. Her mother's parents, too, had died when Tess was still a toddler.

"Why does everyone in this family die so young?" she said.

"Just rotten luck is all." The general's voice was soft. "I was stationed at Ft. Irwin in California back then, and I knew the boys when they were growing up—your father, James, and Travis. Your grandparents died when the boys were still fairly young, though there's an age gap between them. I think James might have just turned twenty at the time. Travis was maybe eleven or twelve. Their parents hadn't planned for it, of course, so there was no will, no instructions."

"How did they get by?" Tess knew her father had been resourceful, but couldn't imagine what it would be like to take responsibility for a younger sibling after losing her parents.

"Ted and Joanie—your grandparents—had life insurance, and they'd been doing pretty well so they had some money set aside. The boys were taken care of financially. But I was concerned about them, so I petitioned the court for guardianship, which it granted. The boys continued to live in the house, but I kept tabs on them. I was so proud of Travis when he joined the military. Of course, I was proud of your father, too, for getting him through the teen years. Sally—your mom—helped, too, even before she and James got married."

"What does this have to do with me?"

The general chuckled. "Sorry. I got caught up in my own story. I just wanted you to have some background, Tess, so you get a feel for who I am and understand my position here. I've been on the board of directors of your dad's company ever since he started developing computer games in your grandparents' garage. James asked me to be the first director, in fact, even before he asked his own dad, your grandfather. Here's the thing; I'm sure you know that your parents left the company to you."

"I know it's in some kind of trust fund until I turn eighteen. Uncle Travis controls my shares until then."

"Exactly right. But Travis is missing."

Tess thought about the implications. "Which means the shares come back to me."

"Well, technically they're yours anyway, but until you turn eighteen you still don't control those shares, which means you can't vote unless the board of directors approves. Or, the board could appoint an interim guardian."

"Which you don't want because you might not be able to control which way the shares are voted."

"You're quick, Tess. How'd you learn that?"

She shrugged. "Guess I paid more attention to dad's dinner table talk than I thought."

"Good for you. That helps. I won't have to explain everything. There's a board meeting coming up, which is why I'm here and why I was supposed to meet Travis."

"You want me to come if he doesn't show up before then."

"Yes, I do."

"But I don't know anything about running dad's company."

"I don't think you'll have to vote on any issues. All I want to do is buy some time until we find Travis."

"And if we don't?" Tess swallowed hard. She didn't want to consider the possibility.

9

Travis shivered. Glad he'd thought to take a coat that morning, he hugged his arms and reassessed his situation for the hundredth time. From all outward appearances, his prospects wouldn't excite a Vegas bookie. He'd been grabbed by pros. They'd snatched him with military precision, and had spared little expense. Whoever was behind it had money and resources. Probably the same people who had tried to get to Tess a couple weeks before. He didn't know who they were or what they wanted. He had no idea where he was or how long they would keep him here. They'd taken all his personal possessions—wallet, cell phone, keys—except his watch. He wondered if they'd overlooked it, or let him keep it as part of some psychological game they wanted to play.

He could handle the games. Part of his training for SICC had been special interrogation techniques, psychological torture and even Psy Ops. Psychology had been as potent a weapon in Afghanistan as an M16 or an IED. He'd dangled rewards and wielded punishment depending on what he and his team wanted to accomplish. Make friends, do favors, provide cash and resources when you wanted to build trust and create allies. Bully, threaten, harass and intimidate those you wanted to keep in line. Six years of navigating his way through the intricate ethnic, tribal, religious, and political intricacies of the relationships in tribal Afghanistan had given him plenty of experience. But perhaps nothing had prepared him for psychological games than growing up as the little brother of one of the all-time genius game theorists in the world.

He'd worshipped James, wanted to *be* James. He'd devoured James's comic book collection during the hour after school before James got home, and later James's graphic novels. He'd begged James for a mini-version of James's skateboard so Travis could come to the skate park with him on weekends, even knowing that he'd spend most of his time running errands for James and his friends instead of boarding and learning new tricks. They'd teased him mercilessly, sent him on fool's errands, made him the object of their jokes and pranks. He never gave up, and knew that James had secretly respected him for it. It had never been about skateboarding, or mimicking his brother. It had been about getting close to James. He'd never been as good as James on a board anyway. When James had taken up laser tag, though, Travis found a game at which he excelled, something he did better than his smarter, bigger, stronger, older brother.

Barstow, California, had felt like the last outpost on Earth, a small piece of civilization before the desert consumed everything that wasn't scaly, spiny, poisonous or all three. Hotter than Hades in the summer and colder than a witch's tit in the winter, at least after dark, the environs around the town were among the most inhospitable on the planet. And the town itself didn't have much going for it—a handful of mom-and-pop and fast food restaurants, a movie theater and not much else in the way of what you'd call culture. But it did have one of the biggest train yards west of the Mississippi. A perfect place to stage battles.

Travis's small size, stealth and speed served as advantages in the day-long games, and his unerring aim had made him an effective combatant that James and his friends had soon fought over when selecting teams. He'd taken those same skills into the army and used them to root out Al Qaeda members in the northwest provinces of Afghanistan.

Travis shook the memories out of his head and made another tour of his prison cell. The watch they'd let him keep had an illuminated dial. He'd tried to use it as sparingly as possible since he couldn't remember the last time he'd changed the watch's battery. He pushed the button and held his wrist out in front of him. The blue-green glow barely permeated the murk. He moved quickly around the space's perimeter, eyes scanning everything at the edges of the glow.

Rough rock walls about ten or twelve feet apart rose and arched to meet each other about nine feet off a packed dirt floor littered with gravel and small stones, some as large as his fist. At one end, a rusted steel grate stretched the width of the tunnel, the bars at the edges embedded in the rock wall. A hinged section the size of a French door was latched and locked. Fifty feet in the opposite direction, a rockslide or cave-in had blocked the tunnel save for a small black space near the roof about two feet in diameter. The craggy walls, though irregular, revealed nothing on his first two passes.

On the dirt and gravel floor, two parallel iron rails ran the length of the tunnel, continuing on past the steel grate at one end and disappearing under the pile of rock and rubble on the other. Oxidation had dusted them with a russet patina, an indication of how long it had been since an ore cart had rolled through. A few of the wood ties under the rails had dried and split in places, but having no weather to contend with, most had survived the years with almost no sign of aging.

The glowing dial blinked off, plunging the tunnel into total darkness. Travis shivered again, blew on his cupped hands and swung his arms a few times before hugging them around his chest. He guessed the ambient temperature at around fifty degrees, maybe a little lower. He faced the real danger of hypothermia if he didn't keep moving. He shoved his hand in his coat pockets, stuck an elbow out until it brushed the jagged wall and walked toward the mouth of the tunnel reviewing what he knew.

They'd dumped him in an old, abandoned mine. Here in the western half of the country odds were this tunnel had been mined for gold, silver or some other less precious metal, maybe copper. Without an actual map to check, he figured a silver, gold or copper mine within a few hours radius by jet could put him in any of about ten states and a couple of Canadian provinces. Even if he found a way to pinpoint his location more accurately, he had no way to communicate it to would-be rescuers in the outside world.

Waiting was the worst part. He could handle whatever games they threw at him, could even handle physical torture if it came to that. But the waiting would eat at him unless he kept his mind active, working the angles, coming up with a plan. First he had to be patient and see if they kept any sort of routine schedule. Images of the Barstow train yard flashed through his mind again. James and his friends had ganged up on him mercilessly in their war games at first, sidelining him early so they could focus on each other. Until Travis learned not to let them play him or lure him out of hiding places. Until Travis learned patience. Rather than stalking his prey, Travis had learned to find the vantage points and wait for the others to come within range. When they eventually did, he took them out silently, never giving away his position. The thrill of winning had been addictive.

His stomach growled now, reminding him that he hadn't eaten breakfast that morning. He had reserves of strength, and if he conserved his energy to stay as warm as possible, he could last several days at least. But if they didn't feed him soon, without fuel his body would succumb to the cold more quickly. Dwelling on it wouldn't do any good. He forced himself to think of something else.

Time to take another look around his prison to see if he could find a way to break out.

10

Senator Jeremy Latham brushed a hand through the mane of silver hair, sweeping it off his high forehead like the crest of a wave. The phone rang as he strode into his expansive office in the Russell Senate Office Building in Washington. Those of his aides who hadn't gone home yet were tied up in meetings with aides of other senators, wrangling over wording of legislation that had his fingerprints on it. He snatched up the receiver without pausing as he rounded the corner of his desk.

"Latham," he snapped.

"The package is secure," said a muffled voice.

Latham automatically glanced around the office, taking in the plush Oriental rug, the polished antique mahogany furniture, the heavy damask curtains framing windows darkened by a night sky, looking for anything out of place.

"I told you never to call me on this line," Latham said gruffly.

"You weren't answering your cell phone," the voice said.

Latham fingered the phone cord and rolled his eyes as if he might spot some patience hiding on the high ceiling. "I just came from a subcommittee meeting over in the Capitol building. There's no cell service in the subway tunnel."

"You don't have to be patronizing, *sir*. I'm just doing my job."

Offending people was just fine with Latham. The rank stupidity he encountered on a daily basis staggered the mind. Reminding people of their place in the world—in the food chain, more like—should serve as a warning and keep them on their toes. Too many ignored the hint, or missed it completely, and the unsuspecting usually were summarily eaten or simply shoved aside by those more powerful.

"Your *job*," Latham said between barely clenched teeth, "is to follow instructions. If I tell you not to call me on this line, don't dial this number. If I tell you to report in at a specific time and you can't reach me on a secure phone, then you wait and try again in a few minutes. Is that clear? I don't know where your superior finds people like you."

"Excuse me, sir, but I was with Cy—"

"No names!" Latham barked. "For god's sake, use your head! What did I just tell you?"

"I'll call you back, sir," the voice said quietly.

Latham slammed the receiver down, breathing heavily. He closed his eyes and rubbed the back of his neck. Easing into his desk chair, he slowed his breathing and consciously relaxed his muscles starting with his toes and working his way up. He'd gotten as far as his torso when the disposable cell phone in his suit coat pocket chirped. He pulled it out and pressed the talk button.

"Report," he said.

"We intercepted the subject at oh-seven-forty and seized him without incident. No witnesses. We transported him to the prearranged location, where he's now secured."

"He's had no contact with anyone?"

"Other than the apprehension team, no. No one spoke to him during transport, and he didn't seem interested in starting up a conversation."

Latham glanced at the gold Patek Philippe watch on his wrist, a $50,000 gift from an ardent supporter and campaign contributor.

"He's been confined for, what, about six or seven hours now?" He went on without waiting for an answer. "Let him stew overnight."

"What about food and water?"

"Do what you want. As long as you keep him out of action until after the board meeting."

"Why not just kill him?"

"Because we need him," Latham snapped.

"Fine. I'll take care of it."

"See that you do."

Latham ended the call and slipped the phone in his pocket. He leaned back and stared at the ceiling for a moment, envisioning a global chessboard in his mind, the pieces representing governments, world leaders, tribal warlords, weapons programs, intelligence agencies, and more. Some of them he controlled directly and some indirectly. Outcomes were what mattered, outcomes beneficial not to America or some foolish notion like patriotism, but to Jeremy Latham and the men he represented. What mattered was the balance of power, and only he and a handful of others could control that.

No one, not the president of the United States or the leaders of the European Union or the president of China, to name a few, knew how little they had to do with how events played out on the world stage. The most powerful countries in the world were mere game pieces for Latham and his group to move about at whim to suit their own goals—money and power. That's what it came down to, wasn't it? The world belonged to those with money and power. Without them, a person had nothing.

A faint smile came to his lips as he stood up and walked to the ornate liquor cart in the corner. He chose a cut crystal decanter of Scotch single malt whisky, poured some into a matching tumbler and raised the glass to his nose. Scents of sherry, oak, raisins, almonds and peat smoke wafted up from the glass. He raised the glass higher still in a toast—to money and power.

11

The distant drone of a small airplane engine floated into the silent classroom. A scarlet flush crept up Tess's neck into her face, ticking off the rising degrees of her discomfort.

Madame Villeneuve grimaced and gave a little nod, her gaze shifting from Tess to the rest of the class. *"D'accord. C'est ça. Quelqu'un d'autre?"*

A couple of students chimed in with answers simultaneously, and the classroom's normal volume resumed.

I leaned toward Tess. "What is wrong with you?" I hissed. "We covered this material before I left yesterday."

Spine rigid, face forward, Tess refused to answer. I sat back and picked up the conversation, trying to catch up on my notes. I'd barely started when the bell rang. I gathered up the papers, textbook and pen, stuffed them into Tess's backpack and slung it over my shoulder. She stood, still stiff with embarrassment, and jerked away when I took her arm.

"Just walk and get us out of here," she mumbled. "I'll manage."

"Fine." I turned to go. A slight tug on the backpack strap told me she'd grabbed on and I heard her shuffling out behind me.

In the hall, Tess's hand on my shoulder, I slalomed through the throngs of constantly moving students, intent on getting to Johnson's music class on time.

Tess tugged me into a lower gear. "Oliver, slow down!"

Grudgingly, I shortened my stride. She slid her hand down my arm until it rested on my forearm and came up next to me.

"You're mad at me," she said.

"No, just disappointed."

She went on the defensive. "You're not the one who has to know everything. No one's calling on you in class."

"You're wrong, Tess. I do have to know everything. I have to know all the stuff they teach you, and all the stuff your teachers leave out just in case it comes up on a quiz or a test. That's my job. If I don't make sure you understand all the material—all of it— then it's my fault, not yours if you don't do well."

She gave me the silent treatment.

"What's the problem, Tess? You've been acting weird all morning."

"I have a lot going on, that's all."

I put my hand on hers and pulled her aside to avoid a group of freshman boys dashing by.

"You always have a lot going on." I paused. "Look, I know you're worried about Travis."

"What I'm worried about," she blurted, "is that he won't let me go to tolo."

I frowned and shifted to edge sideways through the music room door ahead of her. Inside, the decibel level dropped about 75 percent.

I lowered my voice. "That's, like, a Sadie Hawkins-type dance?"

She nodded and shuffled her feet as I led her slowly to a chair at an empty table. I eased into the chair beside hers.

"That's what you argued with Travis about yesterday, wasn't it?"

She bit her lower lip and nodded. "There's a guy I want to ask."

"And your uncle doesn't approve."

"He doesn't even want me to go."

I was probably shooting myself in the foot, but my mouth started moving before my brain had a chance to work it out. "I'll talk to him."

"What good will that do?"

"He's worried he can't protect you. Where's the dance? In the commons?"

"Yes, but we don't stay there all night. I mean, we have pictures at someone's house first, then we go out to dinner somewhere. We might spend some time at the dance, and then there's usually a party at someone's house after."

"Let me think about it. I'll figure something out."

"Really? You really think you can convince him?"

"I'll do my best."

At the front of the room, Mr. Johnson rapped a conductor's baton on the edge of his desk. "All right, class, let's get started."

I didn't bother with notes. Johnson's course was mostly an exercise in listening, and Tess could handle that. Historical context I could pick up from the textbook later. I spent most of the class wondering how I was going to convince Travis to let Tess go to this tolo thing. More interesting was why I'd want to help her go out with some high school dork in the first place. Then again, it shouldn't have mattered to me one way or the other. I had no designs on Tess. I mean, I was a grad student—at least I had been before my grandparents spent the trust money that was supposed to be for my education—and she was only a junior, in high school no less. So that meant my concern was fraternal, platonic. Crap, I was turning into a boring, conservative adult like Travis.

Assisting Tess was supposed to be a simple job, something that would help me pay the rent without resorting to wearing a funny hat, a button that said, "Hi! My name is Oliver!" and asking people if they wanted ketchup with their fries. When had life become so complicated?

Since I'd already dipped a toe in these waters, on the way to the commons at lunch I demonstrated my good sportsmanship and irreplaceable value by sticking my whole foot in.

"So who's this guy you want to invite?" I kept my tone nonchalant.

"To tolo? Tim Daley."

"Nice guy? Is he cute? Why am I asking? Of course he is or you wouldn't want to ask him."

"You're smarter than you look."

"Ha, ha, very funny. I'd ask you to point him out, but you probably don't know what he looks like."

"Ha, ha yourself," she said. "Aren't you clever."

If I were smart I wouldn't have gotten myself into this situation. And if I were clever, I'd figure out how to get one of Tess's friends to give me the skinny on Tim Daley. I snaked through the crowds of kids milling in and around the tables jockeying for seats. Her hand resting lightly on my shoulder, Tess stayed close and kept pace as I maneuvered.

"You know I have to check this guy out before I go to bat for you," I said.

"You're kidding, right? No way. You are *not* going to interview my date."

"Yeah, well, you're not going unless I convince Travis."

I spotted Matt sitting at a table off to the side, empty chairs next to him suggesting he'd come down with flu, or social leprosy. I angled toward him anyway. As far as I remembered we still liked him, and since my high school years were behind me I was immune to clique syndrome.

"Found a couple of places for us," I said over my shoulder. "Come on."

Matt didn't look up when we took seats next to him, eyes and fingers glued to the touch screen of his smart phone. He grunted when I said hello, but his concentration didn't waver.

"Hey, Matt, what are you doing?" Tess said.

He turned away with another grunt, shoved his feet out in front of him and crossed his ankles. He slouched in the chair, lunch on the table in front of him untouched.

I leaned down next to her ear. "He's busy playing *Never Bitten*. Can't talk. What do you want for lunch?"

"The usual."

"Turkey sandwich, whole wheat, Jack cheese, avocado, lettuce, no tomato, hold the mayo?"

"You remembered." Like sun breaking through clouds, her expression lightened for an instant then fell back into shadow. "Oh, right."

Her disappointment took a swing at me, but only landed a glancing blow. Of course I remembered. An eidetic memory meant I could recite most of our conversations since the day we met word for word.

"I'll be right back," I told her.

Only a couple of kids stood in line at the sandwich station, so I didn't wait long. The girls ahead of me chatted amiably about a friend who'd hosted a party the weekend before while her parents had been out of town. Someone had posted it on Twitter and the resulting crowd had trashed the house, stolen several bottles of liquor, and been rousted by the police because of the noise. According to the pair in front of me, the girl hadn't even gotten in trouble with her parents. I wondered if there were any adults in that house even when the parents were home.

I ordered and paid for two sandwiches, and when I turned, a commotion broke out at the table where I'd left Tess. Too far away to hear the exact words, the gist of the confrontation seemed pretty clear. A kid I recognized from the baseball team thought Matt's feet were in the way and kicked them under the table. I left the line and hustled back.

Matt jumped up and shoved the kid. "Back off, asshole!"

Even over the normal din, Matt issued the command loudly enough to turn heads.

Nearly a foot taller than Matt, the kid stepped forward and shoved back, hard. Matt stumbled into his chair. More heads turned and several people ran toward the table as a chant broke out, "Fight! Fight!" As the kid towered over him, Matt leaned to one side and dug into a backpack on the floor. I shouldered my way between a couple of guys who'd stood up to see better and opened my mouth to tell them to cool it when Matt jumped up on the table.

"I said back off!" Matt screamed.

The kid looked up at him and laughed. "Yeah, or what, dork-face?"

"This, you dick!" Matt yelled. He waved a pistol in the air.

"Gun!" someone shouted.

"Matt, what are you doing?" Tess cried. "What's going on?"

I elbowed more kids aside in my haste to get back to her, adrenaline now sending my heartbeat into double time.

"Matt!" I yelled. "Don't do it!"

Matt held the pistol over his head and pulled the trigger. The shot sounded like a stick of dynamite going off in the big, high-ceilinged room. For an instant, the commons went silent, then a girl screamed, and another, and the room erupted in pandemonium. Kids nearest the courtyard doors burst through outside, and a crowd pressed toward the hallway that ran perpendicular to the far end.

"I warned you!" Matt screamed. "Would you listen? No, because you're all stupid, dumb, dick-heads! I'm not gonna take it anymore, you hear?"

His rant registered in some corner of my consciousness, but I'd already sprinted the rest of the way to the table while Matt turned a slow pirouette. I reached Tess when Matt's back was turned. The blood had drained from her face, turning her kabuki white. Shock froze her in place. I crouched next to her, yanked her off the chair onto the floor and shoved her under the table.

"Stay there!" I whispered hoarsely.

Slowly poking my head out from under the table, I raised my eyes over the edge. Matt continued screaming, but the shouting and bedlam in the crowd nearly drowned out the words. The kid who'd confronted him elbowed his way toward an exit in a panic.

"Come back here, you bastard!" Matt shrieked. "I'm not done with you!"

Without thinking, I stood up, grabbed the round table by the edge and lifted it straight up, tipping the whole thing over. Matt went up in the air as his feet went out from under him. The gun fired again as he waved his arms wildly to get his balance. I stood the table vertically on its edge, and gave it an extra shove into Matt's body as he fell. Rolling the table out of the way, I leaped over Tess and landed on top of Matt. His breath left him with a whoosh. Sitting on his chest, my eyes and hands went for the gun still in his fingers.

Pinning his wrist to the floor with one hand, I twisted the gun out of his fingers with the other. Tears of pain sprang into his eyes and as he looked at me, sudden comprehension changed his expression from fury to horror.

"Oliver? Oh, god, oh, god, I'm sorry, I'm sorry," he mumbled. "What have I done? It's the app, man. I didn't mean to do it. It's the app."

12

Tess lay on the cold concrete floor, shaking like Jell-O in an earthquake. The uproar surrounding her battered her in waves. Screams still echoed from the far edges of the room, and she could only imagine the stampede caused by the students' panic. Deeper voices shouted now, telling the students not to be alarmed, and to walk, not run. How could they not be unnerved? Matt had just fired a gun in the commons. *Matt had a gun!* Amid all the shuffling feet and loud voices, Tess heard Matt's voice close by, alternately babbling softly and keening like a small child with a stomachache.

Something hard pressed into her hip, and her fingertips went exploring, closing around a smooth rectangular object that fit into her palm. A cell phone, but not hers. *Matt's.* Keeping her hand by her side she slipped the phone into the front pocket of her jeans without thinking. Deep down a little voice told her that taking the phone was wrong. The commotion in the commons drowned it out.

"Oliver?" she said tentatively. She reached out her hand. Strong fingers closed over hers.

"I'm here, Tess. It's okay. Everything's going to be okay."

"What's wrong with Matt? Is he hurt?"

"He's okay. He's just—"

"Drop the weapon!" a voice boomed, so close that Tess jumped. "Drop it now!"

"Okay, okay," Oliver said. "I was just keeping it safe."

"Put it on the ground!" the voice said. "Do it now!"

"It's down, okay?" Oliver said.

"He didn't do anything!" Tess said, her voice shrill in her ears.

"Now slide it over, slowly. All the rest of you, don't move. And everyone keep quiet."

Tess followed the scraping sound as the gun traveled across the floor from left to right. She finally recognized the voice; it belonged to John Kelly, the school's huge security guard.

"That's good" Kelly said. "Get comfy, 'cause we're gonna sit here and wait for the cops."

"Oliver didn't do anything," Tess said again, controlling her emotions this time.

Oliver muttered, "Except maybe save your life."

Rubbing her elbow where it had smacked the floor when Oliver pulled her down, Tess ignored the comment.

"If that's you John Kelly, you have to listen to me," Tess said. "Matt's the one who pulled a gun. I think he needs help. He just went crazy."

"And you saw all this, did you?" the security guard said.

"I *heard* it, which is almost as good," she said. "Oliver was getting me a sandwich when it happened. He—"

"Uh-unh. Don't say another word. You can tell it all to the cops."

Approaching footsteps clacked on the hard floor. Tess realized that the room had gone quiet except for Matt's whispered refrain, "Sorry, so sorry; the app made me do it."

"What's going on, John?" a new voice said. Tess knew this was Greg Olton, the assistant principal. "Students are saying someone shot a gun in here. The building is in lock-down."

"Someone fired a gun all right," John said. "Not sure who yet."

"Matt did!" Tess said. "Listen to him. He's saying how sorry he is. He didn't mean it. He just went nuts when Joe Pistarro pushed him."

"Like I said, we'll wait for the cops."

"Are you all right, Miss Barrett?" Mr. Olton said. He took her arm and helped her up.

"I'm fine. Really."

Mr. Olton led her to a chair. She sat, rubbing her hands in her lap, wishing she could see what was going on. Tears sprang to her eyes, and she blinked them back. A thought like that hadn't entered her head in a while. Not only had she not felt sorry for herself in the last week or so, she'd actually been moving through her routines as if blindness was natural to her. Well, there was nothing natural about having two useless orbs in the front of your face that did nothing but leak saltwater. She swiped at her face with the back of her hand hoping no one saw her.

Two patrol officers arrived a minute or two later, followed by two detectives a few minutes after that. The officers organized students still in place into groups of witnesses—those who'd seen the altercation from start to finish, and those who'd seen only bits and pieces. They cleared a couple of tables, for interviews, and then had Mr. Olton and John Kelly send the rest of the kids back to their classrooms. Announcements had gone out over the school intercom, and by now several teachers had arrived to help calm and escort students out of the commons.

One of the detectives introduced himself to Tess, and asked if he could ask her some questions about what had happened. He spoke in a gentle tone and seemed to genuinely care about her feelings. The problem was she didn't know how she felt. She was angry with Oliver for dragging her off the chair onto the floor, but part of her was touched that he'd thought her life was in danger. And she was even angrier with herself for freezing up when Matt had fired the gun. Just because she'd been in the middle of a firefight up in the mountains two weeks earlier with bullets flying everywhere was no reason for her to panic every time she heard a loud noise.

Tess also worried about Matt, about what would happen to him. He'd be expelled, for sure, and his shot at college, let alone the scholarships he'd seemed a shoo-in for, had probably vanished in the puff of smoke that issued from the barrel of his pistol. His behavior had been so un-Matt-like that she had a hard time reconciling what he'd done with the person she'd known all through middle school and high school. She conveyed this to the detective. He nodded and told her not to feel badly. He said it was pretty common for people in these situations to say they never expected someone they knew to snap the way Matt had.

But Tess felt there was more to it than that. Matt hadn't just been pushed to a breaking point. He'd been teased before, something that was bound to happen to a nerdy guy like him. Not that she thought he was a geek. He was just smart, and had other interests besides things like sports or cars. Guys like Toby and his friends didn't know what to do with that, so they made fun of it, attacked it. Matt was small, not exactly athletic, but he was tough. He shrugged off the taunts. He made light of the teasing, even turning it on his tormentors, belittling their shortcomings with an acid wit that made her laugh. And he'd been key to helping her and Oliver decipher the clues that had led them to discover a software program her father had hidden in fragments on memory devices in several places. No matter what Matt had done, she owed him her friendship and loyalty. But she didn't know what she could do to help him out of this jam. Bringing a gun to school was serious enough. Firing it...

When the detective finished asking questions, he left her alone at the table. She heard low voices around her, and imagined that students were being interviewed at other tables scattered around the commons. She had no idea where Oliver was, or even whether the police had taken him away. She fidgeted, and caught herself chewing on a fingernail several times. Each time she put her hand in her lap it would somehow make its way to the top of the table and eventually to the corner of her mouth.

Some time later, another policeman came to her table and introduced himself. He spoke more gruffly than the first, and his questions were more direct, more probing. She didn't know why, but he made her feel guilty.

"I've answered all these questions," she said finally. "I went over this with the other detective."

"I know," he said, sounding human for the first time, "and I'm sorry about that. But we like people to go over events again while they're still fresh in their minds. Sometimes they remember things the second time through that they didn't think of at first."

Tess mulled the thought silently for a moment. She didn't think she could forget what had happened, but when she ran through it again in her mind, other details came into focus—the smell of gym locker and sweaty socks when Joe Pistarro had first accosted Matt, and gunpowder after the sharp report; the scent of Oliver's shampoo when he'd pulled her to the floor; the sounds of her heart banging against her ribs and blood singing in her ears. None of which was pertinent to the detective's questions.

Matt had been taken away shortly after the police had arrived, still muttering about the game app. But the police held the rest of them for another hour before conceding they'd questioned everyone who'd actually seen what had happened. Oliver finally came and found her, and silently walked her out to the car. Her fingers on his shoulder felt the tension in his body.

"I'm worried about Matt," she said.

"Yeah, well, you could've backed me up a little more in there," Oliver replied.

"I did! I told them you didn't do it. You heard me. How can you say that?"

"The big guy—what's his name? John? He saw me with the gun in my hand, so the cops treated me like I was the suspect. They grilled me for almost two hours—like about why I didn't have a student ID, and why I was even here at school at all if I wasn't a student."

"Hey, sorry, but I did say Matt fired the gun."

"You're right. I apologize. It's just... I don't like cops asking me questions. It makes me feel like I should confess everything I ever did, like the time I snuck a cookie off a plate when my grandmother wasn't looking."

"Chunk," she said, a memory flashing through her mind. "You know, in *Goonies*?"

"You saw that movie? It's so old."

She nodded. "On TV, when I was a kid. I loved it. I told you, my dad and I were into all that buried treasure, secret code stuff."

Oliver opened the car door for her. She ducked her head, got in and buckled up. A few moments later the driver-side door opened and Oliver climbed in next to her.

"What are we going to do about Matt?" she said.

"There's nothing we can do. He's pretty much screwed."

"Didn't you hear him, Oliver? He said it had something to do with that game he's been playing."

"The app made me do it? Come on, Tess, you really think that's the defense he should go with? Might as well plead temporary insanity and be done with it."

"People are always saying video games make kids more violent."

"You believe that? Television and video games might desensitize us to violence, but there's no proven link."

"Still, we need to find out more about that game. We don't even know who makes it."

"That's easy enough to find out. I'll call Derek. He should know. Hang on a sec."

Tess and Oliver had met Derek Hamblin a couple of weeks earlier when Travis had pulled Derek into the intrigue that had nearly gotten Tess and Oliver killed. A brilliant "coder" like Tess's father had been, Derek had helped Travis figure out the meaning of the fragments of software that Tess kept finding. But when Derek had learned Tess might be in danger, he'd done what he could to help her.

"Derek, it's Oliver... Yeah, good, we're good... Say, listen, Tess and I were wondering if you knew who put out that new game app everyone's addicted to... MondoHard? You're kidding... You're not?"

"Uncle Travis wouldn't do that," Tess said. "He wouldn't let the company put out a game that could hurt people!"

"Shush! I can't hear. What's that, Derek? ...We're on our way now."

13

Cold had seeped through tissue, muscle and sinew, down into his very bones. Travis groaned involuntarily from the pain as he stood and straightened stiffened joints. He'd managed a few hours of sleep between bouts of exercise to keep warm. The last time he'd closed his eyes, however, he'd intended to get only twenty or thirty minutes of shut-eye. Instead, sleep had pulled him down deep for nearly two hours, and his body now paid the price. He stretched and flashed the lighted dial on his watch. Not quite six in the morning. As if suddenly aware of the time, his stomach rumbled with hunger.

He felt his way to the center of the tunnel and slowly worked his way through a series of martial arts forms. They couldn't be called *poom-sae*, *taolu* or *kata* because they didn't adhere to one style or another. The army had taught him that all was fair in war, which meant the close-quarters fighting style they taught was about how to kill, maim or disable an enemy combatant as quickly as possible. Barring that, they'd taught him how to survive.

He moved slowly, concentrating on breathing and balance, treating the forms almost like the balletic motion of *tai chi*. As he moved, he thought of the last time he'd been this cold. To the best of his recollection, it had been his second winter in Afghanistan. Sill new to the ways of the tribal people in the mountain villages northeast of Kabul, Travis had spent two months trying to befriend a man that the Strategic Intelligence Collection & Containment (SICC) unit believed was second-in-command to a local warlord. The man was chief of his *khel*, or family group, and distrustful of strangers, al Qaeda and the Taliban, in that order. Travis had been a stranger, but he spoke Pashto, so he'd spent weeks just asking questions and listening.

When the *malik*, the tribal elder, had grown comfortable with Travis's presence, Travis had asked him what he wanted most for his village. The man had said simply, "Water for our crops." The answer had surprised Travis. The winter had been cold—in the teens at night and the 20s during the day—with a lot of snowpack. All Travis had had to keep him warm was the traditional dress of woolen *salwar qmis* over layers of cotton robes. He would have given a couple months' pay for thick socks, insulated combat boots, a decent coat and a good pair of gloves. The village had plenty of water, just no way to store and distribute it. In the spring when the ground had thawed, Travis had helped the villagers construct an irrigation system that collected snowmelt and channeled it into ditches to be used when crops were planted.

The memory made him smile as he moved through his forms. Despite the fact that the primary purpose of the SICC unit was to identify and assassinate enemy targets, he and his teammates had done a lot of good works in Afghanistan. Within minutes, his core had warmed considerably, and within twenty minutes, he'd started to break a sweat. He stopped. The chill would affect him more quickly if his clothes were damp.

To keep busy, he explored his "cell" once again, methodically starting at the hole atop the rockslide. With an unerring sense of time, a colony of bats had funneled through the opening the previous evening at dusk, at least by Travis's watch. The cloud had navigated neatly through the barred gate at the other end and disappeared into the blackness beyond. During the night, Travis had heard their chirrups as they'd returned, singly or in groups, having eaten their fill of insects. He'd been able to widen the opening somewhat, but there was no sense in breaking his back trying to move the really large stones since that direction led deeper into the mine.

Carefully picking his way down the slide in the dark, his feet found level ground again. He knelt until his groping hands found one of the steel rails in the dark. His empathy for Tess and her situation grew steadily. Finding his way in the pitch dark was frustrating, maddening. To be sightless all the time...? Travis had difficulty imagining it. His hands moved along each side of the rail stopping when they reached a tie to grip the heads of the spikes and test them for looseness. After ten minutes, he found one. Splintered by rot, the tie had relaxed its hold on a spike, allowing Travis to wiggle it a fraction of an inch. He pried and pulled at it with his fingers, almost numb now from the cold. The spike barely budged, but it did wobble a teeny bit.

Travis cupped his hands and blew on his fingers to warm them. He stood up again to loosen knee and hip joints creaky from stooping so long. For an instant, the walls appeared to move. Freezing in place, his eyes roamed right and left. Suddenly, the walls flickered again. He whirled around and faced the steel gate across the tunnel. Far down the dark tube, the rock walls glimmered dimly. Someone coming. Travis squatted with his back to the wall and waited.

The light grew brighter, illuminating the walls of the tunnel closer and closer until its source rounded the curved tunnel walls, a flat, white disc shining so brightly its intensity blinded him. He shielded his eyes from the direct glare of the spotlight beam and tried to make out the figure behind it. Someone tall, judging from the height of the spotlight above the floor. Whoever carried the light kept it aimed at Travis's face, intentionally blinding him. Travis swung his gaze away and looked the other direction to let his eyes adjust. At this distance, the light now revealed details about his prison he could not have seen by the glow of his watch face. Blue seams ran in jagged lines up the rock walls like veins standing out on his arms after lifting weights. A sure sign of copper.

"Who are you?" Travis said as he faced the tunnel mouth again, careful to keep his gaze down. "What do you want?"

His questions were met with silence. The only sounds were the rustle of paper and muted clanks of something bumping the bars of the mine gate. The light retreated. In a few moments, whoever held it turned and walked away, disappearing around the bend in the tunnel.

While the flickering illumination still allowed him some vision, Travis quickly approached the mine gate and investigated the paper sack left there. Inside he found a liter of bottled water and two sandwiches. He bit into one hungrily, not caring what lay between the two slices of bread. After wolfing down two large bites, he chewed more slowly and took time to appreciate the food. A far sight better than the gruel he'd expected, the sandwich consisted of thick slices of hearty multi-grain bread, stacks of paper-thin shavings of rare roast beef, crisp lettuce, mayonnaise and a dash of horseradish. With no idea how long he'd wait before they fed him again, he vowed to hang onto the second sandwich until dinnertime. It wouldn't spoil in the cool tunnel.

After he'd polished off half the first sandwich and washed it down with water, he made his way back to the spot where he'd found the loose spike. He hunkered down, bit into the other half of the sandwich, gripped the spike with his fingers and worried it like a loose tooth.

14

Over millions of years, glaciers repeatedly scoured the Pacific Northwest leaving Seattle with its ridges and valleys, lakes and creeks. Those monstrous frozen rivers flowed down from Canada and once covered what is now the city under two-thirds of a mile of ice. The last of these, the Vashon Glacier, retreated about 13,000 years ago, leaving in its wake the basic contours of Seattle and the Puget Sound region. I knew this not because I had a great love of geology, but because my memory linked the information with a joke a history professor told, a bad one that had made me laugh anyway. That's sort of how my memory works; I remember things that originate with an emotional experience or that elicit an emotional response. Basically, if something makes me laugh, cry or leaves any impression at all, really I'll remember every detail of the context—conversations, clothing, scents, ambient sounds, and more. Memory has its benefits, but the inability to forget can be a curse.

We drove across Lake Washington—one of the valleys scoured out by glaciers and filled with melting, retreating ice—on the floating bridge and up into the U. District—one of the ridges left behind, too. Like a lot of institutions of "higher learning," the University of Washington was located at the top of one of the city's high spots, but the campus had grown so large that it descended the hillside south to the shore of Lake Washington. The U. District ran up the ridge north of campus a bit and down the hill to the east where it ran into the ritzy Laurelhurst neighborhood.

Derek had asked us to meet him in the U. Village shopping center, quite a distance away from the MondoHard building. A large open-air mall, U. Village offered the benefit of easy parking and large crowds of people in which to lose ourselves. The latter point worried me, not that I was afraid of getting lost, but that Derek thought the situation required some cloak-and-dagger theatrics. His caution suggested that Matt's theory was plausible, or that something even bigger was at work. Then again, after all that had happened in the few weeks since I'd met Tess, I couldn't blame Derek for exercising discretion around the two of us. A small war had erupted around Tess and, as her employee, me as well.

After five minutes of asking me what Derek said on the phone, Tess gave up and rode the rest of the way in silence. When we arrived, I circled around the mall and looked for a space in the lot close to a frozen yogurt stand in the middle. The sky dripped liquid pewter as I guided Tess into the little shop. A heater mounted up high tried to blow the chill coming off me back out the door. A couple of university students stood at the counter ahead of us peering through the glass sneeze guard at the candy, cookies, fruit and other ingredients, trying to decide what to pile on top of their yogurt. A uniformed employee stood idly behind the counter while the pair considered their choices. The students appeared Inuit to me, proving, I suppose, that even a pimply teenager can sell ice to an Eskimo under the right circumstances.

"What do you want?" I murmured in Tess's ear.

"I want to talk to Derek," she said through clenched teeth.

"Well, he's not here, so have some frozen yogurt."

"Fine. Do they have black cherry? If so, some of that and some cheesecake. And sprinkle some Golden Grahams cereal on top. Please."

"Wait here. I'll be back."

Grabbing an empty cup from a stack near the door, I scanned the signs by the soft-serve handles to find the flavors Tess wanted. The cup was more like an ice cream maker's pint, designed to encourage over-consumption, and the soft-serve machines dispensed quickly. Though I did my best to regulate the flow and serve a decent size portion, the cup was two-thirds full by the time the last drip of yogurt plopped in. A scale by the register weighed the contents and the cashier rang it up. For what it cost, we could have bought two or three pints of ice cream at a grocery store.

When I put the cup in her hands, Tess raised the cup to her chin and scooped a spoonful into her mouth. Grasping her elbow, I steered her to the door.

"Wait, you're not having any?" she said.

"Too cold to eat anything frozen."

I led her out into the Chinese water torture that is Seattle weather six months of the year. April's weather actually wasn't too bad, with a mix of showers and sunbreaks, those fleeting patches of blue in a cotton quilt sky. Temperatures typically ranged from 40s up to high 50s or low 60s. Being spring, however, vestiges of wintry weather revealed themselves on occasion—blustery windstorms redirecting rain at a forty-five degree angle, dustings of snow every now and then, and skies as leaden as a radiology apron.

"What now?" Tess said, scooping more yogurt into her mouth.

I pulled a napkin from my pocket and dabbed a drip off her chin. "We wait. He'll be here."

No sooner had I spoken than Derek sauntered up in the drizzle, dressed in his usual uniform—black jeans, black boots and a black pea coat. The only thing that ever seemed to change was his black T-shirt. Today's had "The Killers" emblazoned across the front.

My first impression of Derek had been less than positive. About the same age as me, he favored piercings, tattoos and a generally scruffy look while I tended to be a bit more conservative, my dress and grooming showing my Midwestern roots. He'd quickly disabused me of my groundless prejudice, though. He was smart, and when push came to shove, he'd come down on Tess's side.

His head wagged from side to side as he approached, turning when an engine revved. He moved casually, but his nerves were contagious. I eyed passersby suspiciously, wondering why.

"How you doing?" he said as he came up to us.

I touched Tess lightly on the arm. "Tess, Derek. Derek, Tess."

Derek scuffed a toe on the sidewalk. "Nice to meet you finally."

"Yeah, you, too," Tess said.

Derek raised his gaze to Tess's face and his mouth dropped open. Tess had that effect on people; she appeared to look right at them, but because she couldn't see, her eyes didn't quite track people's expressions, didn't quite focus. Derek waved his hand in front of her face.

"You really are blind," he said.

Impatience took a walk across Tess's face and lingered. "He's waving his hand at me, isn't he? Yes, I'm blind. You really are a genius."

"Okay, I deserved that." Derek looked sheepish.

Rain droplets that had collected on the rings in his eyebrows glittered in the light from the yogurt shop. The misty drizzle had slicked his dark hair, plastering curls to his forehead. Tiny drops adorned the tips of Tess's eyelashes, too, making her eyes sparkle. Like lifeless diamonds, though, they reflected the light instead of projecting the radiance from within.

"What's with the stealth mode?" I asked.

Derek again glanced furtively over his shoulder. "You're talking about *Never Bitten*, right? The game app you mentioned?"

"That's the one," I said.

"It's mine," he said quietly.

"What do you mean it's yours?" Tess said loudly. Derek shushed her. "You told Oliver that MondoHard released it," she said in a softer tone.

"I mean I developed it," Derek said. "I came up with the idea. I wrote a lot of the code. I directed the team that came up with the graphics and animation. The game's in beta test. We put the word out anonymously on a couple of blogs and game forums with a link. We wanted to see what kind of buzz it generated before we released it. So, it's still hush-hush as far as the company's concerned." He turned to me. "Why the sudden interest?"

"It's messing with people's minds," Tess blurted.

"She thinks there's something wrong with it," I told him.

"Impossible." He frowned. "We went over it and over it to work out the bugs. Hundreds of man-hours. A lot of late nights, man."

Tess responded hesitantly. "You don't think my uncle could have, well, you know, done something?"

"Like what? Maybe you better tell me what's going on."

"That's a good idea," I interjected, "but could we do it someplace warmer and drier?"

I swiped at the water dripping off the end of my nose. Derek nodded and pointed to a coffeeshop across the lot. Less than five minutes later, we huddled around a table in a corner, wet coats hung on the backs of our chairs. I used a stack of paper napkins to blot some of the water out of my hair. I put a bunch in Tess's hand, which she used to dry her face. She set the damp wad on the table and launched into the story of Matt's peculiar behavior over the previous couple of weeks. When she finished, Derek silently stared at one of the baristas behind the counter.

"People have been trying to pin youth violence on the video game industry for a long time," he said finally.

"This is *real*!" Tess said. "Matt wasn't like that."

"I didn't say it couldn't happen," Derek said sharply. He dropped his gaze to the table. When he looked at Tess again, his expression softened. "You're sure about your friend."

Tess nodded. "He wasn't one of those kids who keep things bottled up. And he had friends who cared about him. He would've talked to someone if something was bugging him."

Derek looked at me, face twisted into a question mark.

"As far as I can tell, she's right," I said. "I've only known the kid for a few weeks, but he didn't strike me as the type to go all Columbine."

Derek rubbed the stubble on his chin. "Look, Tess, your dad was the expert on all this stuff—game theory, PSYOP, subliminal messaging, all those mind games. So I suppose it's possible, even likely, that some department in the company is fooling around with mind control. But I guarantee you we didn't put any of that into *Never Bitten*."

"Is there some way to tell whether someone else did?" Tess said.

"You mean see if someone subverted my code? Added something?" He stretched out a hand. "Let me see your phone. I assume you downloaded a copy."

I dig in my pocket and handed him mine.

"Not yours," Derek said. "It's too old."

Chagrined, I put it back in my pocket and glanced at Tess. She bit her lip, her brow furrowed.

"What's the matter?" Derek said.

Tess flushed. "I took it. I took Matt's phone." She brought a hand out from under the table and held it out palm up as if serving the phone up on a tray.

"Even better," Derek said, taking it from her.

He swiped a finger across the screen. It flickered to life, lighting up his face. With deft strokes, he swiped and touched and typed, his fingers a blur.

After a few moments, he frowned and murmured, "That's not right. That's weird, too." He held the phone up. "Mind if I borrow this for a bit?"

"No," Tess said. "Actually, it would be a relief. I wasn't sure how I was going to explain it. Now, if anyone asks, I don't have it."

"What are you going to do?" I said.

"I need to see if I can track the source code for the game version that's on this phone," Derek said, "see how they changed it. And I'll try to figure out where he downloaded it. I need to tell your uncle about this, Tess."

"He's gone."

"Business trip?"

"They took him." Her voice quavered. "He left this morning and never made it to work. They found his car half a mile from the house."

"Isn't that interesting," Derek said. "They've been covering for him at the office. I heard he's been in meetings all day."

15

Tess let herself into the kitchen from the garage while Oliver got her book bag out of the back seat and followed her. The warm air was thick with scents of vanilla, brown sugar, butter and chocolate. *Cookies.* She'd taken only two steps inside before a voice assaulted her.

"Theresa Camilla Barrett, where have you been?"

"Alice? I, uh, I—"

"I've been worried sick! Someone called to say the school was in lockdown because of a shooting! That was hours ago."

"I'm fine, Alice. Really, I'm fine."

"I've been trying to call you all afternoon, young lady! The least you could do is text me to let me know you were all right!"

"My phone didn't ring." Tess frowned, confused.

"It must have," Alice insisted. "What have you been doing all this time?"

"That's my fault, Alice." Oliver's voice came from behind Tess as he entered the kitchen. "We went to go talk to someone."

"Who? Why?"

"Just a friend," Tess said, turning defense to offense now. "You're not my mother, Alice. Stop grilling me like I'm a murder suspect. I've already been through that once today with the police."

"I'm responsible for you, Tess, when Travis isn't here. But it's *your* responsibility to check in so I know where you are. For you not to call, especially after an event like the one at school today, is not only the height of irresponsibility, it was thoughtless and cruel. I care about you, Tess. I don't just make sure your clothes are clean and your meals are prepared, I actually care about your wellbeing and what happens to you."

Tess felt her ears burn. "I'm sorry, okay? What do you want from me? I didn't hear the phone!"

"You should have called. And you, Oliver, are just as responsible for this situation. You've been told on more than one occasion that I expect to know where Tess is at all times. You should have made sure she checked in."

"Yes, ma'am," Oliver said, sounding meek. "I see what the problem was. Tess's phone needs charging."

"No." Alice's voice was firm. "The problem is that neither one of you took the time to think about anyone else after what happened today."

"Stop it!" Tess cried. "You weren't there. You don't know what it was like!"

"No, and I'm sure it was awful for you," Alice went on, more quietly now. "But just imagine for one second what it was like for me knowing there had been a shooting at school, but not knowing who'd been shot, if anyone had been hurt or killed, and not being able to get any information because the school was locked down. Imagine what it was like still not hearing a word even when the lockdown ended, still not knowing where you were or if you'd been involved in any way."

"I said I was sorry."

Silence filled the space between them for a moment. Oliver shifted his weight behind her and cleared his throat.

"Yes," Alice said, "well, I'm sorry, too. You'd better get started on your homework."

Tess shuffled out of the kitchen down the hall to the library. Oliver tried to help her, but she shrugged him off both times.

"It's my fault," he said softly. "I should have called Alice."

Tess shouldered her way through one of the library's double doors and headed for the study table, hands dusting imaginary furniture as she went.

"I know better," she said, the words tasting bitter on her tongue. "Today was just so weird, and I got so stressed out by that whole thing with Matt that I forgot. I hate it when Alice does that to me. She's always trying to control me. Everyone around here tells me what to do. 'Tess, you can't do this. Tess, you have to do that.' It was bad enough when my mom..."

She left the thought unsaid, knowing if she dwelled on it she'd get teary-eyed. She wanted to hang onto her anger, not let sentimentality turn her insides to mush.

"So, homework?" Oliver said.

He almost sounded fearful, and Tess knew it was because of her foul mood. She didn't care. She was sick of being ordered around, of being treated like a child.

"Where's my backpack?" she said.

Oliver dropped it on the table with a thump and slid it across to her. Her fingers found the right pocket and pulled out her phone. She groped inside another pocket, withdrew a USB cable and plugged it into the laptop already open on the study table. The other end fit neatly into a socket on her phone allowing its battery to charge.

"Well?" Oliver pressed.

"Look, after what happened today none of the teachers are going to expect us to do homework. Why bother?"

"Come on, Tess. Don't be like that."

Tess's head rose automatically at the sound of a knock on the library door. She knew her eyes were aimed in the general direction, but only a clean blackboard registered in her brain. Nothing but blackness.

"Miz Barrett," a male voice said. "Someone here to see you. I figured it was okay I let him in the gate out front."

"Who is it?" Tess said.

"Oh, sorry. It's Luis."

"No, I meant who's here to see me?"

"Right. Tim Daley. Said he's a friend of yours."

Tess's breath caught and her heart hopscotched before settling into a faster rhythm. "You can show him in, Luis. Thank you."

Tess had known Tim since fifth grade. In middle school, they'd developed a minor crush on each other, but, being gawky pre-teens, hadn't done much about it. They'd stayed friends going into high school, and even though they hadn't seen as much of each other when she and Toby had started going out, they'd remained amicable. Instead of getting pissed and jealous, Tim had gone out of his way to support her. He'd been the first person who'd called the house after her accident, not Toby or Addie. Of course, back then she hadn't wanted anyone to see her swathed in casts and bandages, her once pretty face contorted by pain and self-pity. Funny how her looks had faded in importance when mirrors had become useless.

"Hi, Tess." Tim's voice came from the spot where Luis had been a moment ago.

She didn't think her heart could beat any faster without exploding. *It's just Tim, and you're just friends.* She beamed, unable to keep her cheeks from rising up somewhere near her ears. The world around her slipped away until it was as if her uncle's disappearance and the shooting at school had never happened. No more Alice or Yoshi nagging her, no more Oliver, no more school. All that remained was the pounding of her heart and the echo of Tim's voice in her ear.

"What are you doing here?" Her voice sounded breathless, and the question sounded lame. "I mean, I'm glad you came, but—"

"Oh, come on, Tess. I've been calling for weeks, ever since I heard you were coming back to school. You kept putting me off, so I figured I'd just stop by. I wanted to see if you were okay after what happened at school today. That's okay, right?"

"God, yes. I mean, of course. You know you can drop in anytime."

Tess felt her cheeks flush. Now she sounded too eager, like some star-struck freshman.

"Really? That's not the impression I got."

"She give you a hard time?" Oliver said. Tess had forgotten he was in the room. "I'm Oliver, by the way, Oliver Moncrief."

"Tim Daley. You're Tess's assistant. I've seen you leading Tess around school."

"That's me," Oliver said, "seeing-eye guy."

Tim laughed and Tess's face burned red-hot now. "I don't treat you like some dog."

"No, I guess not. More like a go-fer."

Tim's laugh sounded nervous this time, and Tess's embarrassment turned to anger.

"Nice, Oliver," she said. "I think you can go now."

"What about your homework?" He sounded genuinely surprised.

"Tim can help me with whatever I've got left," she said.

"Sure," Tim chimed in. "No problem. Happy to help."

"Don't you have practice with Yoshi this afternoon?"

"I can practice in the morning before school. Stop being such a worry-wart, Oliver."

"You're going to blow off homework, and Yoshi," Oliver said. "Are you positive that's what you want?"

"Go home, Oliver," Tess said. "I'll see you in the morning."

"Fine. But don't blame me tomorrow if your work isn't done right. And no whining about how tired you are because you had to get up early for jiu-jitsu."

Tess fumed, convinced they could see smoke curling out of her ears. "I can handle it. I'll get all my work done. Tim's here, remember?"

"I'm not blind, Tess," Oliver said quietly.

Her mouth opened in shock, but no words came out. A hot boulder sat in her belly.

"I'll see you in the morning," Oliver said.

His footsteps receded as he walked out the door and down the hallway.

16

For the umpteenth time on his way back to the office, Derek ducked into a storefront. A casual observer might have thought he'd gone in purposefully to tick some errand off his list, or that he simply wanted to get out of the rain for a minute. But Derek wasn't interested in casual observers. Looking around to get his bearings, he headed toward the back of the store, listening for the sound of the front door opening behind him. He stopped in front of a rack of clothes marked "Clearance" and shuffled the hangers, pretending to look for and admire some gross looking Hawaiian shirts. He moved around the circular rack until he faced the entrance, and surreptitiously watched both it and the front window for signs that he'd been followed.

Ever since Oliver's phone call, Derek had been spooked. He'd heard about the shooting at the school. Who hadn't? It had been all over the news, but never in a million years would he have connected it to *Never Bitten*. The game had been his baby for two freaking years. He'd written more than half the code and had gone over every line of other people's code a dozen times or more. The app was as close to perfect as anyone could get it, even software genius James Freaking Barrett who, though he'd recently been communicating from beyond the grave, was no longer the head of MondoHard. In fact, Derek defied anyone to find something wrong with the game. Yet Tess and Oliver seemed to think this kid at school might have wigged out because of something in it. If that was true, someone had messed with it.

The bell over the front door of the store tinkled, jangling Derek's nerves. He glanced up to see a kid stroll in with a skateboard in one hand. Water dripped from the deck and ran in rivulets off the ends of his stringy, long hair down his waterproof jacket. Not the enemy. Derek looked past him at the glistening street outside the stippled window. Still no movement except that of passing cars. But he couldn't shake the feeling that *some*one was watching him. He glanced around the store and caught the eye of the heavyset Hawaiian woman behind the register. She grimaced and looked away. Derek flushed and moved away from the rack of shirts. She probably thought he was a shoplifter from the way he'd been acting.

He walked back toward the front of the store, eying the shelves for something he could buy so it wouldn't look as if he'd come in for nothing. He settled on a bag of Hawaiian taro chips, took them to the register. The cashier looked him up and down as she rang up his purchase, took the five-spot he proferred with an audible *harumph*, and made change. He shoved the change in his pocket and mumbled his thanks as he turned for the door.

Outside, he stopped and looked both ways as if uncertain where to go, taking in as many details as he could while he scanned the sidewalks on both sides of the street. He noted pedestrians, their positions, gender and the color of their clothes. Setting off down the street, he tore open the bag of chips and ate a few. A block down, he stepped off the curb and craned his neck down the street the way he'd come as if peering for a bus or a cab. No one darted into doorways or averted their eyes. If he had a tail, he couldn't spot it. He walked another two blocks and caught a bus after a short wait. Two bus-rides later, with some walking in between, Derek made it back to the MondoHard building convinced he hadn't been followed.

Striding into his dim office, he stripped off his wet coat and threw it over the back of a chair. Two other desks sat empty, the teammates who normally occupied them out for some reason. Probably down in the cafeteria getting coffee or soda. Paul, the only one of his officemates still there, glanced up from his keyboard, face painted blue by the light from the big monitor in front of him. Annoyance flashed across Paul's face before he turned back to his work. A poser. Paul couldn't code his way out of a paper bag, but he wasn't bad enough to fire outright. Derek shrugged. He wasn't Paul's boss, and if Paul was given clear enough direction at least he took some of the grunt work off Derek's shoulders.

"Where you been?" Paul grumbled. He pushed black-framed glasses back up the bridge of his nose and blinked rapidly, his eyes magnified by the thick lenses.

"Lunch." Derek eased into the chair in front of his computer.

"Long frickin' lunch."

"Had some errands," Derek said, fingers flying over the keys.

He tuned Paul out, focusing on the task at hand—figuring out what was going on with the app on the shooter's cell phone. First, he checked the app version he had running on his workstation.

He ran the game and found no problems. A quick glance told him that Paul was deeply absorbed in his own work, so he quickly unlocked a desk drawer and pulled out a small touchscreen notebook computer. He kept it for times such as this when he wanted to access networks anonymously while at work. The notebook had a partitioned hard drive in case it became infected with a virus or Trojan, and he knew tricks to disguise its IP address.

He pulled Matt's phone from his pocket and hooked it up to the notebook with a spare USB cord. After downloading the app from Matt's phone to the notebook, he played the game and compared the action to the clean version on his workstation. He noted slight differences on a pad of paper on the desk. Most would have gone unnoticed even by some of the people on his team, like Paul. But he knew every move, every pixel in the app. The changes in the game seemed to guide his play, almost as if steering him. Not in a particular direction in the game, which the others on the project might pick up on, but in an emotional sense. It was almost as if the game was feeding on his mood and driving him into situations that would sustain and amplify it. He found it unnerving, almost spooky.

After a quick check on Paul, he closed out of the app and turned his attention to the phone again. He scrolled through the main menu and pulled up the tools file. With some manipulation, he was able to find the IP address of the site from which Matt had downloaded the app. Switching to his notebook again, Derek executed a search for the address and found a back door into the site. He took a quick look around, careful not to leave any tracks that would announce his presence. From all outward appearances, it duplicated the MondoHard site exactly. For now, he wanted to get in and out quickly, so he downloaded another copy of the app onto the notebook, got out of the site and broke the network connection.

He opened the app and ran the opening sequences of the game. When the same changes appeared that he'd seen on the phone, he closed out of the app, switched to a black screen and began typing commands. He needed to find out what was wrong with the code and where the program had originated, and he knew he didn't have much time. Whoever had messed with the app may have been smart enough to put in a self-destruct command if anyone tried to find code snippets that didn't belong. He opened an anti-virus program that he'd customized and let it run in the background while he started tracing the IP address that he'd found on Matt's phone. Just as the program locked in, Derek heard a shuffling noise behind him. Damn, he hadn't been paying attention.

"What're you working on?" Paul peered over Derek's shoulder, squinting at the notebook screen. He pushed his glasses up with a forefinger then sniffed and swiped the back of his hand across his nose and wiped it on his jeans.

Derek thought furiously as the combined scents of Slim Jim and Axe deodorant drifted past his nostrils and soured his stomach. Selling the truth was always easier than keeping track of a lie.

"I got a fan complaint." He glanced back. "Some kid said his app wasn't working right."

"*Never Bitten*? Impossible, right?" Paul grinned as if he was practicing, his facial muscles unused to the movement.

Derek hated suck-ups, but antagonizing people he had to work with accomplished nothing. He gritted his teeth. Paul wouldn't last long on his team. Derek just needed to bide his time until Paul was gone.

Derek flashed some teeth. "You'd think. But I figured, better check it out anyway."

"Why not toss it back to customer service? Let those weenies handle it."

Derek struggled to turn a frown into something more benign, but Paul had seen the message written on his face and backed up a step.

"Right, it's our program. Well, your program, really."

With a jovial tone to lighten the mood, Derek said, "Yeah, man, it's a matter of pride. We all worked too hard on this. You know how it is; one kid posts a bad review on a game site and we're toast."

Paul nodded at Derek's use of the word "we," and walked back to his desk beaming at his inclusion as part of the team.

Derek breathed a silent sigh of relief and again focused on his work. He checked the location of the IP address that had come up and frowned. Though tempted, he couldn't take a chance on running the trace again, but he double-checked the search result. Matt had downloaded the faulty app from a server inside the building. From a server in the series that housed the main program and database for the app. It didn't match the primary address, but if traffic had been heavy the day Matt had downloaded his copy, he could have been shunted to this IP address.

He turned to the notebook when he noticed that his anti-virus program had stopped running. He peered at the stats box. It couldn't be right. All those files checked for bugs and not a single virus. No corrupted files. Nothing.

He rubbed his chin until another idea struck him. He typed furiously, making up lines of code on the fly, telling the computer what he wanted it to do. When he finished, he scrolled back up and scanned through what he'd written, checking his logic. He nodded. It would work. Drawing a breath, he taped the return key and watched the characters he'd typed dissolve as the program ran.

Matt's version of the game wasn't infected, but *something* about it was different. The program Derek had written would compare the source code of the game on Matt's phone with a copy of the real deal. It would find all the snippets that weren't part of the original game and list them.

While the notebook hummed, Derek started up the game on Matt's phone where he'd left off. The more he played, the more worried he got. Along with his concern, however, came a tingle of excitement. The game anticipated his every move. No, not move, but mood. He varied his style of play, first attacking aggressively with a reckless, take-no-prisoners attitude. The game didn't try to beat him so much as lead him into more situations that would require a similar style and challenge his skills. When he switched to a more defensive posture, the game immediately changed tactics, too, again drawing him in. He almost felt as if the game could read his mind.

Artificial intelligence!

Derek had already built logic capabilities into the app. The game learned from tactics that players used so it would constantly challenge them as they got better. This was different. This app did more than add to its logic base. It sensed the emotional state of the player and used that as part of its strategy. Derek took several deep breaths and forced his heart rate down. He closed his eyes and envisioned an empty blackboard, a little exercise he called his "Jedi mind trick," a way to calm himself and take emotion out of the equation.

When he felt ready he opened his eyes and tried a little experiment. He played the game for a minute or two with normal gestures, noting the response of the game and the tactics the app employed to keep him on his guard. Without changing his breathing or calm state of mind, he swiped and jabbed the screen more forcefully, as if acting angry or aggressive. The game tactics changed.

He stopped play and set the phone down. This was mind-blowing stuff. Derek was the best coder in the company, but he'd never come up with anything like this. This was the kind of software guys at DARPA and the NSA would love to get their hands on. And there was only one man Derek knew of who had the smarts to pull off something this brilliant—James Barrett, the founder of MondoHard. The only problem was that Barrett was dead.

Maybe.

Derek rolled his chair up close to the desk and opened an email program on the notebook computer. Someone claiming to be Tess Barrett's dad James had been in contact with him only a week or two earlier. He still remembered the address of the last email drop box the mystery man had used. He typed a quick message: "*Never Bitten* got bit. You?" His hands hovered over the keyboard for a moment. This was crazy, expecting a cyber-ghost to know anything about whatever had happened to his app. *His* app. Two years of Derek's life.

He hit "Send."

17

Doug and his buddies hadn't shown themselves for the past day, and Austin didn't know what to make of it. He'd expected to be waylaid in the halls or ambushed in the boys' bathroom, but he hadn't seen hide nor hair of any of them. "Hide nor hair..." That was good. Maybe it should be "neither wing nor fang." And just maybe now that he'd shown them the power of Wolfsbane, his alter ego, they wouldn't mess with him anymore. He actually skipped down the hall at the thought and glanced over his shoulder to see what Huey and Dewey, his Secret Service detail, thought about that. Austin refused to use their real names—Hugh and Dennis—just on principle. He didn't need babysitting every second of the day. They didn't seem to mind, or even notice the nicknames he'd given them. Expressionless, they trailed behind at a respectful distance, but not so far that they couldn't be by his side in mere seconds if a threat materialized.

With the end of Rothbottom's history class only minutes earlier Austin was finished for the day. The last bell of the school day always lightened his mood immeasurably, and now he made mental plans for what to do with the remainder of the afternoon. That new girl, Laura Snyder, a transfer from a day school in New York City, had been showing some interest lately, even going as far as slipping him a piece of paper at the beginning French class on her way to her seat. Austin had surreptitiously opened it, astonished to see that she'd given him her Facebook handle with the words, "Message me." He figured he'd do just that once he retrieved his book bag and laptop computer from his locker.

Halfway down the hall he slowed, gaze caught by the sight of something dangling from the bank of lockers on one wall. Like white ropes, or streamers. He drew closer, his heart in his throat and a chunk of lead in his stomach. No, not rope, but some sort of thick, creamy substance that slowly dripped down the face of the lockers in strings. He broke into a run, heart hammering, fear gripping his intestines and squeezing until he thought he'd double over in pain. He didn't want to see...

"No-o-o!" he howled.

Footsteps pounded down the hall behind him as he pulled up in front of his locker, the face of it coated with dripping white foam that oozed through the vents. He could smell it now—whipped cream. He spun the dial on his lock, shaking so badly that his fingers flubbed the combination twice before the cams inside lined up and the hasp clicked open. He yanked up the latch and pulled the door open. A flood of whipped cream whipped cream gushed from the opening, landing onto the floor in large plops and splashing his shoes and clothes. The goo had soaked into everything in his locker—books, notebooks, backpack, and his laptop. He stretched a hand toward the computer.

"Don't touch anything!" a voice said behind him. "That's a crime scene."

Austin whirled on the two Secret Service agents. "Where the hell were you when this happened!" he screamed. "Everything's ruined!"

The agents stood motionless, stony-faced. Austin knew perfectly well where they'd been—camped outside the door of his classroom, protecting him. From what? They hadn't intervened yet in any of the bullying and harassment Austin had received at the hands of Doug, Blaise and Donnie. What was the point of having an armed security team if it didn't keep him safe and unhurt?

He howled again, in pain and rage, the sound opening classroom doors and attracting curious students and teachers into the hallway. Dewey murmured into his shirt cuff, already reporting the incident to his superiors. Austin groaned inwardly. Within minutes the Secret Service would inform his father, an interruption in the great man's day that Austin would hear no end of at home later.

"Big Ed" Thorson, the corpulent dean of students, waddled toward him as fast as legs the thickness and length of tree stumps would allow, giving him a rolling gait that made Austin think of the blow-up punching bag he'd had as a kid that kept popping back up after he hit it.

"What's going on here?" he blustered as he came up to them. His gaze roved across the two agents to the cream-filled locker that now resembled a squished Twinkie, and finally settled on Austin. He pursed his lips and his breath wheezed in and out like a bellows. His eyes narrowed. "Did you do this?"

Austin snorted. "Like I would trash my own locker. Give me a break."

"Watch your tone with me, young man," Thorson said. "Do you know who did?"

"Of course I do, but I can't prove it."

"Calm down, please." Thorson leaned toward the open locker, nose wrinkling in distaste.

Huey put an arm out chest high. "I wouldn't get too close, sir. It's a crime scene now."

"What? A little prank like this? Messy, I'll grant you, but a crime?"

"The boy's laptop is in there," Dewey said. "Looks like it's a total loss. Given its value, this isn't just an act of malicious mischief. We've called in some of our investigative support personnel. We thought you'd prefer we handle it that way than call in the District police."

"What are *they* gonna do?" Austin said.

"Check for fingerprints to start," Dewey said.

"In that mess?" Austin yelled. "You can't get fingerprints off of whipped cream!"

Huey fixed him with a hard stare. "No, but we might pull some off the locker door."

Austin turned away in disgust and muttered, "Whatever. How long do I have to stay here?"

"As soon as forensics gets here and we brief them we'll be able to drive you home."

Thorson nodded as if he had a clue then frowned when he realized that students and teachers still crowded the hallway.

"Back to your classrooms, everyone!" Thorson said in a loud voice. "There's nothing more to see here. Go back to your classes, people!"

As if a spell had been lifted, the corridor suddenly swelled with the murmur of voices and sounds of shuffling feet as milling students slowly funneled back into their classrooms. Gradually, the noise died down, leaving the hall quiet once more.

"Okay, fine," Austin said. "I guess I have no choice, as usual. Can I, like, wait in the library or something?"

Thorson swept his suit jacket away from his big gut like tent flaps and put his meaty hands on the shelf where his hips should be. "If you have no more classes today, that would be acceptable."

"Great," he said with all the enthusiasm of a root canal patient. "That's where I'll be."

Dewey threw a look at his partner. Huey caught it with a nod and trailed a few paces behind Austin toward the school library.

Austin tried to ignore the footsteps on his heels, and once inside the library he slipped into the stacks and quickly weaved through the rows of shelves, leaving Huey parked near the entrance. Finding an empty study table, he slouched into a chair, shoulders sloped and head bent by the weight of the foul mood that blanketed him.

He pulled out his phone and turned on the game app that had frustrated and enthralled him for the past few weeks. Playing furiously, he moved his avatar through the urban terrain, picking up weapons and fending off attacks by roving bands of werewolves, dive-bombing vampire bats and leering zombies. But no matter how quickly he moved, no matter how many weapons he collected, each time he tried to better his record he got bitten by one of the creatures in the game and died.

About to give up after one particularly grisly battle with a horde of creatures from all three monstrous species, he noticed that the game hadn't ended. Instead of the life-force bar draining to zero as his avatar, Wolfsbane, lay dying in the street, blood pouring from his wounds, the bar pulsed faintly with a dim green glow. The other creatures had left him for dead. Austin watched the screen with bated breath, certain that Wolfsbane would suffer one last killing blow. A swipe of a werewolf's clawed hand. The rush of wings and fangs of a vampire. The swing of an axe from one of the gruesome undead. But nothing happened. Until the life-force indicator blinked brighter and more strongly.

He rubbed his chin. The object of the game was not to get bitten. Once bitten, you were as good as dead if death wasn't instantaneous. He'd never seen anything like this before. Austin hit "Save" and closed out of the game to think about what had just happened.

18

Does anyone understand teenage girls? I didn't. Since my exposure to the species had been limited I turned to the Internet for advice. I read about changes in the adolescent brain, about puberty, about the psychological and social development of teenagers, their sense of identity and self-esteem. I learned about how their capacity for relativistic thinking improves along with their cognition and hypothetical and abstract thinking. I boned up on their sexual development as well as the formation of their sexual identity, their relationships, both romantic and with peers, and their culture.

The wisest bit of information I came across suggested that pre-adolescent girls are like puppies. But once girls become teens they turn into cats, and gradually, as they head into adulthood, some of their feline traits moderate, and they slowly become mostly human once again. The research left me no closer to understanding Tess than I had before, but rather with a bunch of useless facts and suppositions that I was doomed to recall every time I became frustrated with Tess's behavior.

I gave up and went to bed. Sometime during the night, I woke in a cold sweat from a dream. I hit the replay button before the details sank back in the depths of my subconscious and recalled Tess getting angry with a host of faceless men, picking up Matt's gun off the floor and shooting each of them with unerring accuracy. Falling back to sleep took a long time.

The alarm woke me again at six. I debated rolling over and ignoring it. The events of the past few days, not to mention the dream, made me less than eager to spend time with Tess. And while I needed a job, surely safer and saner jobs existed out there. Flipping burgers, maybe.

A sharp rap on the door cut short my mental job hunting. I glanced at the clock again, thinking I must be imagining a visitor at this hour. More likely a neighbor bumping against the wall, but the knock came again.

"Hang on!" I yelled, swinging my legs out of bed. I grabbed a pair of jeans off the floor and yanked them on, hopping on one foot to maintain my balance. I peered through the peephole as I zipped them up. Farouk, one of my landlords.

He peered at me and shifted his weight when I opened the door.

"Farouk, do you know what time it is?"

He looked indignant. "Of course I do. I'm on my way to class."

For the first time I noticed the strap slung across his chest holding a heavy bag behind him. Farouk was a medical student at the university. He and his roommate Farid, both of them from Dubai—or was it Abu Dhabi? I could never remember which—had used family money to buy the big house to live in while they went to school. A previous owner had divided the house into apartments which were popular with students like me. Though Farouk and Farid weren't related, they looked as if they could have been brothers. To tell them apart, I'd heard several people in the building call them Frank and Joe, which I assumed was a reference to the Hardy Boys. Though rude, the nicknames were apropos. Both of them loved to snoop.

I put my hand up to my mouth and tried to stifle a yawn. "What can I do for you, Farouk?"

"I want to be sure you aren't late with the rent this month."

I frowned. "I'm not late."

He nodded impatiently and scrubbed an imaginary window a foot from my face. "Yes, yes, you are not late now. And you won't be, of course. Which is why I am asking you to pay early."

"That doesn't make any sense. I've always paid you on time."

"But this month there is damage to the door. I'm thinking maybe you are having troubles."

"What do you mean? What kind of troubles?"

"Money troubles."

"I said I'd pay for the door." I couldn't argue the damage—someone had kicked it in and ransacked my apartment a week earlier. "What makes you think I have money problems?"

"You haven't enrolled for next semester, and your faculty advisor says you haven't T.A.'d in weeks."

"I've been busy." I liked Farouk, but it rankled that he was asking for rent nearly two weeks before it was due. I'd never been even a day late. But that was before an estate attorney had called me to let me know the trust fund that financed my education, my very existence, had been sucked dry by my profligate grandparents.

"Besides," I went on, "I have another job that pays more than the T.A. position. Lots more."

Farouk's very black, very thick eyebrows rose. His intelligence had been good, but not infallible, apparently.

"And what is this new employment?"

"Personal assistant."

He stifled a laugh. "You actually assist someone?"

"A blind girl, whose family is very, *very* wealthy."

He dismissed the thought with a wave and a sneer.

"Your kind of wealthy," I added. The comment brought him up short.

"I doubt that," he said, but his expression didn't match his tone.

"The girl's father is—was—the founder of MondoHard."

He appraised me for a moment as if the lighting in the hall had just changed dramatically. "And you assist this girl. With whatever she needs."

I nodded. "In fact, if you keep me here much longer, I'll be late for work."

"Of course. I'll expect your check as usual then."

He actually bowed. Well, not obsequiously, but he definitely inclined his head in a show of respect. Before I could respond, he turned and hurried down the hall. I shut the door resolving to drop the Barrett name more often.

A glance at the kitchen wall clock brought me back to sober reality. As I'd told Farouk, I had a job, a better job than a minimum wage gig in fast food. And I had to hustle if I was going to get there on time.

Light traffic on I-90 across the lake gave me room to maneuver the BMW around the slower moving cars. Even in the best of conditions, Washington drivers found reasons to slow down. I pride myself on being a careful driver, even with a 450-horsepower twin-turbo V-8 under the hood, but too many drivers on the road guided their vehicles like prissy schoolmarms, cautious to a fault. Courteous, too—you'd never hear a native honk the horn, only those from out of state—which often led to dangerous situations. In manners lay madness. Rules of the road were proscribed for a reason. I made good time, anyway, without busting the speed limit—well, maybe cracking it, but not shattering it.

With the remote for the gate, I breezed right in, for a moment thinking how easy it would be to breach security. All someone had to do was follow me, take the remote and... Before I could follow that line of thought to its logical and probably painful conclusion I spotted Luis patrolling the grounds and instantly felt better. Security appeared to be just fine.

Alice stood at the stove as I let myself in the door from the garage. She glanced over her shoulder at me when she heard the door then leaned over and shoved a plate in the oven. She pulled off an oven mitt and laid it on the counter.

"Good morning, Oliver," she said, dusting her hands on her apron. "I just put some pancakes in the oven for you and Tess. I have to run. I have a million things to do today. Contractors are coming in to give me bids on window cleaning, and I noticed that a couple of the thermal windows in the living room have broken seals. They'll have to be replaced."

"Sounds like you have a lot to do," I said. "Good morning, by the way."

She untied the apron and brushed the back of her hand across her forehead. "I'm sorry, Oliver. You don't need a summation of my to-do list."

"That's okay. Where's Tess?"

"She didn't get up when her alarm went off. I had to go in and wake her, so she was late to practice with Yoshi this morning. I would imagine she's showering and getting dressed by now, though. I'll warn you—you may be in for a rough day."

"Why? What happened?"

"Nothing happened that a little more sleep couldn't have cured."

"She stayed up late?"

Alice nodded. "It was my fault, of course. I let that boy— Tim?—stay after dinner. They did homework—at least that's what she told me—and then watched a movie. I should have sent him home much earlier."

I shrugged. "We'll manage. You made plenty of coffee, I see."

"Coffee's the least of your worries." She saw my furrowed brow and shook her head. "I better not say anymore. Maybe she'll be fine. Just... be prepared, that's all."

She hurried out. I walked over to where she'd been standing, picked up the abandoned oven mitt and opened the oven. A surge of heated air scented with pancakes, browned butter and sausage wafted out of the opening, tickling my nose and caressing my cheeks. I closed my eyes and breathed in the smell. It reminded me of Sunday mornings at my grandparents' house—the other grandparents, the ones who raised me after my father ran out on me. I didn't think of him very often because I'd never known him.

For a moment my internal compass spun wildly, and I lost all sense of time and place. Alice wasn't grandmotherly in any form, but she mothered Tess in her own gruff way, a manner which reminded me of how my grandmother had parented me. She'd been firm but fair, and while she hadn't been overtly emotional I'd always felt loved, cared for. I wondered if Tess knew how lucky she was.

I took a plate out of the oven and set it on the counter at one of the two places that had been set with utensils, napkins, glasses of juice and mugs for coffee, tea or hot chocolate. Alice also had put out butter, a small pitcher of syrup and a bowl of fresh blueberries and strawberries. I spooned a mound of berries on top of the pancakes and poured on some syrup. Tess showed up just as I tucked into my first bite, wet hair combed straight, cheeks pink and freshly scrubbed, unseeing eyes shining.

"Alice?" she called as she felt her way into the kitchen.

"*Mmfp*," I said. Washing down the food with a swig of juice, I tried again. "It's me, Oliver. Alice said she had things to take care of. Want some pancakes?"

A dark cloud crossed her face when she heard my voice. But she brightened at the mention of pancakes and paused to sniff the air.

"I thought that's what I smelled," she said. "Yes, I'd like some pancakes, please."

"There's a place for you at the counter. Second stool." I got the other plate out of the oven while she made her way to the counter and set it down in front of her.

Her fingers mapped the locations of her plate, the pancakes on it, the glass of juice and her place setting. She put her napkin in her lap and picked up her fork.

"Are you still mad at me?" I said, unnerved by her silence.

She stopped cutting pancakes with her fork. "Seems to me you were the one who was mad. Could you pour some syrup on these, please?"

Gathering my thoughts as the thick syrup slowly spread across the surface of her stack of pancakes, I finally said, "Sure, I was a little upset you wouldn't let me do my job."

She ventured a smile. "I told you we had it covered. You need to lighten up once in a while. Stop taking this so seriously." She took a bite of her pancakes.

I bit back a retort, literally chewing the inside of my lip to keep from reminding her that she wasn't the one who needed the paycheck. Through clenched teeth, I managed a pleasant, "So, you had a good time last night?"

"I had a wonderful time last night." She sounded a little too breathless for someone who only watched a movie. "It was so nice to see Tim. We've been friends for, like, forever. Well, since middle school, but I hadn't really talked to him in ages. It was so interesting to hear what he's been up to recently. I mean I knew he liked to joke around sometimes, but I didn't realize he joined the drama club. He's starring in the spring production of *Twelfth Night.*"

"As Viola?" It popped out before I could take it back.

She made a face in my general direction. "Of course not. As Orsino."

I'd just met Tim, but he struck me as the sort who might play Sir Toby Belch for the laughs, or maybe Sebastian, Viola's twin brother. But Duke Orsino?

"Hey, that's great. And you finished your homework, right?"

"God, you sound like Alice. And don't tell me it's your job. I'm sick of hearing it."

Before I could reply the sound of footsteps on the kitchen's tile floor jerked both our heads up as Marcus strode in.

"Good morning," he said, heading for the coffee brewer. "Thought I'd find you here."

He poured some into a mug, blew across the rim and slurped, wincing when the hot liquid scalded his lips. His normally crisp, fashionable attire looked a little rumpled, almost as if he'd slept in it. Though his eyes were bright as his gaze darted around the room, bags darker than the mocha skin tone of the rest of his face drooped beneath them. He held himself erect with his usual military bearing, but his shoulders stooped slightly, bent with weariness.

"Have you found my uncle yet?" Tess demanded.

"No." Marcus shook his head slowly. "That's why I'm here, of course, to give you an update. He's been gone long enough at this point that we felt it necessary to file a missing persons report with the police. We wanted to keep this in-house, but there would be questions if we didn't do everything we could to get him back. Both local and state police have issued a BOLO—be on the lookout—for him. But since we don't know how he was taken or by whom, we can't give the authorities any kind of description of a vehicle or the people responsible."

"What *are* you doing?" I asked.

He stepped up to the counter and set the mug down. I glanced at Tess and saw her wrinkle her nose so fast that I almost missed it.

"We've been working closely with the company's security team chasing down anyone who's sent a threatening note to either Travis or your father in the past two years," he said. "I know this is frustrating, but we're chasing every lead we can think of."

I focused on Marcus as he spoke and gently inhaled through my nose. A sour smell overwhelmed the usual tropical coconut scent of whatever grooming products he used.

"You will find him, though, right?" Tess spoke firmly, but her lower lip quivered.

"Yes, we will," Marcus said. "I'm sure we'll have him back in a few days. Even though we haven't received a ransom demand, we have some theories."

"Like what?" Tess said, echoing my own thoughts.

"Nothing I can discuss with you at present. But we're working on it, I promise you."

"Just get him back," Tess said. "Please."

"We're doing our best. I'll keep you posted."

"Thank you, Marcus."

Tess's conciliatory tone surprised me, but Marcus didn't seem to notice anything amiss. He gave a short nod and walked out with his coffee. I watched him go and turned to ask Tess what was up. She appeared to stare at her pancakes with narrowed eyes.

"Is he gone?" she muttered.

"Yes."

"Did you smell it? Just like last time."

"Yeah, pretty rank."

"How did he look?"

"A little disheveled. Tired. Not the fashion plate he usually is."

"Something's going on. I'm telling you he's up to something. You have to find out where he's been."

"What? Like, ask him?"

"No, stupid. Do a little research. He smells like manure, metal and rotten eggs, and something else I can't quite put my finger on. Something burning. Look up places where you're likely to find that combination."

"You're kidding, right? Think maybe you could narrow that down a little?"

"Sure," she snapped. "The metallic scent isn't ferrous. More like copper, so try that."

"Yes, ma'am. I'll get right on that just as soon as I drive you to school, take notes in all your classes and run through your homework with you after school."

"You don't have to be so snippy."

"Look who's talking. Finish your pancakes. We've got five minutes."

"I'm not hungry anymore." She shoved the plate away. I should have let it go crashing to the floor, but reflex kicked in and I caught it just before it slid off the slick granite countertop.

19

Derek swilled another gulp of his triple venti mocha and made a face. Already cold and it wasn't even seven in the morning yet. The lack of sleep was killing him. After months of burning the candle at both ends to get the app ready for release—developing it, writing it, testing it—now this. Not only did the changes to the program appear capable of reading emotions, but controlling them, too. Or at least encouraging an emotional state.

Since getting into his office well before dawn, he had been trying to isolate the program, but even when he pulled out the snippets of code that didn't belong in the app as he'd started to do the day before, he couldn't make sense of them. Somehow, the snippets were like strands of DNA, and when combined with the app program—*his* program—they formed building blocks, instructions, code that even self-replicated.

When he'd gone back into Matt's phone to look for places where the strands interacted with the app, he discovered that the program had spread. The app now controlled the phone's front- and rear-facing cameras, its audio and GPS, and could track his pulse and measure the conductivity of his skin—how sweaty his palms were as he held the phone. The more data it collected, he realized, the faster it could learn. With GPS and photos, the app could read the phone user's exact location at any given time and guess his or her preferences from visual cues. The app would know where and what he liked to eat, what kind of clothes he wore, his favorite music, who his friends were—everything about his life. Derek was stunned at the ramifications. The app could begin to predict what he would do at any given moment. And by encouraging a certain set of emotions, it could not only predict but also influence, even dictate, his choices.

The data were going somewhere, being collected and analyzed by some huge bank of servers somewhere. Probably a supercomputer bigger than IBM's Watson. With dawning horror he shut off Matt's phone, fumbled open the cover and ripped the battery and SIM card out of it. He hadn't been careful enough. He wasn't supposed to have Matt's phone. The police were probably looking for it, and they'd be asking him a whole lot of questions about how he got it if they knew it was in his possession. But that was the least of his worries. He broke into a cold sweat.

If he was right about the artificial intelligence behind his hijacked app the data were being collected here at MondoHard. Someone in the company, someone he probably passed in the hallways every day, had designed and developed the DNA code that mutated his app into the alien thing it had become. Not just a "someone," but a team, like the one he'd had working with him. And they'd done it in tandem with the development of *Never Bitten*. They'd had access to everything—his code, his notes, the test parameters...

He grabbed his notebook computer and typed in commands. He needed a better idea of what he was up against. The day before, he'd tracked the infected app to a server inside the company. Now he worked feverishly to find out who had uploaded it to the server. He used every hacking trick he knew to skirt the firewalls and bypass security protocols. He piggybacked on software service modules he knew were part of regular maintenance to hide his tracks.

Sweat moistened his brow and trickled down his temples into the stubble on his cheeks. He hunched his shoulder and wiped it off on his T-shirt. He couldn't take time to stop. He had to get in and out of the system quickly. He was in the server now, checking its logs, making it appear the check was routine. And... *There!* He found the upload notation. Grabbing a pencil and piece of scrap paper, he jotted down the pertinent information—time stamp, IP address of the computer where the upload had originated, user ID. He finished the log check and signed out of the server.

Now he turned his attention to the admin files in the HR department. Though they should have been even more secure, they were far easier to breach than the server. He used a department vp's employee ID and an old password that was still good. On his end, even if someone grew curious and tried to trace his computer, his activity would lead them back to a hacker in Kyrgyzstan. Derek quickly found the files he wanted, but frowned at the information on his screen. According to the file, the computer used for the upload was located outside Dave Bradley's office—the company's head coder and vice president in charge of all software programming. Anyone could have used Bradley's secretary's terminal. Whoever it was had used a fake employee ID, one that HR assigned to temp workers.

Derek signed off and leaned back, considering what he'd learned. Slowly, it dawned on him that the people behind this hadn't needed any of his work on *Never Bitten*. He opened the file of code snippets his special program had identified in the tainted app. A glimmer of a theory on how the bits of code worked their magic dimly lit up the back of his brain. He had the feeling that the AI program would work almost anywhere on any software program. They'd had the benefit of surreptitiously working on it alongside the development of *Never Bitten*. And they'd seen his app as the perfect way to distribute their Dr. Frankenstein. But why? What purpose did it serve to create little monsters all over the place? Fear coursed through him like an electric current. He had to watch his back. This was major. Whoever was behind this had caused a regular guy like Matt to take a gun to school and shoot up the cafeteria.

His phone whistled, signaling an incoming text. The sudden sound sent his heart leaping into his throat. He clutched his chest and looked at the phone ruefully, checking the display. The sender's number was blocked. Taking a deep breath to stop his hands from shaking, he opened up the message.

Not me. The threat's inside.

James—or the person pretending to be him—had finally responded to Derek's email. He quickly hit "Reply" and typed out a response before the guy vanished.

Inside MH? I figured that. If not you, who?

Derek waited, but his phone stared at him silently, the screen blank. The guy was like a ghost. Frustrated, he set the phone down and reached for his cold latte, nearly knocking it over when his phone whistled again. He snatched the phone off the desk and opened the text.

AI is mine. They stole it. Don't know who. Be careful.

Derek's fingers flew across the screen as he typed furiously.

What do they want? How do I find them? How do I get in touch with you again?

This time the phone remained mute. He wanted to throw it against the wall, smash it, as if that would prevent all this from happening, as if it would protect him—hell, protect all those kids who'd already downloaded copies of *Never Bitten*—from the threat *inside* and the madness someone wanted to let loose on the world. Like that would happen. Sure, toss the phone and like magic everything would be hunky-dory.

Suck it up!

Derek took a deep breath. He suddenly knew how Tess had felt a week earlier when the weight had been on her shoulders, when dark forces had been arrayed against her to prevent her from finding the strings of code that the ghost had said might save the world, to kill her if necessary. He could do this. He was the best damn coder MondoHard had ever had next to James Barrett. He could find a way to keep the AI DNA from infecting *Never Bitten*. He smiled at the irony—like looking for the cure or the antidote to being bitten by a vampire, werewolf or zombie. He'd designed a way to do it, a way to survive, in *Never Bitten*. A secret way. So, there had to be a way to beat this. And he was probably the only person in the world who could do it.

His eyes fell on the calendar hanging on the wall over his desk and focused on the date circled in red. *Crap!* The app was going live in less than two weeks! If he didn't find an antidote to the AI mutation before then, millions of people would be susceptible to its influence.

Think!

His gaze darted across his workstation, littered with electronic gear. He needed to buy time. He glanced at the calendar again, counting the days he had until the official launch of *Never Bitten*. Too few. No matter how many times he counted it came out the same. Staring at the calendar wouldn't make any difference. Yet the longer he looked, the more he felt that the answer was staring back at him. And then he saw it.

He grabbed his phone and his car keys and ran out of the office.

A little more than twenty minutes later he pulled into the parking lot behind Tess Barrett's school. He didn't trust texts or email anymore. He needed to convince her in person. Waiting in the lot seemed risky, so he grabbed a hoodie from the back seat and pulled it on, then climbed out of the car and calmly followed a group of students entering the building, hands in his pockets, eyes downcast, shoulders slumped.

He could easily fit in among these kids. It hadn't been that long since he'd been one of them, struggling with the homework load, the petty dramas, the pressure to get into college, the peer pressure. He'd barely made it through alive. Hacking had kept him sane, focused, but he'd almost gotten caught and sent to jail. Two years of college had convinced him that higher education wasn't meant for him. Fortunately, his computer skills had gotten him noticed in the right chat rooms, and James Barrett had come knocking with a job offer.

He shook off the memories and scanned the crowded hallway. He'd never find them this way. Letting himself get carried along with the flow of bodies moving down the corridor, he saw the vast space of the commons through doors to his left. He cut across the current, weaving through the small open spaces until he could break out of the stream and into the relative calm of the cafeteria. Rows of tables marched down the floor, surrounded by mostly empty chairs. Scattered here and there a few students sat eating breakfast or doing homework, noses buried in books. Two tables away, a lone backpack sat on the floor next to an empty seat.

Quickly moving toward it, he scouted the area nearby for its owner. No one stood close. He walked by the table, barely slowing to bend and scoop it up. Slinging it over one shoulder, he headed back the way he came and let the throng of students in the hall swallow him up. He moved along with the stream headed toward the administrative offices and stepped to the side when he saw a sign that said "Attendance" on the wall by a large opening. A girl with a bored expression sat behind a counter.

She noted his presence with a barely interested, "Help you?"

Derek swung the backpack off his shoulder, dug inside, pulled out a textbook and held it up.

"Yeah, this belongs to Tess Barrett. I promised I'd give it back to her. Can you tell me where her first period class is?"

The girl sighed and pushed herself to her feet. "Hang on, I'll check." She pressed herself against the edge of the counter and peered at a flat screen monitor as she typed something on a keyboard. "English. Room 310."

"Thanks."

He turned away as if he knew where he was going and stepped into the flow once more. Before he taken a half dozen steps he saw a sign that said "300 Corridor," so he veered off in that direction and down the hall until he found the right classroom. He poked his head inside but didn't see Tess, so he stood a few feet away from the door and scanned the throng of students passing by. Within minutes, Tess and Oliver came down the hall. He stepped away from the wall to intercept them.

Oliver looked at him in surprise. "What are you doing here?"

"We need to talk," Derek said in a low voice.

"Derek?" Tess had a bewildered expression on her face.

He took her arm and pulled her aside. "You were right about the app. It's messed up."

"The game? I knew something was wrong. Poor Matt."

"Yeah, yeah, poor Matt." Derek nodded impatiently. "You've got to stop the launch."

"Me? What do you mean I have to stop it?"

"Travis is still gone, right?" Derek explained. "That means you're in charge. You've got to convince the board to postpone the launch date. I need time to find a way to beat this thing."

"Why? What is it? A virus?"

Derek glanced up and down the hall, but no one paid them any attention. "It's an AI program. It thinks and adapts. Worse, I think it can predict and promote certain behavior."

"When's the launch date?"

"Next week?"

"I'll never convince the board without proof. What have you got?"

"Nothing concrete," Derek said. "I've got snippets of code that don't belong in the app program, but they just look like gibberish. I don't know how it works yet. I have an idea, but you have to buy me some time."

"They won't listen to me."

"They *have* to listen. It's *your* company, Tess. You have to try."

She sighed. "Fine. I'll try."

"When is the board meeting?" Oliver said quietly.

"This afternoon," Tess replied.

Oliver looked peeved, and Derek thought he was going to say something, but a bell rang.

"We have to get to class," Oliver said, taking Tess's elbow. "We're late."

"Yeah, well, thanks," Derek said. "I'm supposed to be at work anyway."

Oliver nodded and steered Tess toward the classroom door.

"Hey, wait," Derek said. "You still have that burner phone I gave you?"

Oliver glanced back. "Sure."

"Call me later and let me know how the meeting went."

20

The low murmur of voices filled the room, charging it with electricity. The effect was the same as the air in a thunderstorm, ionized by strong electric fields, creating paths through the sky for lightning strikes. Tess swore she could smell ozone. The cool, smooth surface of the etched glass table under her fingers reminded her of the times she'd been in this room with her father. She could still see the blue tint of the conference table top and the silver of its brushed stainless steel base, the blond ash paneling on the walls lending some warmth to the almost cold sterility of the rest of the room. She sank into the soft, plush leather of her swivel chair, still pale gray, she knew, offset by its shiny stainless steel frame.

The voices belonged to the eight men seated in matching chairs around the table. Oliver, who sat silently by her side, made nine. She heard his chair creak slightly as he swiveled it, likely for a glimpse of the breathtakingly beautiful view behind them. The conference room was on the top floor of the MondoHard building, and its curved glass wall afforded a view of Lake Union, Queen Anne Hill, the Olympic Mountains to the west and on a clear day, Mount Baker to the north in the Cascades. Today—she could tell from the hint of sun's warmth on her back through the insulated triple-pane, solar-filmed windows—was one of those days.

She felt a presence lean in next to her, bringing with it familiar scents of old leather and cedar.

"General Turnbull," she said.

"Thanks for coming," he murmured. "Very good, by the way. My cologne?"

She shook her head. "No, sir. You don't strike me as the type to wear cologne."

"Then what?"

"Just your specific smell, sir. I think maybe you wear after-shave on occasion, but I'm guessing it's a combination of the soap you use and your deodorant. Yoshi taught me."

"I'm impressed. It's a valuable skill. Well, I guess I should find a seat. The show's about to start." He chuckled. "Enjoy the fireworks. Ah, and you must be Oliver. I'm Jack Turnbull."

"General? So then you must know Travis. Duh, of course you know Travis. You're on the board."

"I used to be his boss," Turnbull said. "Now he's mine. Stop worrying, Tess. You'll do fine."

She hadn't realized that she let her feelings show. Closing her unseeing eyes, she focused on letting her muscles relax, first big ones in her legs, shoulders and arms then smaller ones like those in her face. Seeing her father's face in her mind, she remembered that he'd told her about snowboarding competitions when she was younger. *"The boys will try to beat you, Tess, not through skill, but through your emotions. They know you're a better boarder, so they'll try to undermine your confidence. They'll tease you and bully you. Don't let them get to you. Don't show them a thing. It'll drive them crazy, and they'll be the ones to lose confidence. Poker face, Tess. Don't let them see your cards."*

She took a deep breath.

"You okay?" Oliver said.

"I'm fine," she said, opening her eyes. The world was still black, a blank slate, but she knew staring at people with sightless eyes unnerved some of them.

"You knew about this meeting before Derek showed up this morning at school," he said. "Why didn't you tell me?"

"When? I found out two days ago. In case you forgot, a lot has happened since then."

He responded with silence, and for a moment she felt a twinge of guilt for snapping at him. She pushed it aside. It wasn't her job to tell him everything that was going on in her life.

"I think we can get things started here," General Turnbull said in a loud voice.

The murmur of other voices quieted as if someone twisted a volume knob on a radio, and stopped altogether.

"I move that the quarterly MondoHard board of directors meeting be called to order," the general said.

"Second," another voice said.

"All in favor?"

A chorus of "Ayes!" sounded around the room.

"I assume everyone has read the minutes of the last meeting," the general went on. "Discussion? No? Motion to accept the minutes?"

"Before we get too deep into this meeting," someone interrupted, "I'd like to know what she's doing here."

"'She' happens to be James Barrett's daughter," Turnbull said.

"I know perfectly well who she is," the voice said. "What I want to know is what she's doing here."

"I own this company, sir," Tess said, cheeks hot with anger. "And who are you?"

"Tom Cuthbert, CEO of Edge Capital. And you don't own this company, Miss Barrett. You *will* own a portion of it when you turn eighteen. More importantly, you don't run it. If my information is correct, you've never even held a job here."

Cuthbert spoke quickly, and the points he drove home made her doubt herself. She replayed her father's words again, transporting her to a half-pipe in her mind where a dozen stupid, arrogant boys thought they could stomp her ego into bits by trash-talking her skills on a stick—until they saw her shred every run.

"All of that is true, Mr. Cuthbert," she said. "Someday, however, I *will* run this company. My uncle runs it for now. Since he's unable to attend this meeting, I'm here in his place."

Another voice interjected. "This is Reginald Drexler, Miss Barrett, president of Commonwealth Bank. Where, exactly, is your uncle?"

Tess felt her chest tighten and her throat constrict. Where was Uncle Travis? He should be here, handling all of this. She wasn't ready. Again she heard her father's words. *You've got this, Tess. You can do it.*

"I don't know," she said firmly.

"You don't know," Cuthbert repeated, "yet you expect us to believe he empowered you to stand in for him?"

"You can believe whatever you want." Tess shrugged. "The fact is I'm here. And what better place to learn the business than right where I'm sitting?"

"Most people start at the bottom and work their way up to earn that seat," Cuthbert said. "Jack, this is highly irregular. Shouldn't we have been informed that Travis wasn't able to make it? We could have rescheduled."

"What's the problem, Tom?" Turnbull said. "Travis couldn't be here, so he sent Tess. She's the majority stockholder; he acts on her behalf anyway as both her guardian and president of the company."

"And all my initial objections still stand."

Oliver cut in. "May I say something?"

"Who the hell is he?" Cuthbert said.

"Oliver Moncrief, sir," Oliver said. "Tess's assistant"

"I wasn't talking to you," Cuthbert snapped.

"He's exactly who he said he is," Turnbull said, his voice even and calm. Tess even thought she heard a hint of a smile in it. A little boardroom spat was probably nothing compared to what he'd seen in combat.

"He doesn't even have a notepad or a pencil," Cuthbert grumbled. "How can he be the girl's assistant if he can't even take notes?"

"I don't need to, sir," Oliver said. "My memory is pretty good."

"Pretty good?"

"General Turnbull: *I think we can get things started here. I move that the quarterly MondoHard board of directors meeting be called to order.* Gentleman to your right: *Second.* General Turnbull: *All in favor?* Everyone: *Aye!* General Turnbull: *I assume everyone has read the minutes of the last meeting...* Should I keep going?"

"I think that will do, Oliver," Turnbull said.

"*Hmpf,* a parlor trick," Cuthbert said.

"No, sir," Oliver said. "Eidetic memory. I literally can't forget."

Tess fidgeted, and sat on her hands so she wouldn't chew her fingernails. She wanted to get to the real reason for being at this meeting, but she knew she had to bide her time if the men around the table were going to take her seriously.

"Go ahead, son," Turnbull said.

Oliver continued, speaking quietly. "Mr. Cuthbert, if I were you, sir, I'd seriously reconsider your position on Tess's presence. I don't see a lot of diversity around this table, which in this day and age just begs for a shareholder suit accusing the board of gender discrimination. That could cost the company hundreds of millions in profits."

The room broke out in a babble of heated conversation.

"I can fight my own battles," Tess hissed at Oliver. Though furious that he'd intervened, she smiled inwardly at the way he'd done it.

"Settle down, people!" Turnbull said over the jabber of voices. As the room quieted he went on. "I don't think anyone was threatening to file a lawsuit, just pointing out a need we have on the board. Now, shall we continue, gentlemen? All right then, first order of business is the defense contract for the mini-drone. I'd like to open the discussion with an update on the project. In the past few weeks, it appears that we've worked the bugs out of the system. Dave, would you explain?"

"Dave Bradley here, Miss Barrett, head of software development. As you know, gentlemen, the project has been plagued by an adaptable virus, one that mutated as fast as we tried to eradicate it. We've developed an anti-virus program that appears capable of preventing the bug from changing. At this point, we're cautiously optimistic that we've overcome the project's major obstacle."

Tess heard the creak of Oliver's chair and felt him lean in close.

"What's this 'we' business?" he murmured. "Derek wrote that program."

"Shh," she whispered. "Bosses always take credit."

She turned her attention back to the meeting.

"... isn't exactly a ringing endorsement," Cuthbert was telling Bradley.

"The company has invested far too much in this project to back down now," the general said. "We have just weeks before the defense subcommittee's decides whether or not to continue funding it. I've seen what this drone can do, gentlemen. We need it. This country needs it."

"You saw it a year ago," Drexler said. "Since then it's produced nothing but headaches. Dave, is this really the fix you've been looking for?"

"We think so," Bradley said.

"You think?" Cuthbert interjected. "Not good enough. I want to hear it from Travis. He tested the prototype. He knows how it's supposed to work. We need him here, damn it."

"We're too close to quit now, gentlemen," Turnbull said.

"Fine," Cuthbert relented. "But if you can't demonstrate a working prototype for the subcommittee by the deadline and they pull the plug, we shut the project down. It's costing us too much money."

"We can live with that, I guess," Turnbull said. "Moving on."

Tess couldn't contain herself any longer. She kept thinking about Matt, and shuddered to think that the same thing could happen to thousands of other kids.

"Before you go to the next item on the agenda," Tess said, "I'd like to introduce some new business."

Her request was met with silence, and she was afraid they wouldn't give her a chance.

"I guess we could give you a little latitude," Cuthbert said grudgingly.

She took a breath and let it out. "It concerns the new game app, *Never Bitten.*"

"That's my department," Bradley said. "Well, not directly. It's on the gaming side of the company, but since I oversee all software development, it's my purview. What about it?"

Tess wanted to just blurt out the story, but knew that if she didn't handle this properly, they'd never listen. "I have reason to believe there's something wrong with the game."

"What do you mean?" Bradley demanded. "It passed product testing with flying colors, and we've received no complaints in beta tests with consumers."

"I'm sure you all heard about the school shooting yesterday," Tess said, keeping her voice as calm as possible, even though her knees were shaking. "That was my school, and the boy involved is a friend of mine. He would never have done that without some outside influence. So I had the app tested. It's contaminated with software code that wasn't in the original program."

"What code?" Bradley said. "A virus? A worm? Why haven't I heard about this?"

Tess shook her head. "We don't know what it is yet, but if there's even a chance the game could cause someone to lose control like what happened to my friend, it's too big a risk."

"Who's 'we'?" Bradley said. "I'd like to talk to this expert of yours."

"You can't afford to delay the launch," Drexler said. "Third quarter profits depend on revenue from that game and advertising associated with it. If financial analysts get wind that we're postponing the release on top of the problems we've had delivering on the defense contract, they'll crucify us and send the stock price into the dumper."

"Is that worth the risk of someone dying?" Tess said. "I was there! You don't know how frightening it was to see a normal, well-adjusted kid like Matt just lose it like that!"

"Now, now," Cuthbert said, "I'm sure you're friend had some deep, underlying issues you didn't know about."

"I agree," Bradley said. "I'll have our team comb through the source code with magnifying glasses to see if you're right. But I highly doubt it. We need to stay on schedule with this."

"You have to listen!" Tess said, fighting the rising panic inside. "If you release this, millions of people could be affected."

"You're being alarmist," Bradley scoffed. "Show me a study that says video games cause violence and I'll show you one that says they don't. Besides, even those that do say there's a link don't suggest the games can control gamers' emotions, just slowly influence them over time."

"Tess," Turnbull said softly, "you might be taking this to the extreme. Let Dave's team check the source code. If it there's something wrong, they'll fix it. If it's clean, though, they have to release the game. It's too important to the company's bottom line."

"I disagree, sir," Oliver piped up. "As I suggested earlier, as a publicly held company you have an even greater responsibility to consumers, not just shareholders. Even one death, if it's linked to your product, can cost you dearly."

"I'll make sure it doesn't happen," Bradley said. "*If* there's a problem, we'll find it."

"There's definitely a problem," Tess said.

"Prove it," Bradley shot back. "Bring me proof, not just some story."

Tess gritted her teeth. "Oh, I will. I promise you that."

21

The blister on the side of his thumb from loosening the rail spike had popped and now bled. His fingers were so numb from the cold that Travis hardly felt the pain, but the metal grew slick with blood and hard to grip. Without letting go, he stopped for a moment to catch his breath and started in again. He wasn't about to quit now. He gripped the spike tighter and rocked it. As the bleeding slowed and dried the spike actually grew stickier so he loosened his cramped fingers some as he toggled the spike back and forth like a switch.

He'd screwed up bigtime. Not just because he hadn't anticipated this possibility—he'd thought their focus was on Tess, had never even considered he might be in their sights. No, he'd screwed this up from the very beginning. From the moment he'd accepted Jack Turnbull's assignment—protect the family—he'd handled every situation like a rank amateur, not a Special Forces soldier in an elite black ops division.

First, the debacle on the mountain a year earlier that had taken James and Sally out of the picture and blinded Tess. Then the endless problems with the micro-drone he'd first tested in Afghanistan. If he hadn't destroyed the only prototype, all those legions of design and software engineers at MondoHard would not have had to spend the past year reinventing the wheel. So many of the drone's design details had been in James's head. And the bizarre worm that had infected the operating software had been the icing on the cake. If not for Derek's genius the past couple of weeks they wouldn't have a chance of getting the prototype ready before the defense subcommittee's deadline. They still might not if Travis didn't get himself out of this jam somehow.

But his biggest screw-up had been Tess. Well, not Tess herself, but the way he'd parented her for the past year. He didn't know how James and Sally had managed, even with just one kid. Hell, Travis didn't know how James had managed to parent him at such a young age, how James had managed to keep him out of trouble and in school until he was old enough to join the army. Parenting was hard. He'd given James a lot of credit for many things, but never for being a great father. And now that it was his turn, all he could do was mess up.

True, he'd walked into parenthood totally unprepared, but what parent didn't? Also true, he'd been saddled with a teenager his first trip out the chute, not a newborn that couldn't think or provide for itself. But that meant he had the benefit of all those years of terrific guidance from Sally and James. So why couldn't he connect with Tess? They circled each other like a couple of wary wolves fighting for territory. Travis understood what it was like to lose parents. He wasn't insensitive to Tess's feelings, to what she endured every day. Why couldn't she see that? All she saw were his rules, his overprotective efforts to keep her safe. Nothing short of prison could keep any child safe—the world was a scary and dangerous place—and even prison would dampen a kid's spirit to the point of irreparable harm.

He sighed. He would just have to suck it up and accept the fact that Tess was bound to hate him no matter what he did. His job was to protect her, and he would keep that promise to James and Sally if he died trying. Because one thing he knew with absolute certainty was that the threat against the family was real. *Someone* wanted to sabotage the company, steal its secrets, possibly both. Some people suspected Travis himself. Maybe they weren't far off.

He thought about the board meeting, and wondered if Tess was terrified or holding her own. He knew Jack would maneuver her into position to sit in for Travis, but the board would insist she not vote. They would wait until either Travis showed up, which appeared unlikely anytime soon, or the court appointed her a new guardian, effectively blocking any meaningful decisions.

Travis frowned. There wasn't anything very important on the agenda that he could recall. He kept going back to the question of why they'd taken him. Why now? They still had done nothing to intimidate him or get information from him. No interrogations under blinding lights. No beatings or waterboarding. They'd done nothing but warehouse him. The same silhouetted figures had brought him food again. Another sandwich twenty-four hours after the first hadn't been enough to sustain him—he was burning body fat quickly trying to keep warm—but it had taken the edge off his hunger. Unless... *They were trying to derail the drone project, keep him out of the picture long enough to prevent the prototype from being thoroughly tested before demonstrating it to the defense subcommittee. That had to be it!*

The thought chilled Travis more than the cold emanating from the tunnel's rock walls. If his bid to renew the defense contract failed, it could cripple the company. The company had poured too much money into the development of the second prototype due to all the snafus. Unless MondoHard could sell a working model to the military to recoup that investment, the company's investors would bail. He couldn't let that happen. After all the work James and Sally had put into the company, it couldn't fail. Not on his watch. He tensed at the thought, a molten river of anger and frustration coursing through him. Unconsciously, his hand gripped the spike even tighter, and with a roar he pulled on it until the tendons on his neck stood out and his eyes bulged.

His arms quavered with the strain, and the hard, packed earth finally released its grip on the cold steel. Travis drew the spike out of the ground like Arthur pulling Excalibur from the stone, and raised it over his head in triumph. Now he had a tool. His hope rekindled, he stood on creaky joints and walked to the bat gate, working out the kinks in his back and legs as he went. He pressed the button on his watch that illuminated the face and held it out to light his way. Slowly, he inspected the gate, especially where the bars were anchored in the rock wall. Some moisture had seeped down one wall, corroding the metal. The rust and corrosion meant whoever had installed the gate had used a less expensive type of steel. Travis had expected a material more along the lines of manganese steel used to produce heavy machinery like tanks and bulldozers.

His nostrils flared, detecting the faint echo of something rotten. He wished he had the little drone he'd tested in Afghanistan, with its ability to distinguish odors. But his nose was good enough to identify sulfuric acid. The moisture had leached some sulfides from the soil on its way down through the ceiling and wall of the tunnel. The resulting acid had no doubt hastened the metal's corrosion.

The length of re-bar welded to the grate that served to anchor the grate to the wall was so rusted it sat loosely in the anchor hole drilled into the wall. The bar below it also had corroded, though not as badly. Shining the weak light across the gate, Travis felt his excitement grow. The weakened bars were less than a foot from the hinged side of the door built into the grate. Aiming the glow from his watch at the anchor hole, he stabbed at the rock around the corroded bar with the rail spike. Sparks flew as steel struck rock. Travis screwed his eyelids nearly shut to keep the flying rock chips from hitting an eye and blinding him for real.

Savagely, he hammered at the rock and steel with the point of the spike with all his strength, chipping the edges of the hole a millimeter at a time. His breathing grew labored and sweat broke out on his forehead and dripped into his eyes. He swiped it away with a sleeve and continued pounding the wall around the hole until his arm felt like lead. Mouth parched from the effort, thirst forced him to stop. *Foolish.* Expending that much effort simply drained his reserves that much faster. And overheating would lead to rapid cooling in this environment.

Locating the water they'd left him, he sipped slowly, rationing it carefully. When his heart rate settled down, he squatted next to the grate where he'd been working, gripped one of the cross bars and pulled. The metal groaned as the gate shifted a fraction of an inch. He pushed it the other direction, putting his weight into it, trying to bend the corroded re-bar anchored into the wall. Again, it shifted a fraction, but the re-bar anchor showed no sign of weakening. He had a lot more work to do, but he'd made progress.

He rested another five minutes, gripped the strap of his watch in his fist so he could aim the dim light at the wall, and chipped away at the hole with the spike. Working more methodically this time, he conserved his energy. Slow and steady would win this race. The steady rhythm of his pounding mesmerized him into a kind of stupor, and his movement grew as automatic as the ticking armature of a metronome. After a while nothing existed except the loud *whang* of metal on rock, as regular as his pulse. Even the pain in his hands and legs and back faded into another place as the hypnotic swinging of his arm became his sole focus.

Sometime later, and without warning, the little light on his watch winked out, plunging the tunnel into total darkness. Travis had completely lost track of time. He didn't know if it had been minutes or hours since he'd started. For a moment he panicked, but he forced himself to breathe deeply and rein in his fear. Darkness was his friend. Darkness had provided cover under which he'd been able to strike his enemy undetected in Afghanistan. Darkness had provided shelter when he and his team had needed rest and refuge. For years, darkness was the environment in which he'd operated best, tracking and stalking his kill like a heat-seeking missile.

But this was different. This was complete blindness. He held his hand in front of his face. *Nothing.*

This was Tess's world.

22

"Come on," I muttered. "Let's get out of here."

I took her elbow and helped her stand, turned and waited until I felt her fingers find a spot on my shoulder and give me a gentle tap to let me know she was ready. I returned a few curt nods as we walked out, but most of the men in the room ignored us. I was a hired hand—the "help" as they used to say down south—and Tess was female, status that rendered us both insignificant, unimportant. I wanted out of there as quickly as possible not to spare Tess any more humiliation—despite their best efforts, she'd held her own pretty well—but because if we stayed any longer I might've hit somebody.

The tension in Tess radiated up through her arm and out the tips of her fingers. I could feel their imprint on my skin through my shirt.

"They didn't even listen," she said. Her voice trembled with anger.

"Oh, they listened," I growled. "They just didn't want to hear what you had to say."

"What are we going to do?"

"Get proof." I stopped in the hallway and pushed the button to signal an elevator. "Derek never should have sent you into that meeting without it."

"I had to be there anyway. And Derek doesn't have anything yet."

"Then he shouldn't have asked you to speak to the board. They made a laughingstock of you, Tess. And now it's going to be twice as hard to convince them, even with proof."

A set of elevator doors opened with a soft *ding*. I led Tess inside. Down the hall, General Turnbull broke away from a group of board members and hurried toward us. He raised his hand.

"Hold the elevator," he called.

I let the doors close without even making an effort to stop them.

"Was that—?"

"Turnbull," I finished for her. "He wasn't much help in there. Let him get his own elevator."

"Well, we didn't exactly let him in on it ahead of time," Tess said. "Maybe I should have."

"Look, he's either an ally or an enemy. He didn't act like much of an ally in there. How much do you know about him, anyway?"

Tess chewed on a fingernail.

"I thought so." I looked up at the blinking numbers. "Our floor's next."

The elevator slowed and stopped with a soft bump on a garage level. Tess's fingers crept to the top of my shoulder. They trembled as she followed a half step behind me to the car, and I heard her sniffle.

"Where are we going?" she said as she lowered herself into the passenger seat.

He turned her head away, but not far enough to hide her swiping at her cheek with her sleeve.

"I don't know yet." I shut her door and rounded the hood to get in behind the wheel.

"I don't want to get home too late," she said in a small voice after I started the engine. "Tim's supposed to come over later so we can do math homework."

Again with the boyfriend. She was breaking my heart, not to mention cutting into my hours. What we needed was a break from all of it—from the psychopathic app that made kids shoot up school cafeterias to Travis's disappearance to stuffy company board meetings. And, yes, from the new boyfriend, too. Suddenly, inspiration struck. I pulled out of the parking garage with a clear destination in mind. A black SUV pulled out right behind me—our security detail for the day, though I couldn't remember who was on duty. Red, maybe.

Twenty minutes later we pulled into a gravel drive not far from Tess's house that curved up to a long, low-slung stable. At the far end was a large fenced-in riding ring, and beyond that a smaller covered ring for riding in inclement weather. I parked close to the big sliding door at the end of the stable. Glancing in the rearview mirror, I was glad to see that the SUV had hung back without turning into the drive, and now parked on the shoulder of the road.

"Wait here," I said as I got out. "I have to check something."

"Where are we?"

"You'll see. Just wait. I'll be back in a minute."

I hurried into the stable before Tess grew impatient, and quickly found the manager mucking out a stall.

"Mrs. Forrester?"

She stopped and leaned on her fork, peering at me from under the brim of a baseball cap embroidered with the stable's logo.

"Do I know you?"

"I'm Oliver Moncrief. We met on a couple of other occasions."

She shook a finger in my direction. "Hang on. Just about got it. Yep, you were with Suki Hashimoto. Both times. Or was it three? How'd that work out?"

"I got a few good rides out of it," I grinned.

"Figured, seeing as how she's been here with, oh, two or three boys since. What can I do you for?"

I explained what I wanted. She looked doubtful, and glanced at her watch.

"Tell you what," she said. "It's slow right now, so I'll give you half an hour. Free, if you help me finish mucking out these stalls."

"It's a deal."

I hustled out to get Tess while Mrs. Forrester saddled up a horse. She wrinkled her nose as I helped her out of the car. I sniffed the air—earthy, with the grassy scent of straw. The odors were stronger in the stable—horse sweat and the sharp scent of urine mixed in with the smell of straw and earth.

"I smell horses." Tess said.

Mrs. Forrester led a dark bay mare from its stall. It nickered softly as they approached.

Tess took a step back. "What's going on, Oliver?"

"You are going riding," I told her.

"I'm not dressed for it or anything!" she blurted.

"You're dressed just fine," Mrs. Forrester said. "All you need's a helmet, and we've got extras lying around."

"But I can't," she protested. "Oliver, tell her. You know I'm—"

"Blind?" Mrs. Forrester said. "Swee' Pea, here, can see just fine. And she doesn't give a hoot what you're wearing."

The mare nickered again and nuzzled Tess's hand. Tess tentatively stroked the mare's muzzle. Swee' Pea blew into her hand in response. A hint of a smile lightened Tess's face as she moved her hand up to the horse's cheek and then its strong, graceful neck. Swee' Pea stood motionless, pressing her nose and forelock into Tess's side as Tess stroked her neck.

A few minutes later, a helmeted Tess sat astride Swee' Pea, hands white-knuckling the saddle's pommel as I led the horse to the covered ring.

"She won't bite," I said. "And she won't buck you off, either. Relax."

Tension drained out of her, shoulders coming down from around her ears, and legs swinging more naturally with the horse's gait. She leaned forward, taking one hand off the pommel and running it up Swee' Pea's neck. Twining her fingers in the horse's mane, she leaned farther still until her nose touched Swee' Pea's glossy coat. She breathed deeply. When she straightened, a smile spread across her face that made me glad I'd thought of this place. She looked happier than I'd seen her since I answered Alice's ad for a personal assistant.

"I've never done this," she said sounding surprised that she enjoyed it.

"You've never ridden a horse? I thought that was a mandatory phase in every girl's life—ballerina, gymnast, equestrian..."

"Not this girl. I was a tomboy I guess. How'd you know about this place? I mean, I've seen it a million times. Well, I used to see it. It's the stable near my house, right?"

"Yes." I hesitated. "I dated a girl who rides here. That's how I met Mrs. Forrester. Mrs. Forrester volunteers her time to a school for the blind, and the owners of the horses donate them for an hour or two a week so the blind kids can ride them."

Tess was silent for a moment. Finally, she said, "So, are you still dating her?"

"That girl? No, not my type."

"That's too bad." Somehow she didn't sound all that sorry. "Well, I'm glad Mrs. Forrester remembered you. This is nice."

She stroked Swee' Pea's neck. For the next fifteen minutes while I walked the horse in a slow circle around the riding ring, Tess and I just talked about nothing in particular—likes and dislikes, favorite subjects, teachers good and bad, best prank on a schoolmate, best summer vacation trip... I made her laugh a couple of times with college tales of derring-do. She recounted similar stories, all pre-accident I noted. She brightened as if she'd thrown off some invisible film that filtered out some of the spectrum of light that shone from within. For that short bit of time, the outside word didn't exist—no missing uncle, no deadly game app, no condescending board members, no security team... Well, not breathing down our necks anyway. A quick glance confirmed that the SUV was still parked out on the side of the road.

With about five minutes left, I told Tess to take her feet out of the stirrups, and swung up onto Swee' Pea's rump behind the saddle. Reaching around Tess, I gently took the reins from her hands and made a circuit around the ring, explaining what I was doing as we went. Then I put the reins back in her right hand, had her find the stirrups again with her feet and let her guide Swee' Pea. I loosely wrapped my arms around her waist, and with my chin over her shoulder gave her course corrections and encouragement.

After a couple of circuits, I hopped off and let Tess ride Swee' Pea back to the stable, walking alongside with my hand on the horse's bridle just in case. Just outside the stable door sat a wooden structure built almost like three small open-air stalls with no doors on the front, and covered with a raised roof on posts. A ramp led up to a platform in back running the length of the stalls. The smell hit me right about the same time I remembered that the stalls were meant to compost the heaping contents inside.

Tess squirmed in the saddle, and held her nose with a sour expression. "Oh, god, that's awful. What is it, Oliver?"

"Horse manure. It's a composting shed."

She suddenly went still, looking more thoughtful, and gave a tentative sniff. "That's it."

"What's it?"

"That smell," she said, leaning forward in excitement. "It's what I smelled on Marcus. Not just manure, Oliver. Horse manure. He's been on a ranch."

"Maybe he was here," I said.

She shook her head vehemently. "No, not here. There's no metallic smell here. No rotten egg smell, either. You have to help figure out where he's been, Oliver. I'll bet you anything that's where we'll find Uncle Travis."

She was right. I recognized it now. The last two times we'd seen Marcus, he'd been around horses recently. Not just horses, but a stable where he'd picked up the smell of manure, probably on his boots. But I couldn't wrap my head around what that meant. Why would Marcus look for Travis in a stable or on a horse ranch? And if Tess was right, then Marcus either was covering for Travis, or he'd been in on the kidnapping. My unease grew. I'd clued Red in, more to humor Tess than anything. Now I wasn't so sure. I didn't know who to trust anymore.

23

The cell phone on Derek's desk *feeped*, signaling an incoming e-mail. He cursed himself for not setting his phone on silent. The last thing he needed now was more distractions. Most of his day had been spent tweaking and making final edits on the software program he'd written to neutralize the worm that had plagued the mini-drone that MondoHard was building for the military.

His entire career at the company had been in the video games division until company president Travis Barrett had plucked him out of his comfortable obscurity in the legions of programmers at the huge conglomerate a few weeks earlier. Travis had roped him into figuring out what was wrong with the drone project, and Derek had taken the bait. The challenge had appealed to his ego. But now the pressure was on to finish, to fix what had gone wrong with the project for the past year before the bureaucrats in D.C. pulled the plug. In the meantime, Barrett had vanished, and someone had sabotaged his game app. Could it get any worse?

He tore his attention away from the computer monitor and glanced at the subject line.

Complications

Oh, crap, what now? The sender's line was blank; he knew if he opened it all he'd see was an IP address that led nowhere. His mystery man. Pulse racing now, he knew he had no choice. He logged onto his secure notebook computer, opened his email and read the rest of the message.

You've got problems. T. gave the app to someone who shouldn't have it—Austin Dunn. You better find answers quick.

A rising tide of panic welled up in his chest, threatening to drown him. A link floated on the message screen like a life ring. His hands dove for it, fingers swimming across the keyboard. The link pulled up a drop box, and Derek quickly typed a reply.

Who's Austin Dunn? What answers? Where? How do you know this? Why are these MY problems? Why can't you fix them? Wall!

He hit "Send" and waited. Paranoia set in with the next wave of panic. Derek forced himself to breathe slowly, leaned back in his chair and stretched, casually glancing over his shoulder. Across the room, Paul sat with his back turned, absorbed in his own work. His other two office roomies had gone out for a late lunch and hadn't come back. Hell, all three of them were out to lunch mentally, but they were decent coders if he told them exactly what to do. He sat up and glared at the small notebook screen, willing it to reveal a new email. His phone beeped suddenly. He grabbed it and set it on vibrate then opened the incoming message on his notebook.

Only so much I can do from here. Lucky to find out this much. I'm counting on you.

Derek knew further questions would only result in equally enigmatic answers. His shoulders drooped as he closed out of the window. Why him? Why was everyone suddenly turning to him for answers? He was just a gamer who'd happened to luck into a job that let him do exactly what he wanted most of the time. But the more he thought about it, the more he realized that he was more than that, a heck of a lot more. He was the best damn coder at MondoHard, for sure. And in his younger, dark-side days, he'd held his own against some fearsome wizards in hackerdom. He wasn't some pansy-ass poser like Paul. He was the real deal.

So, act like it.

Okay, so first things first. Find out who this Austin Dunn was. Easy enough. Derek ran an online search. To his surprise, the name popped up almost immediately in every search result on the first page. He linked to one page and saw some story about a kid in D.C. Next link, same kid. Derek read the story more closely. The kid was the son of Vice President Josiah Dunn. Okay, so the kid was famous, but not so famous that Derek had ever heard of him before. Maybe Dunn was famous among middle school girls who read *Teen* and *People* magazines. So what was the big deal? So, Travis gave the kid a beta copy of the game. That didn't mean it was one of the infected copies. And even if it was and the kid went a little nuts like Matt had, what would it do other than get him kicked out of school? Might not help his dad's political career, but the vice presidency was a dead-end job anyway.

Still, Derek didn't want *anyone* to have a bogus copy of *Never Bitten* until he figured out what was wrong with it. One, it would kill his rep if people thought he had anything to do with the bogus version. And two, the more he learned about what the AI infection could do, what kinds of biometrics it could track, the more he worried about much influence it could exert over someone playing the app. He'd already started on a fix. Problem was, he'd had to devote most of the day to debugging the other major fix Travis had tapped him for. Well, he'd done enough for the day.

He glanced at his cell phone display and was surprised to see that it was long past quitting time. He *had* done enough. Time to return to this little project. But first, he needed something to nosh on. His stomach growled at the same time he realized he'd worked through lunch. He spun his chair around.

"Yo, Paulie," he said. "I'm starved. Want to split a pizza?"

Paul clicked a few more strokes on his keyboard and turned around to look at him. "No, thanks, man. Appreciate the offer, but I just wrapped up for the day, and I am outta here."

"Hot date?"

Paul blushed as he stood up and peeled the windbreaker off the back of his chair. "Not really. Dinner and a movie with some friends."

"Cool. Just thought I'd ask."

"Sure. Thanks again. See you tomorrow."

Derek waved as Paul turned for the door. "Yeah, goodnight."

He swiveled back to his desk, picked up his phone and speed-dialed a pizza joint that delivered. As soon as he'd placed his order and disconnected, the phone vibrated in his palm. He checked the display nervously, wondering if Mystery Man had more bad news. But this time it was a text message from Tess. He opened it.

Board won't nix launch. We need proof. Bradley "looking into it." Help!

The idea of pizza suddenly didn't seem so good. His stomach knotted. He needed more time. James Barrett had spent years working on artificial intelligence. Derek knew the stories. He'd spent his early years as a hacker reading up on Barrett, learning everything he could about him. Even when he'd gone dark-side for a year or so, he'd kept tabs on what Barrett was working on. It was probably what had kept him from stepping so far over the line that he couldn't come back to the light. It had definitely influenced his decision to join MondoHard. But Derek had less than two weeks to learn what James had developed—what someone had stolen—and figure out how to outsmart it. It couldn't be done.

Derek slumped in his chair. He could figure it out eventually. He knew he could. But in two weeks? No way. If Tess hadn't been able to buy time from the board, though, what was left? *Proof.*

Sure. Tess was right, proof that the app had been tampered with would buy time. But it had to be solid. Derek knew he couldn't rely on the little he'd gleaned from his earlier digging. A few random copies downloaded from one of the servers? They'd simply say it was a hardware glitch and pull the server off-line. He had to find evidence that incriminated whoever was behind this, something that would nail them.

He glanced at the text again. Bradley was on the board of directors. And now he knew Tess was aware of the bogus app. The terminal outside Bradley's office had been used to upload the infected version to the server. Derek had a hard time believing a board member and the head of software development would try to sabotage his own company. But he'd seen some pretty weird stuff in the past few weeks. Near as he could tell, there was a battle going on inside the company that practically no one knew about. Even Travis didn't seem to know who he was up against. Derek had made his choice, picked his side. If Bradley'd had anything to do with what they'd done to *Never Bitten*, he'd be covering his tracks, and soon. Pizza would have to wait.

He checked the time once more—already past 7:30 at night—tucked his notebook computer under his arm, grabbed an extra external hard drive off a nearby work table, and headed out. The halls were quiet, the way he preferred it. While he had no doubt that plenty of people still slaved over projects at their desks, most had gone home for the evening. He'd already been there for more than fourteen hours, but he didn't feel tired. Adrenaline fueled him now.

He worked his way up two floors and across the building to the section in which Bradley's office resided. Derek had been in the vicinity only once, to drop off some work for another project manager soon after he'd started at the company, but he remembered being introduced to Bradley in the hall as he came out of his office. While Derek had heard murmurings in offices on the floors below, this floor was almost deathly still. He wasn't surprised; the bosses had gone home while workers bees continued to drone in the hive below. It made his present job easier.

Surreptitiously checking both directions as he approached Bradley's office, he slipped inside and headed straight for the large mahogany desk. He circled behind it and sat down, placing his gear on the desk. He glanced underneath the desk to see if the CPU was turned on, but didn't bother pulling out the keyboard drawer. To be safe, he tried not to touch anything. He opened his notebook and connected it to Bradley's computer with a USB cord. He knew Bradley's computer would be password-protected. The guy headed up one of the biggest software divisions in the country—he knew how important security was—and Derek didn't want anyone to be able to detect that he'd tried to log on. Instead, he used some tricks he knew to clone Bradley's encrypted hard drive onto the spare he'd brought along. He figured that Bradley probably stored most of his files in the "cloud," but Derek could track a lot of his email and probably get into most of his files by checking the temporary files on the CPU.

While the CPU's files copied to Derek's external hard drive, he pulled up a key-logging program he'd customized and tinkered with it. In his hacking days, he'd used "rootkits" to hack into encrypted systems, but over time operating system security had gotten better. Now he used a special "bootkit," a more powerful version of the rootkit. He'd hacked into IT's system and gained administrative access to every computer in the company his second week on the job. Old habits die hard. Now all he had to do was used that access to do "routine maintenance" on Bradley's computer and install the bootkit in the process. Once installed, it was undetectable.

Just to be sure, he double-checked that IT hadn't installed any new security patches since he'd last tested the bootkit. The company intranet was slow for some reason, and he caught himself before he started to drum impatiently on the desk with his fingers. He wiggled them over his keyboard instead, willing both the file transfer and the network connection to go faster. Finally the check of the IT updates stopped running, and Derek quickly scanned down the list. He saw nothing that concerned him, so he used his admin access to insert the bootkit on the CPU's drive.

He'd been so intent on his work that he hadn't paid attention to his surroundings at all, but gradually the sound of voices penetrated his focus, and he jerked up in alarm. Listening intently, he heard what sounded like an argument. The voices weren't that close. He checked the progress of the hard drive transfer—almost done. Heart pounding, he raced to the office door on tiptoe, opened it a crack and peered out into the hall. Bradley and another veep Derek vaguely recognized stood next to the elevators in heated conversation. *Crap!* Bradley could head for his office at any second! He was trapped!

Derek raced back to the desk, slid the notebook and external drive off the top and crouched next to the chair. Silently, he willed the files to transfer faster. *Come on, come on! Almost there!* The voices grew louder, closer. Derek caught only fragments.

"...what do you want me to do?" the veep said. "Stonewall?"

"She's a kid!" Bradley said, "with no authority. What're you afraid of?"

"Losing my job."

"Don't forget who your boss is," Bradley menaced.

Their voices dropped to murmurs for a moment, and Derek focused on his computer screen. The progress bar hesitated, blinking, and finally hit the end. *Success!* Derek shut the notebook and quickly yanked the cable out of Bradley's CPU and the notebook, unplugged the external drive and stuffed them both in his pocket. He held his breath as the voices stopped right outside the office door. Peeking over the top of the desk, is heart nearly jumped out of his chest as he saw it open. He ducked his head and slowly sucked in another deep breath, sure the thumping in his chest would give him away. Bradley would discover him in a matter of seconds.

How the hell was he going to explain what he was doing under Bradley's desk? His thoughts raced.

"...no, you have to see this first," the veep said.

"Now?" Bradley was clearly annoyed. "All right, fine. Let's do this quickly. I have to be somewhere."

The veep's voice replied, but from farther away. They'd gone! Derek released the breath he'd been holding and quickly tiptoed to the door, notebook clutched in his hand. He poked his head around the doorframe. Bradley and the other man disappeared into an office down the hall. Derek slipped out into the hall and practically flew in the opposite direction, ducking into the nearest stairwell.

24

Tess didn't think she'd ever been so confused in her life. For two days she'd ridden an emotional rollercoaster, not knowing from one minute to the next what was around the next bend or over the next crest. Events cascading around her had made it hard to tell what was normal anymore. Matt's frenzied outburst at school had been horrifying, more so because it had been so unlike him. Her uncle had disappeared, and she couldn't help thinking that the man in charge of her safety and security was responsible. Her first board of directors meeting at the company she would soon inherit, and maybe eventually run, had gone disastrously wrong because no one would take her seriously.

The only bright spot had been the chance to ride Swee' Pea. Horses had never interested her. She'd always been into more physical pursuits—snowboarding, her jiu-jitsu, tennis in the summer. But the rocking motion in the saddle had been almost hypnotic. The feel of the horse's power beneath her, wrapped in gentleness, had instilled her with awe. Swee' Pea somehow understood her, sensed her emotions, her thoughts. Tess had almost freaked out when Oliver had climbed on behind her. It had seemed so random, so weird until she realized that he wanted to teach her how to control the horse. After that she'd actually kind of enjoyed his presence. Comforting somehow. She knew that assisting her—even taking her horseback riding—was Oliver's job, but sometimes, like yesterday, he acted more like a protective big brother.

Though all of that whirled through her mind, she couldn't focus on any of it—not homework, not Yoshi's practices, not the horrible things that had happened. All she could think about was Tim.

Yoshi slammed her to the mat for the gazillionth time that morning. Tears sprang to her eyes and she cried out in pain. Once again she'd lost focus, thinking about everything but the task at hand. Now she was bruised and sore. It wasn't fair, but she had no one to blame but herself.

"Enough!" Yoshi barked. "Big waste of time if you don't concentrate."

Tess bit her lip to keep from crying, but the tears overflowed anyway. "I'm sorry! I just can't do this."

"Yes, you can. You *choose* not to. You think someone who attack you will wait while you daydream all day? You somewhere else today. Waste my time."

"I said I was sorry." Wiping her eyes on the sleeves of her *gi*, she slowly pulled herself to her feet. "Why are you being so mean?"

"Yoshi no different today than any other day. You the one who is different. You need to use stones more. They help center you."

Tess hadn't even thought about the flat, smooth stones—rose quartz and blue obsidian—Yoshi had given her weeks before. She'd been able to tell them apart not just by their shape and feel, but by the energy they seemed to radiate. Crazy, but the rose quartz always felt warmer and more soothing. The cool blue obsidian seemed to clarify things in her mind and make it easier to put her thoughts into words.

"I will," she said hesitantly. "I've just had so much on my mind lately."

Yoshi grunted. "Is boy, I can tell. You need to clear your mind when you are here. Next time you come, you bring 'Tess' with you. Now go."

She waited. Normally, Yoshi would point her in the direction of the door. Today, she heard his bare feet softly pad away, probably heading for the small locker room to shower and change. She wanted to scream at him, but she knew it was useless. Raising her leaden arms, she shuffled the opposite way, gently patting the air to ward off any potential collision, sniffling as she went.

By the time she showered and dressed, Tess had calmed down some. After a final check with her fingers to make sure buttons and zippers were fastened and hair brushed and in place, she headed downstairs. She was still so angry she wanted to hit something—or someone—but she wasn't sure at whom she should direct all that anger. It melted away the closer she came to the kitchen, replaced once more with thoughts of Tim—his laugh, warm voice and encouraging words. She tried to picture the way he might look now—green eyes more knowing and less naive, the shock of reddish-brown hair maybe a little shorter in front so it didn't fall over his eyes so much, freckles splattered across his nose faded a bit, face lengthened, jaw squared and shoulders broadened in the year since she'd last seen him.

"Good morning."

Oliver's voice brought her back to earth. Lucky she hadn't walked into a wall. Her fingers brushed the kitchen doorframe and she stepped through.

"Good morning," she said, her excitement building. "Did you get all the things I asked for?"

"What things?" Alice said from across the kitchen. "What did she ask you to get?"

"Just some balloons and stuff," Tess said, her heart sinking.

"It was no problem, really," Oliver said. "I was glad to help."

"Balloons...?" Alice said. "What are you up to, Tess?"

She thrust out her chin. "I'm going to invite Tim to spring tolo."

"Oh, Tess, you know Travis won't approve," Alice said.

"Uncle Travis isn't here! He can't tell me what to do if he isn't even here."

"But you know what he'd say if he were," Alice replied. "I just don't want you to be disappointed."

"I told Tess I'd talk to Travis," Oliver said quietly. "I think I can convince him, especially if I offer to go along."

Alice heaved a sigh. Tess thought she might say something more, but the distant gong of the doorbell intruded.

"Odd," Alice muttered on her way past Tess. "Marcus should have let me know we had a visitor."

When Tess could no longer hear Alice's footsteps in the hall, she faced the center of the room. "You're sure you got it all? Everything I asked for?"

"I told you I got it," Oliver said. "I'm not a complete moron. I made the poster just like you asked. It's all in the car."

"You don't have to be snippy."

"Look, Tess, you hired me to assist you. You wouldn't keep me around long if I couldn't follow simple instructions."

"I thought you wanted to help me. I thought you were my friend. It's just a job to you."

"I said I'd help and I will. But I don't have to like it."

Tess was still thinking of a reply when she heard two voices approaching, both raised in argument.

"...she's been through enough," Alice was saying as she entered the kitchen.

"Why don't we ask her? Good morning, Tess."

"General Turnbull," she murmured. "What are you doing here so early?"

"You left so quickly after the meeting yesterday I never got a chance to speak with you."

"There was nothing to say," Oliver said, an edge in his voice. "You left her hanging out there like a slab of meat for the wolves to feast on."

"Careful, son," Turnbull said. "You don't want to pick a fight unless you can finish it."

"I'm not looking to fight you, sir. I'm looking out for Tess. She deserves better than what you gave her in that meeting, which was a whole lot of squat."

"I admit things could have gone better, but you could have given me a little warning you were going to shanghai the agenda to talk about this app—what was it, *Never Bitten*? What was that all about?"

"We didn't have time to tell you, General," Tess said. "There's definitely something wrong with the program. And it may have caused my friend to bring a gun to school."

"Who told you there's something wrong with the software?"

"We'd rather not say, sir," Oliver chimed in. "It could—"

"I'll warn you again, son. I appreciate your loyalty to Tess, but this doesn't concern you."

"Begging your pardon, *sir*, but the hell it doesn't. It became my business the day I started as Tess's assistant, and has continued through several attempts on her life, and mine, too."

Tess jumped in quickly before the fight escalated. "It's a person we trust, and he thinks the app was sabotaged by someone inside MondoHard."

"You should have told me this sooner." Turnbull finally sounded concerned.

"Why should we trust you?" Oliver said.

"Oliver!" Alice said sharply. "Be careful. You're on thin ice. General Turnbull practically raised James and Travis after their parents died. He's family."

"Thank you, Alice," Turnbull said quietly, "but we're getting off point, here. Tess, I still need you—the company needs you. The board wants to reconvene. Cuthbert got wind that Travis may have been abducted and is pushing to replace Travis and cancel the defense contract. We need to stall him."

"The board won't listen to me! You saw what they did."

"They have to. You own the shares."

"But you told me it's all still in trust until I'm eighteen."

"We'll make them take it to court. We need to buy more time to find Travis."

"Why don't you leave her alone?" Oliver said. "You're just using her."

"It's her company, son," Turnbull said quietly. "She either fights for it or watches it go down in flames. It's up to her, not me. I'm just trying to help her save it."

Tess felt torn. All she wanted to do was think about what dress to wear to tolo and where she should take Tim to dinner before the dance.

"Why me?" she cried. "Why do I have to save the world? Isn't that what parents are for? Oh, that's right; I don't have any! Oliver, I want to go to school now."

"Tess," Alice sounded shocked, "be reasonable. You haven't even had breakfast."

"I'll get something at school. Are you coming, Oliver?"

"Right here," he said, taking her elbow. He guided her toward the garage.

"What should I tell the board?" the general called after her.

"Whatever you want," she said. "I don't care."

"Tess Barrett!" Alice barked. "Don't you walk out on General Turnbull."

"It's all right," the general said. "Let her go. She needs—"

The door to the garage closed behind them, cutting off the rest of his thought.

Two minutes later Oliver accelerated her mother's car smoothly onto the main road outside the gate. Tess leaned back in the plush leather seat and closed her eyes. The view was the same with eyes open or closed—nothing but darkness. But images raced through her brain—fleeting pictures of faces and places that already had faded in the year since her accident; sounds of voices, those of her parents mixed in with Alice's and the general's, and explosions and gunfire ripping the night into pieces; whiffs of scents ranging from roses to coconut to horse manure.

She'd been through so much in the past year, but they still wanted more from her. All she wanted was her old life back. Like that could ever happen. She wanted her mother to be there when she got home from school with a hug, a cheery greeting and a cookie still warm from the oven. She wanted her dad to come home from work and ask her how her day had been. She wanted to *see*.

Oliver's voice intruded on her thoughts. "Are you okay?"

145

"Peachy, thanks." She regretted her tone as soon as the words left her mouth. "Sorry."

Oliver was quiet the rest of the way to school, which was fine with Tess. She had plenty on her mind. When he parked, though, he broke his silence.

"We're pretty early. Did you want to get something to eat?"

She nodded. "Yes, please."

She got out of the car and waited for him. When he took her hand and put it on his shoulder, she voiced a question that had nagged her on the ride to school.

"You'll still help me, won't you?"

"Sure. It's what friends do."

She couldn't help a half-smile. "Smart-ass."

The morning dragged on forever. The more Tess wished lunch period would come more quickly, the longer her classes seemed to last. Finally, the bell signaled the end of her agonizing wait.

In the crowded commons, Oliver found them sets at a table and went to get them a bite to eat. A minute or two later he put something on the table in front of her.

"Turkey sandwich," he said. "And your friend is here."

"He is?" Her head whipped one way and the other as if she could actually look around and see him. "Go tell him to wait. No, tell him I have a surprise for him. Then you can get it out of the car. It's in the car, right?"

"Yes, it's in the car. I'll tell what's-his-face to come over. Back in a bit."

Tess bit back a retort and squirmed in her seat. A few moments later she sensed someone's nearby presence and stopped fidgeting.

"Tess? It's Tim. Oliver said you have something to show me?"

All of a sudden, Tess could hardly breathe. She opened her mouth to say something, but nothing came out. Her ears burned as she strained to get enough oxygen into her lungs.

She squeaked his name. "Tim!" Clearing her throat, she tried again. "Yes, I do. Have something to show you. Well, I don't have it, exactly. It's in the car. Oliver's getting it."

The words came in a rush, and now her whole face was on fire.

"Are you okay?" Tim said. "You look like you've got a fever or something."

"I'm fine. I'm just... it's warm in here, that's all."

As usual, the sheer volume of conversations combined to create a dull roar in the cavernous room, and she and Tim had to raise their voices to hear one another. Tess felt sure the people around her were staring and listening in.

"So," Tim said, sounding awkward, "can you give me a hint? No, wait. You said Oliver was getting it? I think I know what it is. OMG, Tess, you didn't."

Fear suddenly gripped her. "Oliver's back?"

Of course Oliver was back. Tess could hear murmurs and catcalls spread from the table outward like ripples in a pond.

"You don't like them?" she said, her stomach dropping through the floor.

And then Oliver was at the table. "These are for you, Tim."

"Oh, gee, um, thanks."

Now the murmurs turned to hoots and laughter. Tess imagined the poster Oliver had made: "TIM, TOLO? TESS." Her face felt as if it was on fire.

"I'm sorry, Tess," Tim said. "I had no idea you... I mean I didn't know you could..."

Tears stung her eyes, but Tess wouldn't let them see her cry. Not here, not now.

"What? You didn't think I could dance? Because I'm blind?"

Tim started in again, less hesitant this time. "No, it's not that. I never thought you'd go. You've been such a hermit the past year. I really am sorry, Tess. Katie already asked me if I'd go to the dance with her, and I said yes. But thank you for thinking of me. And thanks for the balloons. They're... nice."

Nice? That's it? Tess tried to tune out the laughter, the rude comments, but she was mortified. She'd just made a complete fool of herself.

Oliver leaned in and murmured in her ear. "Come on, Tess. Let me get you out of here."

Wordlessly, she pushed her chair back and stood. Oliver took her hand in his. Instead of letting her put it on his shoulder, he held it tight and led her through a door outside. Laughter echoed behind them until the door cut it off with a metallic *clank* as it slammed shut. Tess walked to the car in stunned silence. How could she have been so stupid? She hadn't even broached the subject of tolo with Tim, never asked if he was going or even interested in going.

Oliver didn't let go of her hand until he opened the car door for her. Now that she noticed, it seemed odd but had been strangely comforting.

He slid into the driver's seat. "Tess, I—"

"Don't say a word. Not one word."

"I was just going to ask if there was somewhere in particular you wanted to go. Me? I'd be thinking about going for ice cream after something like that."

She couldn't quite force a smile, but she appreciated the attempt to lighten her mood.

"Sure. What the heck."

He patted her knee. "Atta girl."

As they pulled out of the lot, Tess's phone chirped. She fished it out of her jeans.

"Hello?"

A garbled voice answered hollowly. "If you want to see your uncle alive again, quit the MondoHard board."

Tess went cold with fear. "Who is this?"

"This is your only warning. Turn in a formal letter of resignation by Monday morning, or Travis Barrett is a dead man."

25

Travis had lost all sense of time. Day and night did not exist in the tunnel. There was only darkness, unrelenting, disabling stygian gloom. Only three events gave any signal of passing time: bats left the cave at dusk and returned sometime before dawn; and his jailers brought him food and water after the bats came back to roost and before they left to forage. In between, he no longer could judge how many minutes or hours ticked by. Exhaustion slowly filled his limbs like a rising tide that would eventually drown him. His only recourse was to swing the iron spike blindly in the dark and hope the rock and steel bars gave way before he did.

He worked until he was exhausted, chipping away at the wall, stopping occasionally to brush the rock chips and the dust that accumulated evenly over the dirt floor. When he was too tired to swing the spike with any force he tried to sleep, crouched and huddled against a wooden brace to keep the cold rock walls from sucking the heat out of his body. He managed only an hour or so at a time until the cold forced him to move again, so his muscles generated warmth and directed it to his core.

They'd almost caught him at one point. He thought the dim flickering on the tunnel walls was a hallucination until he realized it must be feeding time. He crab-walked away from the bat gate and hid the spike under some rocks near the slide at the back of the tunnel. But the hulking silhouette behind the light that eventually stopped just beyond the bars of his prison said nothing, merely aimed the flashlight beam at the locked gate and gave it a pull to test it before shoving the usual water bottle and sandwich sack under the bottom bar. Travis knew the man must have heard the sounds of his pounding, but apparently the guard felt confident Travis had no way to get out. He shined the light at Travis, running it cursorily from Travis's head to his toes before turning away and disappearing the way he'd come.

Now Travis stopped for a moment to catch his breath and consider how long he'd been imprisoned. Three sandwiches, three bottles of water—three days. They'd grabbed him on Tuesday, so this must be Friday. And his last meal had been delivered hours before by his reckoning. His stomach growled with hunger, reminding him of just how many hours. He shook himself wearily. He'd been in worse spots. At least no one was shooting at him, as had occasionally been the case in Afghanistan. During his second winter there, he'd been caught in the crossfire of a skirmish between Taliban militants and fighters in a local tribe that wanted no part of either the Taliban's oppressive rule or the Karzai government's interference. Both sides had mistaken him for the enemy, so after beating a hasty retreat, he'd found a small cave in which to hole up for the night until the fighting stopped.

Heaving a sigh, he gripped the bar closest to the anchor rod and pulled as hard as he could, grunting with the effort. Muscles straining until they burned, he was about to give up when he felt the metal give slightly. He relaxed and breathed deeply, feeding his muscles the oxygen they craved. He took one more breath, held it and pulled again, digging in his heels and putting his weight into the exertion. He thought the tendons in his neck would pop, but he kept pulling, and suddenly the metal gave again with a small groan. Drawing on the last of his reserves, Travis pulled harder and the weakened metal slowly gave way. With a screeching sound like fingernails on a blackboard the bent anchor rod fought for a grip in the rock. But as Travis gave a final tug the anchor came loose letting Travis bend the entire grate back on the door hinges.

Travis sank to the floor and sat clutching his knees, breathing heavily. For several minutes he couldn't move, but he knew if he didn't they would find him frozen there. Feeling around with his hands, his fingers grasped the cold iron spike. He rolled over onto one knee and put the spike in his pants pocket. After slowly getting to his feet, carefully stretching knees and back that ached from the strain, he made his way to the back of the tunnel where he'd left the last of the water. The sandwich was long gone. He pocketed the bottle and went back to the grate.

Carefully squeezing his body between the grate and the rock wall he made it through the opening without catching clothes or skin on a sharp edge. He started to pull the grate back into position, but figured they'd quickly realize he was gone. Better to put as much distance between himself and the tunnel as he could in the time he had. He put a hand on the cold wall and walked in the direction the guard had taken after leaving food. His took tentative steps at first, but the floor seemed smooth enough that he quickly increased his pace. After five minutes of walking, he wondered if staying close to the wall had taken him into a side tunnel deeper into the earth. But he had no choice.

After another minute or so, the air took on a different quality, a freshness that had been lacking in his prison cell. And he sensed movement. Not a breeze, exactly. More like a soft breath. Warmer, too, than in the depth of the tunnel. Suddenly his vision was filled with pinpoints of light and he wondered if he was about to pass out. The rock wall fell away, leaving his fingers tracing nothing but air, and he saw the twinkling dots for what they were—stars. He was free. Dark shapes of scrub trees blotted out the stars along the horizon here and there, and the land rose up a rolling hillside to one side and even more steeply up the side of a mountain behind him. Ahead and to his left, stands of conifers poked into the inky blackness, starlight outlining their shapes.

A rutted dirt track stretched in front of him, grass grown in the middle halfway up his shins. He took the water bottle out of his pocket, took a sip and held it up to the starlight. About two ounces left, and no food. He had two choices—head into the wilderness away from his captors or follow the track, perhaps right back into their clutches. Night was probably the best time for him to be on the move. The openness and freedom of the rolling meadow off to his right beckoned in the starlight. He sighed and set off down the dirt road.

26

Tess sat at the study table in the library, headphones on, eyes closed, her face expressionless, her body still as a statue. The eyes closed part made no difference to her I supposed—probably an unconscious habit to help her concentrate—but it helped me by signaling that she was absorbed in her work so I could focus on mine. Though I knew she was blind, whenever her eyes were open they still tried to track sounds and conversations, giving the eerie impression that she could still see. She couldn't help it, she said. It still came automatically. I'd done a little research on her type of sightlessness—the accident had somehow damaged the part of the brain responsible for interpreting signals from her optic nerve, though doctors had found no evidence of it on MRIs. Her eyes were quite healthy and normal. So I wondered if it wasn't a good thing she was exercising the eye muscles on the off chance that whatever was wrong with her occipital lobe might someday be repaired.

She was remarkably calm considering the crappy day she'd had. I don't know that I would have handled rejection to a dance invitation in front of half the high school and a threat to my guardian's life nearly as well. The fact that she appeared to be studying—French or music probably—gave me the chance to get on her laptop and do some research.

We'd agreed that though the caller had not given Tess a chance to speak to Travis or offer proof of life, he most likely was one of the kidnappers. After she'd recovered from the initial shock, Tess had argued, and I agreed, that we now had two reasons to find Travis. Whoever had grabbed him was determined that no one vote the shares of the company held on Tess's behalf, and now his life was in danger, too. Tess also had made a case for finding Travis ourselves, and while I wasn't sure the two of us were the best choice for the job, I had to agree that no one actually responsible for tracing his whereabouts was entirely trustworthy.

Tess trusted Marcus the least. A few days after the gun battle that had nearly killed us both, she'd told me about how Marcus had shot and killed Kenny, another member of Travis's security team, in a supposed attempt to save her. I'd been there, too, but knocked out cold at the time. Marcus had claimed that Kenny was a mole, a traitor, but Tess was convinced that it was the other way around. And even though she hadn't seen what had taken place right in front of her, I trusted what she'd heard and sensed. Which meant our focus was on Marcus.

Twice in the past few days, she'd discerned specific odors on Marcus—horse manure, something metallic and rotten eggs. The rotten-egg smell probably came from sulfur in some form, but there were so many it might be hard to pin down. The emotional context of the snippy way she'd pawned this assignment off on me brought her exact words back. She'd said, "...something else I can't quite put my finger on. Something burning." Burning sulfur smelled more like a burnt kitchen match, fire and brimstone stuff. That smell came from sulfur dioxide. When I put those together I came up with copper mining. Horse manure suggested a ranch of some kind, and my bet was on a working ranch, not a guest ranch. More private. Either way, the odds of finding Travis were as high as winning the lottery. But I had to try.

I narrowed the search by identifying states with a lot of copper production. I figured whoever took Travis wouldn't risk trying to take him out of the country. Most states where copper had been discovered had long since stopped producing it. The only copper mines in Washington had been on the Olympic Peninsula and near Lake Chelan, both long closed. The site in Chelan was now a church retreat, accessible only by boat, and I doubted the Olympic Peninsula boasted many dude ranches. The top five producing states all were in the western part of the country. Ranches would be common in all five states. So maybe they hadn't gone by car.

I sat back and thought about how long Marcus had been gone on each of his "recon missions." Not that long. Eight hours, maybe less, on one. That would make Arizona or New Mexico a real stretch. Utah and Nevada were a little closer, but Montana looked like a good candidate. A couple of hours away by jet. Sitting up, I put my fingers back on the keyboard and initiated another search, pulling up a list of all the mines in Montana. Opening another window, I searched for ranches in the state and compared locations. Most of the mines were clustered around Butte, with most of the others in the northwest part of the state, west of Kalispell. The search turned up hundreds of private ranches for sale, but I also found a couple of sites that listed working ranches that took guests. Most of those were in the central plains. Through trial and error, I found about a dozen ranches relatively close to copper mines.

I reached across the table and touched Tess's arm. Her eyes flew open, that involuntary reaction I still found so disconcerting. She pulled the headphones off.

"I might have something," I said. I explained what I'd done. "The problem is I don't know how to figure out which ranch is the right one."

She cocked her head for a moment, then said, "Follow the money. That's what Dad always used to say."

I turned my head at the sound of the door opening behind me.

Alice poked her head through the opening. "Someone to see you two."

She stepped aside, letting Derek in.

"Sorry to barge in," he said, running a hand through his dark, tousled hair.

"Derek," I said. "Just the man I want to see."

He strode across the room and eased into a chair. "Hey, Tess, Oliver. What's up?"

His eyes blazed with intensity, nervous energy spilling off him like sparks thrown off a hot fire. But he contained whatever he'd come to tell us, letting me start.

"We might have a lead on where Travis is being held," I said. "Could use your help running some searches."

He set his ever-present notebook computer on the table in front of him. "Show me what you've got."

I told him what I'd learned so far and Tess's idea for finding out more. He leaned over to look at the list I'd compiled, and I swiveled Tess's laptop so the screen faced him. He started typing immediately.

"This shouldn't be too tough," he said. "We can probably get most of this from county tax records."

"What's wrong, Derek?" Tess asked quietly.

He didn't stop typing. "That obvious?"

"You wouldn't be here otherwise."

"Good point. Not that I don't like you guys and all." He launched into a story about tracing the upload of the rogue program onto the company servers from a computer outside Dave Bradley's office.

"I can't believe he'd do that!" Tess was shocked. "Mr. Bradley was one of my dad's first employees after he moved the company up here from California."

"Bradley's on the board," I said. "That's serious stuff if he's involved. Someone could have used that computer just to steer attention away from themselves."

"I considered it," Derek said "I checked his computer. Almost got caught."

"Oh, my god," Tess said. "What happened?"

He ran it down quickly for us while he worked. "A little scary, but I got out, so no big deal. The problem is what's on Bradley's computer. Not just the infected version of the app, but a whole bunch of programs that monitor biometrics, GPS locations, web surfing patterns."

"Well, that's it!" Tess said. "You've got proof!"

Derek shook his head. "Like Oliver said, you're talking about a senior vice president and board member. If I accuse Dave Bradley, he'll just say I planted the stuff on his computer. Who do you think they'll believe?"

"They have to believe you!" Tess said. "We have to tell *some*one!"

"I used to be a hacker, Tess. I'm telling you, they'll never listen to me. They'll just fire my ass, and then where will we be?"

"Uncle Travis would believe you." Her face fell. "But he's not here."

"We need more than proof, Tess. We need a way to stop this, or else catch these jagoffs in the act."

"Got anything in mind?" I said.

He glanced up from the screen and scratched the stubble on his cheek ruefully. "No. But I think we better come up with something fast. The stuff on Bradley's computer scares me. It's way worse than Big Brother."

"How much worse?" I said.

"They're not just watching; they're influencing, maybe even brainwashing." He continued to focus on his screen. "Okay, now we're getting somewhere. I think I may have hit pay dirt."

"What did you find?" Tess said.

"Most of the ranches on your list are privately owned. A couple are owned by hotel chains. But this one..." Derek tapped the screen. "This one is owned by a shell corporation. No way to trace the actual owners. But I was able to hack into the ranch's computer and look at the books. In addition to the usual guests—

couples on honeymoon, families on vacation—the ranch hosts a lot of groups for meetings, conferences, that sort of thing."

"You found all that out just now?" The incredulity in Tess's voice matched the way I felt.

"It's not that hard when you know what you're doing." He shrugged.

""So, what's special about these groups?" I said.

"There seem to be an unusually large number of companies with defense contracts that show up. You know, the kind that make planes and tanks and guns?"

"Don't tell me," I said. "A corresponding number of congressmen and senators from Washington, D.C., happen to vacation there at the same time."

"You got it," he said.

"So, whoever owns the ranch has a lot of power, influence and money. Sounds like just the sort of people who would hold Travis to get what they want."

"We have to get him out of there," Tess said.

"Get who out of where?" Alice said quietly as she entered the library.

"Uncle Travis," Tess said, a defiant expression steeling her face. "We think we know where he is. It's up to us, Oliver. If we're right, no one's really looking for him. Not Marcus, and he's in charge of the search."

"Shh!" Alice said. She turned and shut the door behind her. "Keep your voice down, Tess. You don't know who might be listening."

"This is important, Alice! We need to get him back."

"I know that, and I agree. You just need to be more careful, that's all. Now where do you think he is?"

"You agree?" Tess blinked several times. "You'll help us?"

"Of course I'll help. I want him back in charge as badly as you do."

"We've narrowed it down to a ranch in Montana," I said. "West of Kalispell."

"Well, don't just sit there," Alice said. "We've got a lot to do. Dinner's ready, so come eat while I arrange to have your father's jet ready in the morning. Then you two better pack."

"What about Derek?" Tess said.

"Derek has enough to do here," Alice said.

I was still shaking my head over how Alice mentioned ordering up the family's private jet as nonchalantly as the rest of us order a cup of coffee.

27

Austin tumbled out of the rear door of Greg's Beemer, the girls' laughter echoing in his ears as Greg hit the gas and peeled away with a shriek of tires on pavement. He glanced over his shoulder at the dark vehicle sitting on the side of the road a hundred yards behind him. It was hidden behind bright headlights, but Austin knew who occupied it. He gave a little wave and turned onto a driveway blocked by a short iron gate. They'd already passed through the main security checkpoint at the entrance to the Naval Observatory grounds, so practically everybody and his brother knew he was home. He waved again as he trudged toward the gate, knowing that somewhere a cop dressed in a Secret Service Uniformed Division outfit had eyes on him, whether on closed circuit camera or in person. In answer, the gate creaked and opened with the hum of electric motors.

He slipped through before they'd finished opening and headed for the big Victorian house he'd been forced to call home for the past several years. Hurrying now, he passed the front door and onto the walkway the followed the curved, covered verandah around the side of the house. Lights glowed fiercely through the windows of the downstairs rooms, but those on the upper stories remained dark. Austin could see the back of his father's head sticking up above an easy chair in the garden room. Austin hoped he could sneak in the back entry through the kitchen so he wouldn't have to confront his father. With his old man preoccupied, though, Austin decided to come in through a side door by the pool to save time instead of circling around to the kitchen.

Inside, he moved as quietly as he could down a hallway past two lounges. His route would take him through the sitting room next to the garden room where his father sat reading the paper. But Austin figured he could make it through unnoticed and slip up the stairs to his room. He glanced around the room as he crossed the floor. He hated the overstuffed old furniture, the "historic" paintings on the walls, the ornate molding. The whole place reminded him of a museum. Like living at his grandparents' house. You couldn't touch anything.

He'd almost made it to the door into the front foyer and the stairs to freedom when a voice called out behind him.

"Austin!"

He stopped and turned.

"Come here, please." His father stood across the floor in the doorway from the garden room, newspaper dangling from one hand.

Reluctantly, Austin crossed to within a few feet of his father.

His father's brow wrinkled. "Where the hell have you been?"

His voice was quiet, calm—far be it for Josiah Dunn, Vice President of the United States to raise his voice—but Austin winced anyway, as if struck by his father's displeasure.

"You know exactly where I've been," Austin said, straightening his shoulders to look bigger. "Not one minute went by tonight when you couldn't get a rundown from half a dozen of those secret squirrels of my exact location."

"Mind your manners, Austin. I've been worried sick."

"In between campaign appearances? When *do* you find the time, Dad?"

"I'm warning you, Austin. Show a little respect—"

"Or what? You'll ground me? Having Huey and Dewey follow me around all day is bad enough. You might as well throw me in jail, Dad. It's the same thing."

"They're there to protect you, Austin. You know that. They protect all of us."

"From what? They don't do squat. You heard about my laptop, right? Did they stop it? Did they even see who did it? Come on, Dad. That could just as easily have been a bomb. Lucky me it was only Reddi-wip."

"What's gotten into you lately? I don't even know you anymore."

"Maybe if you spent some time with your family instead of playing politics I wouldn't such a huge disappointment to you, and Mom wouldn't be a pill-popping lush."

Austin didn't even see his father's open hand coming. It smacked him hard on the cheek, spinning his head to one side. He felt his skin grow hot where the slap had landed, and he stared at his father in shock.

"That's enough!" his dad said. "Go to your room, now!"

Austin turned away before his father could see the tears that stung his eyes. He stumbled across the room, desperate to get away, to hide his humiliation.

"And Austin," his father called, "next time you pull a stunt like this, I'll have them haul you in on whatever charges they can find and see if a judge can talk some sense into you. I don't care what it costs me politically. You have to learn there are consequences for what you do."

"Yeah," Austin mumbled, "maybe you ought to think about that."

"What did you say?" his father said.

But Austin had already turned the corner out of sight and now took the stairs up two at a time and raced down the hallway to his room. Inside, he closed and barricaded the door with a chair. He couldn't stand it anymore, being on display all the time, everyone watching him, following him. He felt so helpless, so powerless. He looked at the backpack on the floor next to his desk. He still had homework to do. He sat down, but instead of pulling out his books, he retrieved his cell phone and turned on *Never Bitten*.

This was how to feel powerful.

28

Senator Jeremy Latham swiveled his desk chair so that it faced the window and looked out at the lights of the city. Some said New York was the most vibrant city on the planet. It may have been true, but Washington, D.C., was the most powerful. New York had financial power, but money was just a tool, in the same way a nuclear aircraft carrier or a Stryker brigade were tools, nothing more. It took men like him, men with vision and brilliant minds, to wield those tools most effectively. And this town—the capital of the most powerful country in the world—was where those tools could best be put to use.

The hour was late—most of the country had already gone to bed or was on its way—but headlights and taillights still streaked the avenues with red and white. Latham loved this city, with its wide boulevards, its icons of freedom and democracy, its rich heritage. He would die for this city and what it represented, for Latham considered himself a patriot to the core. But his vision, along with that of others like him, was so much broader, so much larger than America. Latham and these others saw the "big picture," the need for a single command structure in the world, a single entity to which all others—countries, ideologies and individuals—would pay fealty. America had grown too wishy-washy. People were tired of war after Iraq and Afghanistan. They wanted the troops to come home. But who would be the world's cop if the U.S. stopped caring?

Latham didn't sleep much himself, didn't see a reason for it. He had too much to accomplish, and more than half his life was behind him. But he considered how far he'd come, and how much more he could still do in the time he had left. He turned back to his desk, its surface lit by a pool of light from a solitary lamp, leaving the rest of the office in shadow. He opened a drawer, took out a prepaid cell phone and dialed a number from memory.

"Yes?" a voice said after a single ring.

"Report," Latham said.

"The subject just returned home and logged onto the app. We've tweaked it based on his game play up to 'aggression' mode."

"You're confident this will work."

"Given what we saw at the high school out here a few days ago, we're very confident."

"We don't have much time," Latham said, the calmness of his voice belying his nervousness. He stopped to evaluate his feelings. No, it wasn't nerves. It was anticipation, excitement, almost. This concept had so much potential.

"He'll be ready. I'm sure of it. He'll be weaponized in time."

"Two days..."

"Stop worrying."

"I'm not concerned," Latham said. "I have other alternatives if this fails. But perhaps you should be. You have a lot to lose, Mr. Bradley."

The man on the other end gave no response.

Latham chuckled softly and hung up.

29

"**G**ood morning, Miss Barrett."

Tess paused with one foot on the bottom of the jet's airstair. "Tom, is that you?"

"Yes, ma'am, at your service. It's good to see you."

Tess laughed. "I wish I could say the same."

She had always liked the pilot her father had hired to take him and the family wherever they wanted or needed to go. In the past year she hadn't given a thought to the family's planes or the staff it took to maintain and fly them. But it made sense that Uncle Travis had kept them for his own use.

"Is Rick here, too?" she said, thinking of Tom's younger co-pilot, remembering the crush she'd had on him when she was in fourth or fifth grade.

"No, I'm sorry he's not. But I'll tell him you said hello. We're taking the little jet today. Be sure to keep your head down once you're inside. Ah, and you must be Oliver. I'm Tom Foley."

"Nice to meet you," Oliver said over her shoulder.

She gripped the railing and climbed the short set of stairs to the open hatch. The little jet was a seven-passenger plane, comfortable enough for short trips, but pretty cramped for any longer than a few hours. She wasn't complaining, though, as she bent over and made her way to one of the plush leather seats.

"So this is what it's like to have money," Oliver said as he sat across the narrow aisle.

"I guess I never really thought about it, but yes, this is some of what money can buy. But money can't buy me parents. Or new friends."

Oliver didn't seem to have a ready answer, so Tess settled back and closed her eyes for a nap. Alice had woken her up too early.

About two hours later, Tom brought the plane down. Tess yawned to relieve the pressure in her ears as they descended, and before she knew it, a slight bump and the roar of reverse thrusters told her they'd landed. The plane rolled down the tarmac, gradually slowing, and finally turned around and taxied.

"Where are we, Tom?" Tess called to the open cockpit.

"Airstrip outside Libby," he said loudly over his shoulder. "Maybe a half-hour's drive from where you want to go. It's a nice strip for a small airport, but the runway's too short for the big plane. That's one reason we took this one."

"The flight was just fine, Tom. We didn't need anything bigger. Thank you."

The plane rolled to a stop and after a cockpit check, Tom unbuckled himself, opened the hatch and lowered the airstair. He climbed down first and waited at the bottom for Tess, with Oliver close behind.

A voice greeted them from the tarmac as Tess carefully stepped down the airstair. "Miss Barrett, Mr. Moncrief, I'm Bob Haskell. Welcome to Libby. I'm your local contact, so whatever you need, you call me. I've got a car waiting for you, fully outfitted. I assume you want to go straight to the ranch first, but based on the briefing I got from Alice Pemberton I've taken the liberty of providing detailed county maps as well as assay maps that show locations of old copper mines. If you'll come this way."

"Thank you, Mr. Haskell," Tess said as he took her arm and guided her to a vehicle.

"I'll get your bags, Miss Barrett," Tom said.

In five minutes they'd loaded the vehicle, consulted the maps and hit the road. Tess enjoyed a few moments of silence, lulled by the steady purr of the engine and hum of the tires on asphalt.

"What kind of car did they give us?" she said finally.

"Range Rover," Oliver said.

Tess couldn't help the sudden intake of breath. She hadn't ridden in a Range Rover since the accident a year earlier. But if they encountered any rough terrain it was probably the best vehicle for the job. If Oliver noticed her discomfort, he didn't let on.

"So, do you have ideas about how we do this?" she said.

"Well, it's not like we'll find him by just waltzing in. They won't have him on display, tied up in a chair in the front lobby, assuming this place has a lobby. But it's worth taking a look and getting a feel for the layout. So here's what I'm thinking. If you don't mind, I propose we pretend we're engaged and are considering having our honeymoon there, maybe even the wedding itself if we like the place enough."

Tess was silent for a moment, trying to decide if she liked the idea of pretending to be Oliver's fiancée. As serious as she'd thought her relationship with Toby had been before her accident, she'd never entertained fantasies of marrying him. And she certainly didn't think of Oliver in a romantic sense. She wasn't sure if she could pull off the charade.

"You think I look old enough to be engaged?"

"Definitely."

"So we'd be there for a tour, basically."

"Sure, and to ask whether the riding the guests do would be suitable for you, since that's something you seem to enjoy." He paused. "Look, if you're uncomfortable with it, we can come up with something else."

She mulled it over. "No, that's okay. I guess it might work."

"Good. We'll give it a shot."

After about twenty minutes, Tess felt the SUV slow and turn off the main highway. Back roads would take them the rest of the way.

"Wow," Oliver murmured a few minutes later. "I wish you could see this, Tess. We're running along a ridge, alternating between thick forests of lodge pines, ponderosa pines, Douglas firs and what I guess you'd call high mountain meadow, kind of sandy soil with grass and scrub. Ahead and down below us is a valley that is almost all meadow dotted with stands of trees. The spring colors are amazing. The valley is a sea of green covered with purple and yellow patches of flowers of some kind. Across the valley in the distance are craggy peaks of the Cabinet Mountain range, some of them still covered with snow. It's just beautiful."

She didn't know whether to laugh or cry. Trying to imagine it the way Oliver described it all she could come up with were memories of spring skiing up in the Cascades when everything was green and blooming in the foothills, but the higher elevations still had enough snow for great boarding in fifty-degree temperatures. She had a feeling this was different somehow.

The five miles from the turnoff to the ranch down in the valley took nearly ten minutes. Tess was content to roll down the window and feel the warm breeze and sun on her face. When the vehicle slowed and the sound of tires on pavement changed to the crunch of rubber on gravel Tess knew they'd arrived.

Oliver gave her a verbal tour as he drove up to the ranch complex—barn and stable buildings off to the left, large main lodge in the middle, and scattered in among the trees a number of half-hidden log guest cabins. He parked, shut off the engine and got out. Tess opened her door and breathed in the mountain air, detecting the sweet, grassy scent of clover mixed with pine and dust. Another deep breath brought more smells—hay, horses, leather and wood smoke. The sun bathed her in warmth, but the little breeze that stirred wisps of her hair, tickling her neck and cheek, never let her get too hot. She could get used to this.

"You ready?" Oliver murmured beside her. "I'll be Joe. Who do you want to be? That character, Cammie Morgan?"

"I can't believe you remembered that. Oh, that's right; you can't forget most stuff."

Tess put her hand out, found Oliver's arm and traced it up to his shoulder. She squeezed lightly and he set off with her in step right behind him. She felt the change in the air as soon as they set foot in the lodge, cooler out of the sun, and tinged with scents of old wood, bacon and a hint of mustiness, as if something in the room collected dust. They took several paces inside before Oliver stopped.

"Good morning," he said.

"Oh, my, are you folks lost?" a woman asked.

"No, we're—"

"It's just that we don't have anyone on the books as arriving today," she went on, "and we're pretty far off the beaten path. So, are you looking for a room?"

"Actually, we'd like a tour," Tess said. "You know, take a look around?"

Silence filled the space around her until it squeezed her chest.

"Are you...?" The woman couldn't finish her thought.

"Blind?" Tess laughed.

Oliver joined in then said, "I'm Joe and this is my fiancée Cammie. We're on our way home from Yellowstone, but we heard about this place and wanted to take a look."

Tess chimed in. "We're trying to decide where to spend our honeymoon, and I recently discovered that I love to ride. So here we are."

"You know, hon'," Oliver said, "this might be a great place to have the wedding. Is anyone available to show us around?"

He was laying it on so thick Tess wanted to kick him, but she smiled sweetly.

"Oh, of course," the woman said hurriedly. "Let me get Mr. Evans. Buck Evans is the manager of the ranch. I'm sure he can help you. Wait here and I'll be right back."

"Seems to be working," Oliver said quietly a moment later.

"You don't have to be so into it," Tess said. "We're not actually getting married."

"I thought girls couldn't wait to get married."

"With the right guy, maybe."

"You don't think I'm good enough for you?"

"I didn't say—"

"Well, hey there, you two!" a man's voice called. He had a bit of a twang in his voice, and Tess couldn't help wondering since this was Montana, not Texas, if it wasn't put on for the guests. Mona here tells me y'all want to take a look 'round the spread. Dadgummit, she was right!" He let out a low whistle. "You can't see a bonfire inside a barn, can you, little lady?"

"Oh, I don't know about that, Mr. Evans," Tess said. "I'd say you're waving your hand in front of my face right about now."

Buck Evans roared with laughter. "Just goes to show you don't have to see to know what in Sam Hill is goin' on. I've got a few minutes of free time. You got yourself a tour."

Oliver took her hand and squeezed it. Evans kept up a steady patter as he led them through the main lodge first, pointing out the large, open great room with panoramic views of the meadows and mountains, the dining room, a smaller sitting room, a library about an eighth the size of the one she had at home, and a little gift shop. Oliver provided physical descriptions when necessary. The musty smell, apparently, came from what Evans said were hunting trophies on the walls—stuffed and mounted heads of moose, elk, deer, mountain goat, a buffalo and even a bear. Tess shuddered, glad she couldn't see them.

From there, Evans took a short path outside to another large building behind the lodge that housed conference facilities. Inside, he showed them a large banquet hall that could be divided into smaller areas, a medium size hall and four smaller conference rooms. All wired, he said, for high-speed Internet connection over a wi-fi network.

"What do you think so far?" Evans said as he escorted them back out into the sunshine.

"Terrific, if we wanted to hold a company meeting," Oliver said.

"Oh, I get it," Evans said. "Y'all are more interested in the accommodations. Well, that's next. We're on our way."

Tess felt warm sun then cool breeze on her skin and guessed the path led through the trees, alternating between shade and sunny spots.

"So, where y'all from?" Evans said.

"Washington state," Tess said, keeping it deliberately vague.

"Y'all look a little young to be gettin' hitched."

"We're planning on a long engagement," Oliver said.

"I plan on finishing school before the wedding," Tess added.

"Well, now, that's smart," Evans said. "You should take your time."

They didn't volunteer any more, and Evans didn't push. He took them to what he called a standard cabin, which Oliver described as a nice size bedroom with a connecting bathroom and small sitting area. The deluxe cabin he showed them next featured a kitchenette and eating nook. Evans explained that the ranch had about a dozen of each, another ten rooms on the second floor of the main lodge, and about a half dozen two- and three-bedroom cabins that were self-contained, more like individual houses.

"Can we see the horses now?" Tess asked after they'd "seen" the second cabin. She wanted to move this along, They hadn't come all this way to look at honeymoon suites.

"Guests have taken a lot of them out on a trail ride," Evans said, "but I can take you to the stables and see if we have staff on hand to show you around."

A five-minute walk brought them to the stable. Tess could tell by the smell of hay, oats, manure, and horse sweat, not to mention the lazy buzzing of flies all around. Inside the relative coolness of the stable, Tess also picked up the scents of leather and liniment. Evans told them how many horses they had, and gave them a summary of the riding programs, including cattle drives, round-ups, trail riding, riding clinics and rodeo riding instruction. He walked them from there to the corral.

"If you'd come a couple weeks ago," he said, "you could've seen spring roundup. That's when we bring in all the mama cows with their new calves for branding before we turn them out in summer pastures."

Tess's nostrils flared. She could still sense vestiges of the wood fires used to heat the brands, along with the smell of burnt hide and flesh.

"I heard a lot of ranches use RFID tags these days instead of brands," Oliver said.

"Really big spreads—forty, fifty thousand acres or more—use radio frequency tags cause they make it easier to track the animals by copter. This ranch is small by comparison, and a visual brand still works for us."

"It just seems so mean," Tess said. She felt fidgety. They'd wasted so much time, and they weren't any closer to finding Uncle Travis.

"I won't say it doesn't hurt, but they live through it."

"Well, I think we've seen enough," Tess said.

"Are you sure, Tess?" Oliver said. "Well, thanks for your time, Mr. Evans."

"My pleasure. Hope you folks decide to come see us when you're ready."

"We should get back on the road ," Oliver said. "We have a long drive ahead of us."

"You can find your way back to your car okay? If so, I have a mountain of paperwork on my desk I need to take care of."

"We'll be fine," Tess said. "By the way, I heard there are a lot of old mines in Montana. You wouldn't happen to have one on the ranch would you?"

Evans hesitated before answering. "As a matter of fact, we do. An abandoned copper mine, but we discourage guests from going there. It's far too dangerous. Even though it's blocked off, the liability if someone gets hurt is enormous. I'd stay away from old mines if I were you."

"Good advice," Oliver said. "Thanks again, Mr. Evans."

"Sure thing. You take care, lovebirds."

"Lovebirds?" Tess murmured.

Oliver shushed her quietly. She found his arm with one hand, made a fist with the other and smacked his shoulder. She'd had enough.

"Hey, what was that for?"

"For suggesting we pretend to be engaged."

"It worked. But why'd you bring up the mine?"

"We had to do something to find Uncle Travis. The tour wasn't helping."

"It helped me, Tess," he said quietly. "They might be holding him here, and I needed to get a sense of how the place is laid out."

She shook her head. "He's not here. I don't smell copper. Marcus wouldn't smell like copper and sulfur if Uncle Travis was here."

"You're probably right. Anyway, your question definitely threw Evans."

"You don't think he suspects we know, do you?" she said.

"I'm not sure. But we better watch our backs."

30

Filtered sunlight dappled the forest floor, and the scent of dry, heated pine needles filled the air. Travis froze, silently drawing a breath and holding it. He opened his eyes to mere slits, slowly taking in the surroundings in his narrowed field of vision. He strained to hear the sound that had woken him from a light uneasy sleep. He lay on his side under the trunk of a fallen tree, obscured by ferns and grass that had grown up around the tree's base. From his hiding place, his eyes searched the undergrowth for signs of intruders. Suddenly, he heard a rustling sound from several yards away, and his intent gaze flicked toward it, scanning the brush until he spotted movement. A little aspen seedling swayed as the rustling sound came again, and Travis exhaled a sigh of relief as a chipmunk came into view from under some leaves.

He slowly unfolded himself with a groan and crawled out from under the tree. Stiff from the cramped space, his body ached, and pain radiated from his hands from gripping and pounding the spike against rock and steel back in the mine tunnel. He stood and stretched, slowly turning and taking stock. He'd spent the night wandering a maze of tracks crisscrossing the backcountry, getting lost a couple of times before using the stars to guide him so he didn't double back on himself. Eventually, he'd found a gravel road obviously more traveled, and had followed it until he saw the lights of some sort of settlement in the distance— too many to be a single dwelling but too few to be a town. Leaving the road for the relative safety of the woods, he'd found his hiding place just before dawn. Exhausted, he'd settled in for a few hours of sleep.

Now, he shook the sleep from his head as he got his bearings. With a huge yawn, he headed through the woods for the road. He knew he should wait until dark to move again, but two things drove him now—hunger and curiosity. If he didn't eat, he would soon start to suffer from exposure. And he needed to find out who his captors were and what they stood to gain from holding him. At the edge of the trees he paused and scanned the road in both directions, listening for sounds of traffic. Satisfied he was alone, he set off at a brisk pace, wishing he hadn't finished off the water bottle during the night.

The road climbed along a ridge. Another higher ridge ran parallel, and the road made a switchback several hundred yards ahead, continuing up the hillside in the opposite direction. When Travis reached the switchback, through the trees he saw buildings on the plateau about a quarter mile above him. As he rounded the sharp curve he saw a trail off to the right that angled more sharply up the ridge. Though a steeper climb than the road, it cut the distance in half, an easy decision.

Five minutes later he came out on the road again a few hundred yards behind the settlement. He paused to catch his breath and size up what lay ahead. Though trees obscured his view of many buildings, he got the sense that it was a guest ranch of some sort. Large buildings off to the right looked like a barn and a stable. One of the two in the center looked like a lodge; the other could be a meeting hall. Small buildings trailing off along the ridge like ducklings following their parents were probably guest cabins.

All of Travis's senses went on high alert now. Though his captors could be miles from here, this was the only sign of civilization he'd seen since his escape from the mine. Nothing that lay in front of him appeared sinister, but he couldn't take the chance. Staying off the road, he listened and watched for signs of life as he made his way through the trees toward the back of the large building closest to him. As he drew closer, the trees behind the agricultural buildings thinned, giving him a clear view of a large livestock watering tank behind what he'd assumed was a barn, some large fenced livestock pens off to the side, and several well-worn trails emerging from the woods from different angles all heading toward what must be a stable.

Rustling of the aspen leaves and conifer branches in the breeze and the calls of several songbirds reached his ears. The same breeze carried the smell of food, and his stomach growled. He stopped to sniff the air, and the smell of meat browning and onions sautéing made his mouth water. He scanned the compound. Seeing no movement, he darted from tree to tree, making his way to the back of the building. The low murmur of voices floated on the breeze. Hugging the wall, he eased over to the end and peered around the corner. Fifty yards away, two men stood in conversation near a back door of the lodge. A large refrigerated truck sat in the road nearby. The smaller of the two leaned on a hand truck. The other was so large that Travis was sure two of him could fit in the checked pants and white chef's jacket the man wore.

Travis ducked his head back around the corner and squatted on his haunches, resting against the wall, biding his time. The sun beat down on him, but he welcomed the warmth after days in the cold mine. Flies buzzed lazily past his head, and a grey squirrel chattered warningly from a nearby tree. Travis glanced up at the sky, noting the sun's position high overhead. He'd slept longer than he'd meant to, but felt as if he could easily stretch out here in the grass and nap for a few more hours. He yawned widely.

Soon after, he heard the truck's engine roar to life and slowly fade away as it drove off. When Travis leaned around the corner again, the cook had disappeared inside, but the door was propped halfway open. He stood, but hesitated before he stepped out from behind the building. Glancing down at himself, he saw that his clothes were dusty and wrinkled from the mine, and his hands were raw and scabbed from the effort to pry the bat gate out of the rock wall. He brushed as much dust out of his clothes as he could, combed his hair with his fingers and crossed the clearing to the open door as casually as if he owned the place.

Stainless steel equipment gleamed throughout the large commercial kitchen. The smell of food cooking was so strong that Travis thought he would faint from hunger. Steam rose from a tilting braising pan on the cooking line. There was no sign of the chef, so Travis walked over to see what was in the big rectangular pan. Ground meat and onions browned and simmered in the pan. Travis turned at the sound of a noise behind him. The cook emerged from a storeroom in the back of the kitchen pushing a rolling cart loaded with #10 cans. He jerked upright, startled when he saw Travis. Though every nerve in his body screamed at him to flee, Travis forced himself to remain calm.

"Help you?" the chef said, frowning.

Travis flashed what he hoped was a rueful grin. "This smells awfully good. I overslept this morning and missed breakfast."

"You missed more than breakfast," the chef said with a curious look.

Travis glanced at the useless watch on his wrist. "Guess I did. Wondered if I could get a plate of something to eat."

"That there's going to be chili once I get all these cans of tomatoes opened and add some spices." The chef rolled the cart to a worktable a few feet away. "Guests aren't supposed to be back here, you know."

"I don't mean to be a bother," Travis said. "It's just that dinner won't be for another couple of hours, and I can't let my blood sugar get too low. You know?"

The cook looked him up and down. "You do look a little pale. S'pose I could rustle up something while you get these cans open."

Travis walked over, took a can off the cart and slid it under the can opener mounted on the edge of the counter while the chef watched. When the cook saw that Travis knew what he was doing he nodded and headed for the walk-in refrigerator.

"You get them all open, you can start emptying them into that skillet," he called over his shoulder.

Travis knew he was taking a huge risk, but as long as the cook wasn't asking questions he figured he was okay. And he needed food. He stole glances at the chef every now and then while he cranked the handle on the opener, popped the lids off and tossed them in a nearby trashcan. The chef had pulled a carton of eggs and some other ingredients from the walk-in, and now stood at the eight-burner stove with a bowl, whisk and sauté pan. Travis tossed the last of the lids into the trash, careful of their sharp edges, and watched the chef whisk ingredients in the bowl and pour them into the hot pan. While the chef tossed the eggs in the pan, Travis rolled the cart in front of the tilting skillet and poured the cans of tomatoes into the ground meat and onions. When he finished, he found a long-handled spoon and stirred the tomatoes into the meat.

The chef brought over a plate heaping with piping hot food and looked over Travis's shoulder.

"That'll work," he said, handing Travis the plate and a fork.

Travis took them gratefully, leaned back against a counter and forked a mouthful of eggs into his mouth. The chef had added little cubes of potatoes, red and yellow bell peppers, some onion, cheese, fresh dill and what Travis at first thought might be ham. But a second look and bite made him ask, "What's your secret ingredient?"

"Smoked trout," the chef answered. "Lot of trout streams around here. We do our own smoking, too."

"Something tells me that's not regular chili, either."

The chef grinned. "Regular enough around here. It's venison."

Travis lifted his plate and said through another mouthful of food, "Thanks for this."

"You earned it. Just drop the plate back in the dishroom when you're done. I've got more prep work to do before dinner."

"Sure thing. Thanks again."

The chef took the rolling cart and disappeared into the storeroom. Travis ate quickly before anyone else showed up. He put his empty plate where the chef had instructed and slipped out the back door into the sunshine considering his next move. Emboldened by his success so far, he decided to do some exploring. If this place was connected to whoever was behind his kidnapping, it wasn't likely that any of the regular staff would know about it, since his captors had held him a few miles away. He nonchalantly set off on a path that wound through the woods past most of the guest cabins. Travis counted twenty, a few of them obviously large enough to house two or three bedrooms.

He reversed course and strolled to the opposite end of the compound, taking a cursory look at the barn and stable. He turned back when he heard voices, figuring he better not press his luck. Eventually someone was bound to recognize that he didn't belong. What he really needed was to get into the office somehow or behind the front desk and see if he could find anything in the files that would give him a clue to the identity of his abductors. He circled around the big building he'd thought was a meeting hall. A sign on the path with an arrow pointing to the "Conference Center" told him his guess had been close. Thinking he might try to get inside the lodge through the kitchen, he rounded the back corner of the conference center and pulled up short.

A man in nice slacks and sweater over a button-down shirt emerged from a door on the far side of the kitchen. Travis quickly ducked behind the conference center and peeked around the corner. Tall and powerfully built, the man had short-cropped brown hair and carried himself with military bearing. He stopped in the clearing at the edge of the drive running behind the kitchen, and his hand dove through the V-neck of his sweater and came back out with a pack of cigarettes from his shirt pocket. He took a lighter from his pants pocket, shook a cigarette from the pack between his lips and cupped his hands around it. His hands came away as a cloud of white smoke billowed out of his mouth.

Travis heard a loud beep from across the clearing, and the man pulled a phone from a holster clipped to his belt and held it up to his ear. After a brief conversation, the man took a quick drag from the cigarette, stubbed it out in the dirt and walked off down the path toward the cabins. Heart pounding, Travis stepped out from behind the building and jogged toward the open door.

31

"You need to be more patient," I spoke for the first time since we left the ranch.

"Why? We weren't learning anything." Tess scowled.

"You don't know that, Tess." I kept my eyes peeled for a side road indicated on the map.

"Well, it's not like they were keeping Uncle Travis in one of the guest cabins."

"You don't know that, either."

I braked hard as the turn came up on my left. The "road" was little more than a grassy track heading for the trees through the meadow. I cranked the wheel and bumped along the new route.

"I didn't tell you this," I said, "but when we turned off the main road to get to the ranch, a line of jeeps sat parked in a gravel lot just off the road. Maybe they're for winter weather. Or maybe they're for military maneuvers or war games for some of the groups that use the ranch. But it would have been nice to find out. We still don't know what we're up against."

"If I stopped and truly thought about what we're up against, I wouldn't have come," she said. "The only reason I did is because we *need* Uncle Travis. We're not soldiers, Oliver. We have no business trying to find out who's behind what happened to Matt. The last three weeks have been like a nightmare, and I can't wake up. But if we don't do this, Oliver, who will?

"Someone's trying to ruin my father's company, maybe even take it over. They tried to kill me—both of us—and they took Uncle Travis. I lost my parents. As angry and crazy as he makes me most of the time, I'm not going to lose him, too."

"Okay, okay. We'll find him."

After a minute she said, "How much farther?"

"Maybe a mile or two," I said, wrestling the wheel as the SUV bounced in the rutted track.

"Think you could have found a bumpier road?"

"You don't like it, I'd be happy to let you drive."

That shut her up for a while, and I concentrated on making the ride as smooth as possible. Or, more like, preventing a wheel from falling in a pothole so big that it broke an axle. From the high meadow, the land sloped down into a gully, up a ridge and down into another gully before climbing again. The track intercepted a gravel road which we followed for a while before heading off onto another dirt track, this one rockier and more rutted as it wound up through some scrub brush and widely spaced trees. It finally crested on a meadow backed by the steep face of a low mountain peak.

A few hundred yards ahead, the snaggletooth jaw line of several dilapidated buildings jutted away from the mountainside, wood weathered to a dull pewter color. Afternoon sunshine poured through broken windows and missing siding, casting misshapen shadows across the overgrown grassy spaces between the structures. Salvador Dali might have painted a scene like that if he'd used more muted colors. Building shapes dictated function. The Wikipedia inside my head pulled factoids out of filing cabinets labeled "Chemistry," "Geology" and "History." The tall skinny structure had likely been the headhouse of a mining shaft. The building next to the crumbled remains of a brick chimney probably had been a smelter. A long, two-story building with evenly spaced holes that windows had once filled likely had housed miners in dormitories. All in ruins now, abandoned for decades, maybe as long as a century.

I pulled up behind one of the buildings and shut off the engine. The sudden silence pressed in ominously until natural sounds rushed in to fill the space—songs of the western meadowlark, mountain bluebird, and varied thrush and the screech of a red-tailed hawk soaring on a thermal high above, and the whisper of the breeze through the grass and windowless buildings.

Bob Haskell had outfitted the Range Rover with everything we might possibly need, from a four-person tent to a three-day supply of food. I opened the tailgate and stuffed a couple bottles of water, a flashlight, a compass and a rope into a rucksack. We'd missed lunch, so I grabbed a couple of energy bars, too. By the time I circled around to get Tess, she'd let herself out and twirled in a slow circle, arms out, breathing deeply through her nose. I closed my eyes and followed suit, trying to imagine how she felt. I picked up scents of clover, pine, earth and dried wood baking in the sun.

"What do you see?" Tess said.

I described the scene in front of us—an old mining camp. Not quite a town, but certainly the basics to house and feed enough miners and other personnel to dig ore from the ground and process it on site. Tess tracked the sound of my voice and came up behind me as I spoke, placing her hand lightly on my shoulder, the signal that she was ready to move.

"We'll check the headhouse first," I said as I finished.

The short walk to the ramshackle building took less than a minute. The roads through the camp had grown weedy with disuse. Nothing suggested anyone had used the camp recently, as a prison or for any other purpose. I'd never felt a place so devoid of human life, and it surprised me. I'd expected a guard of some sort. A shiver ran through me as I truly appreciated the meaning of the term ghost town for the first time. The headhouse door hung askew on a single rusty hinge that groaned as I pulled the door aside far enough to peer inside.

"He's not here," I said.

"How do you know? You haven't even gone inside. What's the matter? Scared?"

"No. The place hasn't been used in decades—thick dust, no footprints. You hungry?"

I pressed an energy bar into her hand, and unwrapped one for myself.

She took a bite and chewed thoughtfully for a moment. "Okay, so now what?"

I turned slowly so she could follow my movements, and walked several paces away from the building. The headhouse stood on higher ground next to the shoulder of the mountain. My gaze panned the other buildings down the gentle slope of the meadow. The faint outlines of a track ran from the headhouse to the smelter. A similar depression disturbed the natural landscape just enough to feel out of place. I traced the indentation with my eyes and saw it wind from the smelter toward the steep rise of the ridge that towered over the camp.

"Come on." I cut across the tall grass to intercept the track on its way up the slope.

"Where are we going?" Tess sounded more curious than concerned. She kept pace easily.

"There's a track leading up to the ridge. I think another mine entrance might be up there."

The track, when we reached it, was an old rail bed that followed the sloping meadow up to the base of the mountain. Though dirt had covered most of the gravel, allowing grass and weeds to grow over it, remnants of some of the old wooden ties poked through like splinters stuck under skin. The rails had long since disappeared, pulled up and used for other purposes—melted and shaped into tools or horseshoes, or used for cattle guards or fence rails. Tess followed silently and stayed with me without complaint though she stumbled a couple of times. As the track curved around a small knoll, an opening appeared in the mountainside.

"Looks like a mine entrance up ahead," I said. I swiped a sleeve across my forehead.

"How much farther?" she huffed, winded by the climb.

"Not far. A hundred yards."

The path leveled out, giving us a chance to catch our breath, and once we stepped into the opening of the mine, the air instantly grew cooler.

I stopped and shrugged the rucksack off my shoulder. Pawing inside it, I pulled out a bottle of water and placed it Tess's hand, and dug inside again for the flashlight.

"This is the place," Tess said, her voice echoing hollowly.

I pointed the flashlight into the tunnel. Darkness swallowed the beam of light just beyond the range of my vision. "And you can tell this how?"

She sniffed. "Smell it?"

I caught a whiff of hydrogen sulfide and something faintly metallic.

"A tunnel, you said?" Tess took a couple of faltering steps inside until her outstretched fingers touched the rock wall. Without waiting for an answer, she headed deeper into the mountain, walking briskly, with only the light touch of her fingers to guide her. The darkness was her element, and I had to trot to catch up.

"Whoa! Slow down. You don't know what might be up ahead."

She laughed and walked faster. "Afraid of the dark?"

I hustled after her. "Come on, Tess. We might run into a shaft any minute. Or a cave-in. Or a guard."

As I drew closer to her, I heard a soft clicking sound that I hadn't noticed before. It took a moment before I realized Tess was making the sound with her tongue. *Echolocation.* She was tracking the changes in pitch of the clicks as they bounced back at her off the walls, ceiling and floor of the tunnel. Like a bat, or a dolphin.

"Something up ahead," she said.

The tunnel wall curved to the right. All I saw was rock and timbers holding up the tunnel ceiling. But I heard what she did—a tinny sound to the echo of her clicks. As we rounded the curve, the flashlight beam glinted off metal blocking the way ahead. A four-inch wide streak of blue ran down the rock wall next to it. Copper. I aimed the light at the obstruction.

"A barricade of some kind," I said. "Like a metal grate. Or a gate. Wait, I've heard of these. It's a bat gate. Designed to keep people out but let bats fly in and out of a cave."

Tess slowed. "How far?"

I counted down the distance as we walked. "Thirty feet, twenty-five, twenty... Where did you learn that, anyway?"

She knew immediately that I referred to her locating skill. "Yoshi taught me. It doesn't always work. Only in small spaces. I'm still learning how to use it."

I walked up to the grate and inspected it under the light. "Jeez, somebody ripped this thing right out of the wall. Recently, too. The supports have been chiseled out of the wall, and the marks on both the rock and the metal are fresh. I can't imagine how long this took, or how much strength it took to pull it out of the wall and bend it back on its hinges."

Panning the flashlight beam beyond the grate, I peered down the tunnel.

"There's a rock slide about twenty yards farther that blocks the tunnel," I told her. "The tracks for the mine cars are still in place, and it looks like there are some empty water bottles and trash back near the slide. Someone's been here. The perfect prison cell, until someone decided to break out."

"Uncle Travis," Tess said, her voice tinged with excitement. "I know it."

"Yeah, maybe. But where is he now? Why hasn't he tried to call you?"

"I don't know!" Her excitement turned to frustration. "He could be lost out there somewhere, Oliver. We have to find him somehow."

"We don't even know if this is the right place. We're guessing here, Tess."

She faced me, sightless eyes imploring me, and shivered in the cold.

I took her elbow. "Come on, let's go back to the Range Rover. I need to look at the map. We need to think like Travis if we're going to figure out where he's gone."

When we emerged into the bright sunlight, I stopped for a moment, blinking against the glare. Tess waited silently, pensive since we'd found the tunnel empty. As we started back the way we'd come I noticed another track heading straight out from the tunnel, more road than rail bed. I wondered where it led. We wound our way back down through the mining camp to the car. Tess sat in the passenger seat with the door open, sun on her face and hair gently waving in the breeze like raven's wings. I broke out two more bottles of water and the maps, gave one bottle to Tess and spread the maps out on the hood. The metal was hot to the touch.

Despite the level of detail in the county road and topographical maps Haskell had provided, I didn't see the trail leading the other direction from the mine entrance. If Travis had taken that route, we would have to follow it to see where it led. That is, *if* Travis had been held in the mine in the first place, and *if* he had escaped. A lot of conjecture on our part. Something broke my concentration. I raised my head and saw Tess leaning out of the Range Rover, head cocked to one side. I heard it then, an engine, a vehicle of some kind, getting closer.

"Oliver?"

"I hear it," I said. "Stay here. I'll go see what it is."

I leaned in the driver's side and grabbed a pair of binoculars from the center console. The sound came from somewhere far on the other side of the camp, so I jogged past the headhouse toward the smelter, keeping the buildings between me and whatever was coming. I rounded the corner of the ramshackle building, pressed the field glasses to my eyes and slowly panned the horizon. In the distance, a Jeep popped into view over a rise on the meadow. It looked similar to the vehicles I'd seen parked up near the highway earlier in the morning. For a time it headed straight for me, slowly growing in size in the lenses. My pulse started to race. As near as I could tell, only one person occupied the vehicle. Then it veered off toward the mountain, and I knew it was headed for the mine.

As soon as it disappeared behind the knoll up the slope near the mine entrance, I ran back to the Range Rover as fast as I could. I jumped in, breathing heavily.

"What is it?" Tess said. "What's going on?"

"Don't know yet," I managed as I punched the start button. "But we're going to find out."

I drove through the camp and pulled up behind the smelter close to where I'd been moments before. Keeping the Range

Rover well out of sight of the ridge where the Jeep had gone, I parked and got out, leaving the engine running.

I leaned back in. "Someone's up at the mine. If Travis was there, that someone's about to find out he's gone. I want a better view, so I'll be about twenty feet away. Okay?"

She nodded, and I hurried to the corner of the building and trained the binoculars on the spot where the Jeep had vanished. It didn't take more than half a minute before the Jeep reappeared, heading down slope at breakneck speed. I had a hard time keeping the glasses steady as the Jeep bumped down the trail. The driver had a phone pressed to his ear. I frowned and pulled my own phone out of my pocket. No signal. We hadn't gotten one since we'd left the main highway earlier. Raising the binoculars again, I got another look at the driver. An antenna poked up from the object in his hand. A walkie-talkie, probably military grade. Lowering the glasses, I saw that the Jeep had nearly reached the distant edge of the meadow.

I ran back to the Range Rover, tossed the glasses in the back seat, and put it in gear.

"Guy just hightailed it out of here," I said as I wheeled around the smelter and took off across the meadow to intersect the track the Jeep had taken. "Looked like he was communicating with someone by walkie-talkie. We're going to follow him and see where he goes."

"Why? What good will that do?"

"Think like Travis, Tess. What would he do if he escaped?"

"Call the police? I don't know."

"These people had to be good to snatch him. He probably didn't see it coming. They've kept him way the hell out here in the middle of nowhere in an abandoned mine. It's dark, cold. They gave him water, but probably not much food. If I were Travis I'd want to know who put me in there, and I'd want something to eat, maybe not in that order."

"You think he went looking for them?"

I gripped the wheel tighter as the Range Rover bounced through the meadow. Tess clutched the seat with one hand, and braced herself with the other on the door.

"It's the kind of man he is. From what I've learned in the past few weeks about your uncle is that this is what he's trained to do. He's a soldier, Tess, a hunter."

She chewed on that for a while in silence, which was just fine with me. I focused on steering the Range Rover on the right path, keeping the Jeep in sight, yet hanging back far enough not to attract attention. Fortunately, the track didn't present a lot of choices, and when we finally reached a junction with a more substantive road, a plume of dust kicked up by the other vehicle showed me which way to turn. Though not paved, this road was wider and smoother than the rutted track we'd just left. I took care not to increase our speed to the point of stirring up the same amount of dust as the Jeep, or catching up to our prey.

The road wound through stands of pines and alders, up a ridge and down into a gully before ascending another ridge. Something glinted in the sunlight through the trees, and I realized the light reflected off a window.

"The ranch is just ahead," I said. "We're coming up on the back side."

"You think he's here? How did we miss him before?"

"I don't know, Tess. I'm just saying it's what I'd do."

"You're not Uncle Travis. You don't know the first thing about fighting."

She was right. We were headed into a nest of vipers, and if Travis was in there, I didn't see how we'd get him out.

"Yeah, well, I'll figure it out," I muttered.

"What are you going to do?"

"Get in as close as I can and see what's going on."

The road leveled out near the top of the ridge where the ranch buildings spread out. I pulled off the road into a copse of thinly spaced trees that provided some cover but gave me room to maneuver. I inched forward until I had a relatively unobstructed view of the back of the lodge building. The Jeep had pulled up in the drive, and the driver now stood next the open door talking and gesturing to three other men. All were dressed in jeans, boots and long-sleeved shirts, and two wore cowboy hats—the attire of ranch hands, not some paramilitary group. I wondered if we were dead wrong. A fourth man emerged from the back of the lodge— Buck Evans, the manager who'd shown us around. The others stepped aside as he approached the Jeep driver.

"What are they doing?" Tess murmured.

"Buck just showed up, and the guy in the Jeep is explaining what happened."

Evans apparently got the picture quickly because he pointed at each of the men and barked orders. They scrambled to comply, running off in four directions. Suddenly they all stopped and eyed two men emerging from a back door, a large man wearing a chef's coat and checked pants appearing to escort the other one outside. The pair looked up in surprise at the men assembled in the driveway, giving me a clear look at the second man's face—Travis.

"Uh-oh," I said. "Looks like trouble."

Travis whirled to bolt back into the lodge, but the big cook stood in his way, confused. The others broke into a run toward them. I put the big SUV in gear and gunned it out of the trees, tires spinning in the pine needles and loose dirt.

"Climb in back!" I said. "Open the door and stay down!"

"What is it?" Tess yelped.

"It's Travis! I'm going in to get him! Now get back there!"

She scrambled over the seat. The Range Rover bounced onto the road, all-wheel drive helping the tires bite into the gravel as I stepped on the gas. Heads turned at the growl of the supercharged engine. I aimed the nose of the SUV between the Jeep and the lodge, hoping to cut off the men headed for Travis, giving him time to get in. They scattered, diving out of the way, but one had already covered half the distance to the lodge. I changed course to get closer to Travis, quickly overtaking the runner. He threw a glance over his shoulder just as I spun the wheel away from him and slammed on the big disc brakes. The force threw Tess's door open. I heard a *thunk* and a grunt as the heavy door swung into the runner and knocked him off his feet.

I leaned out the open window. "Travis! Get in!" I shouted.

His head jerked up, complete shock registering on his face when he saw me, but I didn't have to tell him twice. He sprinted toward us, bent low.

"Go! Go!" he yelled.

I hit the gas pedal again, with more gentle pressure this time, accelerating slowly to give Travis a chance to catch up. He grabbed the top of the open door and ran alongside for two or three strides then gripped the doorframe with his other hand and swung his legs into the back seat. A glance in the side mirror showed he was in, so I tromped on the gas and the powerful SUV roared past the lodge. A group of startled guests on horseback coming in from their day's ride stared at us in surprise as we passed.

That's when someone started shooting at us.

32

Derek frowned at the screen on his notebook computer. He'd been going through the files he'd copied from the computer in Bradley's office onto his flash drive for the better part of the morning. The more he saw, the more disturbed he became. He squirmed in his chair. The contents of the drive made him uncomfortable for two reasons, he realized. First, the level of intrusion on people's lives these programs represented was beyond anything he'd imagined even the government might be experimenting with. The other reason was that he was a little ticked and a lot jealous that he hadn't figured this out before anyone else had.

All of it made eminent sense once he took a look at some of the code. Whoever had written it—and he assumed it had been Bradley—had used an illogical logic tree, if that made any sense. The human brain made leaps in logic from "A" to "L" with no stops at any of the points in between based on experience, or sometimes intuition. Computers took the whole route, and even then didn't always arrive at the correct answer. Until IBM's "Watson," that is. Watson had used the same illogical logic that brains did by searching a huge database of cultural experience and weighing the odds of which possible answer would most likely be right. The results had been good enough that Watson had beaten the most successful contestants ever on the TV game show *Jeopardy*.

But Watson had been a ginormous computer. The genius of this artificial intelligence system was that it accessed hundreds, maybe thousands, of servers and processors in the "cloud." The app itself could easily fit within the confines of a game like *Never Bitten* on a mobile device. Derek knew none of it would have been possible without James Barrett's brilliant knowledge of game theory. That's what had made MondoHard's video games so successful. James had designed games with an uncanny prescience for what gamers would do in any given situation. Building adaptive strategies into the games had been a simple matter of predicting what players would do and changing subsequent action sequences based on how players actually moved. Adding this layer of AI on top made the game seem uncannily intuitive.

Next up on the list of files was the GPS tracker. Derek wanted to see if there was a cache file within the tracking program that might have a list of mobile device addresses Bradley had followed. He figured at least he could warn those people if nothing else. He sifted through the sub-file directory. Sure enough, a cache file lay buried inside the program. He opened the file, but before he could run down the list of contents it shifted down a couple of lines. Which meant data had been added to the file. Which meant the program was active.

Derek slammed the lid of the notebook, putting it to sleep instantly, and reached over to kill the surge protector which would shut down his wi-fi connection and modem. His hand hovered over the switch as he thought it through. He glanced over his shoulder then caught himself. He was at home, not the office, on a secure wireless network that piggybacked on a fiber optic line a local cable company had installed but didn't use. And the GPS program from Bradley's computer was designed to track other people, not Derek.

He opened the computer and backed out of the directory to see who the program was tracking. The interface showed only one mobile device on the tracking screen. Derek pulled up the map where the device was located. Washington, D.C. *Austin Dunn!* Derek watched the dot that indicated the kid's location jump slightly as the satellite refreshed the coordinates of the kid's phone. He knew that if he could watch where Austin went virtually in real time, then whoever else had this tracking program could, too.

He minimized the window and pulled up the files of the copy of *Never Bitten* that had been downloaded to Austin's phone. He'd already been through them once, but he wanted to check them once more to assure himself he wasn't being overly dramatic. Twenty minutes later he'd convinced himself that he hadn't over-reacted. The tweaks they'd made to Austin's program had definitely been designed to incite violence. Someone wanted that kid to go berserk.

Derek pushed himself away from his worktable and pulled his phone from his pocket. He quickly tapped in a text and pushed send. Figuring it would be a while before he got a reply, he rose and went to the kitchen to refill his coffee mug. He'd barely finished pouring when his phone feeped. He fumbled it out of his pocket again and pulled up the message.

Can't help you.

Derek tapped out another message.

Can't, or won't?

A reply came almost immediately.

Can't.

Whoever this guy was, he was beginning to really piss Derek off. Derek's thumbs flew over the virtual keyboard on his phone, typing a withering rejoinder. Just before he hit the send button, he hesitated. Getting mad wasn't going to help, and by now Derek knew the guy well enough to know that he wouldn't respond. He'd probably already signed off. Whoever he was, he acted even more paranoid than Derek felt. He was hiding from something. So, it was up to Derek.

He sipped his coffee and sat down in front of his computer to think it through.

33

Tess shrieked as a bullet smashed through the rear window and whistled past her ear. Strong arms encircled her and pulled her down on the seat. The SUV bounced crazily then settled as it roared away. She held her breath, but there was no more gunfire, only the drone of the engine and crunch of gravel under the tires as they gently swayed and bumped down the road.

"Everybody all right?" Travis said, his voice right above her.

She sat up and threw her arms around him, pressing her face into his chest. "Thank god you're okay!"

"I'm good up here," Oliver said.

"Keep your speed, Oliver," Travis said. "No one behind us yet, but that could change."

Tess realized she was still holding onto her uncle like a scared little kid, and quickly put her hands in her lap.

"I'm glad the two of you are all right," Travis said, "but you're in so much trouble you may wish otherwise."

Tess couldn't believe her ears. "That's it? We come all this way to find you and save you from god knows what, and *we're* in trouble?"

"You can see how dangerous this situation is," Travis said sternly. "If you figured out where I was, you should have sent in a team. That's what they're there for."

Tess fumed. "A team? You have no idea what's been going on while you've been gone. The board is trying to take over the company. Matt was arrested for shooting up the school. The game app Derek developed is infected with some kind of bug that makes people crazy." She heard her voice get higher in pitch as the words rushed out, but she couldn't stop. "You think we should have sent a team? You don't get it! There's no one we can trust!"

She got no response save the growl of the engine and the wind rush as the SUV plowed on.

"Well, except maybe Alice and Yoshi," she said in a small voice.

"She's right," Oliver said quietly. "The only reason we found you is because at least one of your team members set you up. Tess is the one who figured it out."

"Explain, please," Travis said tersely.

Tess took a deep breath while she gathered her thoughts and slowly and confidently related everything that had happened in the past few days. She ended by telling him how she and Oliver had narrowed the possibilities down based on the odors she'd detected on Marcus, how they'd found the mine empty, and followed the ranch hand back just in time. Travis didn't speak for several moments after she finished.

"Did it ever occur to either of you," he said finally, "that I might have let them kidnap me?"

Shock froze Tess's brain for a moment. She couldn't conceive why he'd do that.

"To find out who's behind all that's happened in the past few weeks?" Oliver said.

"I don't know who these people are," Travis went on, "but they're getting desperate. It would have been helpful to have found out more about them."

"Well, did you?" Tess said. "Find out?"

"I didn't get a chance. The chef was nice enough to make me something to eat because he thought I was a guest. I managed to sneak into the office to get a look at their files, but the chef found me, and was escorting me out when you two showed up."

"Lucky we did," Oliver said. "Buck and those men didn't look happy. Who knows what they would have done to you?"

"Buck?"

"Buck Evans, the manager," Oliver said.

"To tell the truth," Travis said, "I wasn't careful enough. They set up an ambush, and I didn't even see it coming. Which is why I don't want you involved. It's too dangerous."

"We're already involved!" Tess said. "In case you didn't notice, they tried to kill me not too long ago. And now they're messing with my friends with this infected game app! What did you want us to do, Uncle Travis? Sit around until they sent you back in pieces?"

He didn't answer. Instead, he asked her a question. "Where are we, anyway?"

"Montana. Not far from Libby. That's where we're going now."

"That's what I figured," he murmured. "How'd you get the Range Rover?"

"Alice," Tess said.

"A guy named Bob Haskell met us at the airport," Oliver said. "Had it waiting and stocked with provisions."

"Alice is good," Travis said. "I'll give her that. She always did run a tight ship."

The conversation petered out, and Tess rested her head on the seat back, suddenly exhausted. The drone of the engine almost lulled her to sleep when the phone in her jeans pocket vibrated. She nearly jumped off the seat. She dug the phone out in time to hear it tell her, "You have one unheard text message." She ran her fingers over the surface to find the right button and played the message back.

"Tess, it's you-know-who." She sat upright. Even though the phone's avatar was reading the message, she knew exactly who it was from—Dad. Only just like the other times, that was impossible. She tuned back in to the message. "...text from your friend Derek. You guys have a real problem on your hands. If you help each other I think you can solve it. Guys are a little slow, I know. But see what you can do. If you don't, bad things are going to happen. Zho."

"Zho?" Travis said. "What the hell is that about?"

"Ex, oh," Tess said, blinking back tears. "You know, like hugs and kisses?"

"Boyfriend?"

"No, it was from Dad. Well, Dad's ghost I guess."

"The same person you got texts from a few weeks ago?"

She nodded. "I told you, Uncle Travis. It's like he's an angel or something, and the only way he can communicate is through text or email."

"And he knows Derek? Of course he does. What am I saying? Derek told me he got texts, too. Better call him and find out what's up. Put it on speakerphone, please. I think we all need to hear this."

Tess told the phone to call Derek, and the voice recognition program auto-dialed his number. He picked up on the second ring.

"I was just about to call you," Derek said.

"I got a text that you might need some help," Tess said.

"Where are you?" Derek said. "Your phone's really noisy. Sounds like you're in a tunnel."

"I put you on speakerphone," she said. "I'm in Montana, with Oliver and Travis."

"You found Travis?"

"Save it for later, guys," Travis said. "What's going on, Derek?"

"Tess, remember I told you guys that I pulled a bunch of files off of the computer in Bradley's office? I've been spending a lot of time going through them to figure out what they did to *Never Bitten*. Travis, you gave a copy of the game to a kid named Austin Dunn, right?"

Tess heard her uncle's sharp intake of breath.

"How did you know?" Travis said sharply. "Wait. Before you answer that, you said this came off the computer in Dave Bradley's office?"

"Yeah. I'll tell you about it later. Or ask Tess and Oliver. They know the story. So, anyway,

you-know-who told me. Here's the problem. The bad guys, whoever they are, *wanted* him to have it. They've been tracking the kid's every movement, and they've been tweaking the game to push the kid into more and more violent play."

"Who is he?" Tess said.

"The vice president's son," Travis said. "I gave him a copy of the game when I was in Washington several weeks ago. Derek, you're sure about this?"

"I know you've been out of the loop, Travis, but trust me, this is bad news. Someone has taken James's work in AI to the next level. It's brilliant stuff, but incredibly dangerous. They can track every movement, every mood and use it to their advantage. If this kid is at all susceptible to suggestion, they can essentially brainwash him into doing whatever they want."

"They're going to make him do something awful," Tess said. "We have to go to Washington."

"No," Travis said. "It's too dangerous. Besides, we don't know that they can make Austin do anything."

"Yes, we do!" Tess said. "You weren't there, Uncle Travis. You didn't see my friend Matt go crazy in the school cafeteria!"

"She's right," Oliver said. "We've seen first-hand how the game app changes people."

"And I don't even think they were specifically targeting Matt," Derek said. "Not like what they're doing to this kid Austin. This kid's ready to blow."

"We can help, Uncle Travis," Tess said. "Austin will never listen to adults, but he might listen to us. We might be able to stop him from doing whatever they've got planned for him."

"I don't know," Travis said.

"Uh-oh," Oliver interrupted. "We've got trouble! There's a couple of SUVs about a half mile back coming up fast."

"Gotta go, Derek," Travis said. "We'll be in touch. Okay, Oliver, get this thing moving as fast as you dare."

Tess was pressed back in her seat as Oliver stepped on the gas.

34

"Tess," Travis said, "I'm going to hand you stuff from the cargo area. Just stuff it anywhere there's room. Which bag is yours, by the way? I might need to borrow a few things."

"It's a North Face backpack. The one I always used to take snowboarding. Black and purple."

Travis surprised himself with the level of calm he projected. Exhaustion rolled over him. The food back at the ranch had helped, but the long hours of pounding against the rock walls in the mine had taken their toll. He couldn't let up now, though. Tess and Oliver had been brave enough to find him and pull him out of a bad situation. The least he could do was make sure they got out safely.

He checked the position of the vehicles behind them, surprised to see that Oliver had made it to the highway at some point during their conversation. Now that Oliver had bumped up his speed to nearly ninety, the SUVs behind them weren't gaining ground as fast. But they had grown closer since the last time he'd looked.

Clambering over the rear seats into the cargo hold, he passed supplies to Tess as fast as she was able to stow them at her feet or in the seat. Tent, camp chairs, camp stove, water, food...it all went forward so Travis could get to the floor panel. He yanked it open, revealing the spare tire. All he wanted was the jack. He removed it from its mount and closed the floor panel. Then he dumped the contents of Tess's backpack on the floor and sifted through them, setting aside what he might be able to use. He looked at the small pile ruefully. Not much there—nail polish remover, a few bottles of nail polish, cleansing pads, deodorant and a small propane tank.

He frowned. "Tess, why do you have nail polish in your bag?"

Since the accident he'd seen her wear it only a few times. She couldn't put it on by herself, and she was embarrassed to ask Alice for help.

"OMG!" Tess said. "I haven't used that backpack in so long. I just asked Alice to pull it out for me. I never checked what was in it."

"Uh, Travis?" Oliver said.

Travis jerked his head up and looked out the back window. Two Jeeps were quickly overtaking them.

"I see them. When they get closer, try to stay in the center of the road so they can't get past. I'll let you know when I want them to pull alongside. Got it?"

"Yes, sir."

Travis quickly screwed a regulator and connector hose into the propane tank, unscrewed the tops of the nail polish and nail polish remover. He stuffed acne cleansing pads into the neck of the nail polish remover bottle and set everything in a corner of the cargo area. A backpack jammed up against them would keep them from tipping in the swaying vehicle. He reached over the seat and touched Tess's cheek.

"Tess, this could get pretty ugly. You up for it? Okay, then, I want you to switch places with me. I've got some surprises for our friends back there. On my signal, hold these up one at a time, and I'll grab them from you. Work left to right."

"All right. I can do that."

She scrambled over the seat, and Travis guided her hands to the small arsenal he'd amassed, watching to make sure she familiarized herself with their shapes. Reaching up, he pressed the button that opened the sunroof and waited for it to slide back. The wind rush filled the interior with noise. He'd have to shout, but he'd make it work.

"Oliver, how far to the air field?" he said.

"I'm not sure. Six or seven miles, I think."

"If you can manage it, get the pilot on the phone and tell him to fire up the engines. Okay, you guys, here we go!"

He grabbed the heavy jack and the jack handle and stood on the rear seat, poking his head up through the sunroof. The SUVs on their tail had pulled up to within a hundred yards.

"Ease up!" Travis shouted.

Oliver slowed some and the Jeeps zoomed up to within a car length. Travis spotted two men in each. The passenger in the lead pursuit vehicle stuck his arm and head out the window and pointed a pistol up at Travis.

"Evasive action!" Travis yelled.

Oliver swerved just as the man fired two shots, loud reports that the wind quickly carried away. Travis grabbed onto the edge of the sunroof to keep from losing his balance, and hefted the tire jack. The Jeep had swerved the opposite direction and now leaped forward to come up alongside the Range Rover.

"Tap the brakes!" Travis called.

As Oliver tapped the brakes, the Jeep shot even. Travis leaned over and threw the heavy jack down on the Jeep's windshield as hard as he could. The glass starred and crazed in a spider web of cracks. Startled, the driver nearly lost control, but straightened it out before running off the road. He lost ground, though, and the second SUV spurted ahead and closed the gap.

"Okay, Tess!" Travis said. "Hand me the nail polish!"

He reached down and took the bottles from her hand. He hurled the first one as hard as he could at the Jeep on their tail. It smacked the windshield and bounced off harmlessly, leaving a few drops of color on the glass. The driver jerked in alarm, but when he realized that Travis was about to throw another one, he grinned and said something to the passenger. The passenger leaned out his window and fired a couple of shots. Travis ducked, then quickly stood up again and threw another of the little glass bottles. This one, too, bounced off the Jeep, but gouged a little chip out of the windshield. The men in the car laughed. Travis just grinned at them and threw a third bottle at them as hard as he could. It shattered, leaving a broad smear of iridescent green polish on the windshield. The Jeep swerved and fell behind, then straightened and pulled up again with a roar.

"Nail polish remover, Tess!" he shouted. "Oliver, let him get up close!"

"You got it!" Oliver yelled.

Tess handed him the bottle. Travis held it below the sunroof opening, out of the wind, and lit the cleansing pad "fuse" with a lighter he'd found with the camping gear. The Jeep pulled up next to them, anger twisting the faces of the two men inside. The passenger pulled himself halfway out the window this time and sat on the frame, twisting so he could aim his pistol over the roof at Travis. Just before he pulled the trigger, Travis threw the flaming bottle of acetone at them, igniting the nail polish on the windshield with a *whoosh*. Blinded, the passenger fired wildly and fell out of the window. The driver jerked the wheel in surprise, and the Jeep swerved and skidded off the road, hit loose gravel on the shoulder and flipped over.

"Whoo-hoo!" Oliver shouted. "Got 'em!"

"It's not over yet!" Travis yelled. He ducked down inside. "Tess, hold that little tank of propane. I'll guide you. Once I get you in position, you have to stay absolutely still. Got that?"

"It's not that tough, Uncle Travis."

Ignoring her sarcasm, he placed one of her hands on the tank and the other on the hose, and then guided her hands so they held the hose next to the window, arms resting on the seat back. He grabbed the spray can of deodorant and the lighter and got ready. Opening the window a crack, he twisted the valve on the propane tank wide open. Gas hissed out of the hose. Blood sang in his ears, and adrenaline bumped his heart rate up. These kids had put themselves in danger to help him, and he was putting them in even more danger by refusing to let these goons take him. But, God help him, this was what he was born to do. His brother James had been destined for the boardroom and the corner office, to fight his battles with intellect and words. Travis was a soldier through and through. He hated to admit it, but he loved the rush and the pride he took in defending his country and those he loved. He almost felt sorry for their pursuers. They didn't stand a chance.

"Okay, Oliver," Travis said, "drift over to the left and let this dick-wad come up next to us. Make it convincing. On my mark, open Tess's window."

"Gotcha," Oliver acknowledged, meeting Travis's gaze in the rearview mirror.

"Keep it steady, Tess," Travis said.

Sweat broke out on his forehead as he watched the remaining Jeep creep up on their rear bumper. Oliver swerved to block them from passing on the left. The Jeep's driver fell for the feint and went right, accelerating to get into the lane Oliver had just left. The two big SUVs roared down the highway at breakneck speed, inches away from each other, the Jeep slowly edging ahead until its nose was even with Tess's window.

"Just a little more," Travis murmured. "Now, Oliver!"

The Jeep's windshield pillar blocked the driver's view inside the Range Rover. Travis gave a little smile as the Jeep continued to inch forward. Extending his arm, he lit the stream of gas spewing from the hose. Just as the driver's open window pulled abreast of Tess's window, Travis sprayed the flammable deodorant through the jet of flame emanating from the hose Tess held. A billow of fire surged across the space between the vehicles and into the driver's window. The driver screamed as the flames engulfed his head, and he wrenched the steering wheel to get away. The Jeep veered off the highway and careened into a copse of trees.

Travis reached over and quickly twisted the propane tank valve closed before Tess lit the car on fire and then heaved a huge sigh.

"Great job, you two."

"They're gone?" Tess said.

"For now," Travis said.

"That was close," Oliver said. "Remind me next time to bring along an anti-tank weapon."

Travis looked at him sharply, then relaxed. There was no way Oliver had any knowledge of what had happened on the mountain the day of Tess's accident. No one knew, except Travis and two members of his security team, Luis and Red, and not even Red knew everything. Despite Tess's concerns about Marcus, Travis trusted those two. They'd never tell a soul what had happened. Oliver's comment about the ATW was just coincidence.

"You did fine, Oliver," he said. "Where'd you learn to drive like that?"

"Took a high-speed driving course for fun a couple of years ago."

Tess and Oliver were silent for a moment as the adrenaline in everyone's system started to dissipate. Travis watched the landscape speed by. The countryside was beautiful. Too bad it had been marred by an attempt on all their lives. He wondered if he could ever truly keep what was left of the Barrett family safe.

"Airport's coming up in about a mile," Oliver said, interrupting Travis's thoughts.

"Let's hope there are no more surprises," Travis said as Tess climbed back into the seat next to him.

"But they'll keep coming, won't they?" Tess said.

"Until we find out who they are and what they want, yes."

"Let them come," she said.

Travis had never seen her look so fierce. He remembered how hard it was being a teen and was glad that she was so strong. She had James's tenacity and stubbornness and Sally's gentleness, but she'd gotten some of the warrior gene, too, from somewhere. Travis had been checking in with Yoshi on her progress, and had been pleased by the reports.

"Oh, they will," Travis murmured. "Count on it."

35

About twenty minutes after we took off, my pulse returned to something approximating normal and my heart stopped banging against my ribs to get out. The mountains, rivers and forests below were beautiful, but I was more than happy to leave Montana behind as we climbed up to altitude. Tess had found herself a pillow and blanket, and had stuffed earbuds into her ears, plugged into the music stored on her phone, and curled up in one of the deep leather seats with her eyes closed.

Travis had gotten up as soon as we'd climbed out of the airfield takeoff pattern and had gone forward to talk to Tom, the pilot. Now he returned to his seat, on a diagonal with mine, and pulled a satellite phone from a cradle in the bulkhead next to him. I turned my head and looked out. The mountains had given way to a checkerboard pattern of fields that now started to darken as the sun fell toward the horizon behind us. Though I pretended to be uninterested, Travis's conversation was impossible not to overhear in the tiny cabin, even with the jet engines trying to drown him out.

"Jack, it's Travis... Yeah, the kids found me... Tess and Oliver... A bit of a mess, but nothing that local law enforcement can't deal with. You might want to look into the ranch where I was held hostage—the 'Flying Eagle.' Manager's name is Buck Evans... Tess and Oliver did a good job, sir. I can't say I was happy they showed up, but they didn't trust anyone else... I know, sir. But you and I both know that if there's a mole, we have to find out where his tunnel leads... No, I'm not headed back yet. We're going to D.C. I did something stupid, and now someone's trying to leverage it... No, I was trying to curry favor with Josiah Dunn. I gave his son, Austin, a game app we've been working on... Yes, that's the one... I know. Tess and Oliver say it's more than a threat, it's a certainty. Derek confirms it. He's been working on a software antidote, but he doesn't have time— What? A political rally? Tomorrow? It's a good thing we're on our way... Yes, Tess and Oliver, too. They didn't give me much choice, and they might be able to help. I'll try to get hold of the vice president, but in case I don't I could use some support on that end. Any chance that you— All right, I understand. I'll check with Tom... Tom Foley, our pilot. He's ex-Navy, might know some guys... I just figured we'd go into DCA... Andrews? The base would be great. Thanks, Jack. I'll have Tom give you a heads-up when we're thirty minutes out."

He looked out the window on his side of the plane for a moment after disconnecting. When he turned back he caught me looking at him.

"You heard what's going on?"

I nodded. "Most of it."

"Vice President Dunn scheduled a campaign rally tomorrow on the National Mall. I'm having a hard time believing it, but if you guys are right, Austin might try something there."

"If he goes nuts like Matt did and does something like shoot into the crowd, someone could get hurt or killed," I said. "Not to mention what the embarrassment might do to his father's campaign."

"We have to stop him."

"We'll do whatever we can to help."

He stared at me as if trying to diagnose something in me, and suddenly broke into a wide grin. "I'll bet most of what you did today was not in the job description Alice gave you."

I glanced at Tess, but she seemed to have tuned us out completely. She might even have been asleep.

"I'd say that's a pretty accurate assessment." I managed a wry smile.

His smile faded and he heaved a sigh. Then he lifted the phone and dialed another number. "Yes, I'd like to speak with him, please. Travis Barrett calling... Yes, I know what day it is and what time it is. It's urgent that I speak with him. When do you expect him back? ... Would you please get a message to him and let him know that I called? ... Have him call me immediately. I'll be at this number."

He rattled off ten digits, listened for a moment and hung up.

Movement caught my eye, and I craned my neck to see Tom clamber out of the cockpit and step into the cabin. He stopped and crouched in the aisle next to my seat.

"Everything okay out here?"

"Okay by me," I said, and glanced at the empty cockpit nervously. "Autopilot?"

He smiled and turned to Travis. "Mr. Barrett, Alice sent along an overnight bag for you with a change of clothes and some toiletries. I left it back in the lavatory if you want to clean up. I also took the liberty of getting provisions during the layover in Libby. Nothing fancy. Just sandwiches, some deli salads and beverages, but at least you won't go hungry."

"Thanks, Tom."

"Did the general offer any support?"

Travis shook his head. "Not really. Looks like we're on our own. I have a feeling that I won't convince either the vice president or his Secret Service detail of the potential threat. That is if I reach Dunn at all. And the three of us are going to have one heck of a time trying to find Austin in the crowd."

"Let me put out some feelers," Tom said. "I might be able to find someone."

"They'd be taking a huge risk, and it might all be for nothing."

He shrugged. "That pretty much holds true for anyone who puts on a uniform. Be nice to improve your odds, though, so I'll see what I can do. On another subject, our flight path will take us down through Pennsylvania on the way into D.C. This bird doesn't have the range to get us there non-stop, so we'll put down in Latrobe and refuel there. The Latrobe airport's fixed base operator is open twenty-four/seven, and the airfield is small, so it shouldn't be too busy. Also, the FBO has a pilot's lounge with showers, which might feel good by the time we get there."

"Sounds great, Tom. I appreciate the thought."

"One last thing before I get myself some coffee. You might want to call your office and let them know you're okay."

Travis looked startled. "It's Saturday night. No one will be there."

"You don't know that. Even so, you should leave a message. The staff worries about you."

"I suppose I don't need to ask how you know this."

"No, sir, you don't. If you haven't figured it out by now, you're probably beyond help." Tom flashed a sly grin. "Now if you'll excuse me, I have a plane to fly."

He turned and poured himself coffee from the tiny galley behind the seat across from me, and ducked into the cockpit. I stared at Travis, curious. To my surprise, he reddened.

"My brother liked to think of everyone—staff, employees—as family," he said. "He always wanted to see the good in people, never the bad. Which is why we have the kinds of problems you two faced today."

I considered him and his words. "I never met your brother, but if this guy who's been messaging Tess is him, he's very aware of all the bad guys in the world. Treating each other a little more like family and a little less like characters in a video game might not be a bad thing."

He blinked several times before responding. "You're pretty smart for someone your age." Waving a hand before I could say anything, he went on. "I'm not talking about book smart. You wouldn't be working on a PhD. if you weren't intelligent. You have some street smarts, too."

"Thanks, I guess."

"Don't let it go to your head. Anyway, what Tom was trying to say was that some people actually care about me as more than someone who signs their paychecks."

I glanced at Tess again, but she hadn't moved.

"She cares," I said. "This is just a tough age."

Travis's gaze followed mine, and he laughed, a short bark without much mirth in it. "I wasn't talking about her, but I'm sure you're right."

I frowned. "Sorry. Someone else?"

The smile on Travis's lips was tight. "Tom was diplomatically referring to my executive assistant, Robyn."

It made sense that she would be concerned, since she probably acted as a firewall to keep distractions and minor issues away from her boss and maintain his schedule. Tom's comments replayed in my head and my eyes widened.

"You like her," I blurted. "And she likes you."

He rose abruptly and made his way back to the lavatory, hunched over under the low headroom. I'd overstepped my bounds. James Barrett and his wife had died in a tragic car accident, and I was definitely not family. I was a hired hand that Tess tolerated because she had no choice.

* * * * *

I woke with a start when the wheels bumped the tarmac. The plane's interior was dark except for a pool of bright light shining on some papers in Travis's lap, and a dim blue glow that spilled from the cockpit into the cabin. The windows were black except for a few bright spots that flashed by as we rolled down the runway and gradually slowed until we turned onto a taxiway and bumped along at ten or fifteen miles per hour. I hadn't slept long. The day's events had kept playing through my mind. Something nagged at me, and I couldn't put my finger on it. Not memories or conversations, obviously. Something was off about the whole situation, and no matter how many times I went over the past few days I couldn't figure out what.

We rolled past the terminal building. Tom pulled the plane up in front of a large building not far away and shut down the engines. Travis looked up with a start and glanced out the window. He noticed me watching him and nodded, then looked over at Tess. She was curled up asleep. Tom opened the hatch, lowered the stairs and climbed down to find a service rep at the FBO. Travis put the papers on the empty seat facing his and stretched with a soft groan.

"This plane isn't meant for trips this long," he whispered. "I'm going inside to clean up. You're welcome to get out and stretch your legs for a bit. It will take us a while to refuel."

I nodded. "What time is it?" I whispered.

Travis looked at his watch and shrugged. "I keep forgetting the battery is dead. Late. Or early, take your pick."

I tipped my head toward the papers in the seat across the aisle. "Already back at work?"

He shrugged. "I couldn't sleep and I had some catching up to do if I'm going to save the company. I also pulled a photo of Austin down off the Web so you'd know what he looks like."

He shuffled through the papers and handed me a sheet of paper with a photo printed on it. I leaned forward to look at it in the light from Travis's reading lamp. Travis eased past me and disappeared through the hatch. I fished in my pocket for my phone and turned it on. It found the network and displayed the local time, 2:57 a.m. Not quite midnight our time. I stifled a yawn, wondering why I was so tired. Soft thumps sounded in the cabin as service crew prepared to refuel the plane.

Tess stirred and stretched. "Oliver?"

"I'm here," I said.

Where are we?" she said sleepily.

"Pennsylvania."

"We're not moving. Is it morning?"

"We stopped for fuel. And, yes, it's morning, sort of. It's early here. Go back to sleep."

"Okay." She yawned, faced the window, plumped the pillow under her cheek and promptly fell asleep.

I went inside the FBO facility and used the restroom, then walked down the tarmac in the dark, the little taxiway lights guiding me. The chill night air braced me, and after ten minutes I felt refreshed. I went back inside to get a soda from a vending machine and boarded the plane to think. About half an hour later, we were wheels up and headed for Washington, D.C.

Due to an air traffic control delay the flight took about ninety minutes, and when we touched down at Andrews Air Force Base in Maryland dawn tinged the eastern horizon in shades of peach. I pressed my forehead against the window as we descended, hoping for a glimpse of Air Force One. Tess was awake, but tuned into her music again. As soon as we landed with a gentle bump, though, she pulled the earphones out and stowed them in her bag. Travis had been napping ever since we left Latrobe, and now he, too, sat upright, alert and focused. As we rolled down the runway, to my surprise I saw not one but two 747 jets painted in the blue and white livery of Air Force One, with the US flag on the tail and Presidential Seal near the nose.

When we deplaned, a black SUV sat on the tarmac waiting for us, a tall man with blond hair dressed all in black standing next to the driver's door. Ten yards away, another man in slacks and a windbreaker over a sport shirt leaned against the hood of an older model Mustang, ankles crossed in front of him, arms folded. His manner was casual as he watched us, but his eyes missed nothing. I came down the stairs behind Travis, with Tess's hand touching my shoulder. Tom, the pilot, descended last, and walked over to the man lounging against the car. They greeted each other like old friends.

The SUV driver came forward to meet Travis as he stepped off the stairs and stuck out his hand. "Mr. Barrett, I'm Rob Bergstrom," he said. "General Turnbull asked me to drive you."

Travis's eyebrows rose a fraction. "He asked, not ordered? Nice of you to volunteer."

"My pleasure, sir. The general helped find me a job when my tour was over. Anything I can do to repay him..."

As Travis and the driver exchanged pleasantries, Tom spoke with the other man in low tones.

After a moment, Tom brought the man over and introduced him. "This is Lee Hanson, an old Navy buddy. Lee, meet Travis Barrett. And this is his niece Tess and her assistant Oliver."

Hanson shook hands all around, and when he got to me, his grip was so strong I thought he might crack a bone or two in my hand. I managed to keep a smile on my face, though.

Travis's expression turned serious. "Gentlemen, I don't know what you've been told, but we have a situation. Vice President

Dunn is holding a campaign rally this morning on the Mall, and we have reason to believe that his son Austin may try some stunt to disrupt it and discredit his father. Tess, do you want to explain?"

"A mobile game developed at my father's company has been sabotaged with a program that makes people do crazy things," she summed up.

"This is nuts," Hanson growled. "You listen to this kid, Barrett? I owe Tom a solid, but this crap is insane."

"Where'd you serve, Hanson?" Travis said.

"In Virginia, not far from here. Naval Special Warfare Group Two, SEAL Team Ten."

"I was Special Forces," Travis said. "You know the drill. How many times did you get orders that you figured must have come from a crazy person?"

"A few," Hanson mumbled. "Okay, a lot. We were deployed in the Mideast. Everything is crazy there."

Travis grinned. "Yeah, I was in Afghanistan. A whole 'nother kettle of fish over there."

"So, how do you want to play it?" Hanson said.

"We go in, find the kid, and extract him before he can do any damage."

"Sounds simple enough."

"Only problem is he'll likely have a Secret Service detail on him," Travis said.

Hanson's eyes widened. "And you don't think they'll be able to keep a lid on him?"

"They'll be looking for threats *to* him, not *from* him," I said. "He's actually got the perfect cover. Which is where Tess and I come in."

"It'll be easier for us to get close to him since we're closer to his age," Tess said. "And he'll definitely talk to us before he talks to adults."

Hanson's mouth hung open. "Wait! You're not bringing these two, are you?"

"Well..." Travis said slowly. "I'd hoped they'd stay out of harm's way."

"We're coming, Uncle Travis. You can't do this without us."

Travis shrugged. "You heard the lady. I suggest we mount up and plan our strategy over breakfast somewhere."

"I know just the place," the driver said.

"I'll have the plane ready when you get back," Tom said, "but if you don't mind, I'm going to get some shut-eye for a few hours."

Hanson crooked a finger. "Barrett, I've got a few things in the trunk you can help me transfer. Or I can follow you. Your choice."

"I assume you're talking about gear. Better we take care of that now than try to do it under the noses of all the security details in D.C."

"Uh, Tess and I will wait in the car," I said. I didn't think I'd be much help handling ordnance.

Travis smiled. "Sounds like a great plan, Oliver."

36

Austin tramped down the stairs in a foul mood. He wasn't sure where it had come from because he'd slept okay. At least he thought he had. The moods had been coming over him a lot lately, and he couldn't really explain it. Okay, so yeah, he wasn't all that happy about their move from what he considered home to Washington, D.C., when his father had gone from being a senator to vice president. And after three years of being under the constant watch of walking, talking mannequins in suits with Ray-Bans and two-way communicators, he was even less happy that the great Josiah Dunn had decided to run for president. But these black moods had gone way past his usual petulance. Hormones, maybe. He was still going through puberty, right? He only had to shave once a week, if that, so he must be. The only time he felt good, it seemed, was when he improved his mastery of *Never Bitten*.

He saw his father sitting at the table in the formal dining room, reading the *Washington Post* and absent-mindedly drinking coffee from a delicate china cup. His father set the cup down and picked up a slice of toast from his plate, never taking his eyes off the paper. After taking a bite, he brushed crumbs from his silk tie and the front of the dress shirt with the monogrammed French cuffs. A suit jacket hung on the back of his chair. This on a Saturday morning, when most normal fathers had on jeans for yard work, or shorts for the golf course.

Austin hated having to sit in the formal dining room and be waited on at breakfast. He didn't know why he couldn't just pour himself a bowl of cereal and eat in the kitchen, or grab a toaster pastry on the way out the door.

His father glanced up as Austin slid into a chair. "Good morning, son."

"Good morning, *father*."

His father frowned. "Watch your tone."

"My name is Austin—a name you gave me, by the way—not 'son'"

"But you are my son. And it wouldn't hurt to show a little respect."

"I'm not one of your constituents, Dad. I'm not old enough to vote, so your political record doesn't mean anything to me, only your record as a father."

"You know what I mean. Respecting your elders is just common courtesy."

Austin felt his face flush as resentment bubbled up from deep inside. "What have you done to earn it? Your accomplishments as a parent bite."

"Austin, that's enough!" His father's voice was sharp. "What's gotten into you lately?"

"Nothing," he mumbled, turning his face away.

A staff member—a college-age guy, not Rachel, Austin's favorite—came through the door from the kitchen and approached him. "Something to eat this morning, sir?"

"Just a bowl of cereal. Whatever you've got. As long as it's not one of those boxes of wood chips that old folks eat to improve their regularity. And a glass of orange juice. Please."

"Right away, sir."

Austin watched him go, wondering why a guy like that would want a job sucking up to people all day. He could be a lifeguard and get all the girls he wanted, or a valet parking attendant and get tips *and* girls. With a sigh, Austin pulled his phone out and turned it on.

Hearing the sounds the phone made, his father lowered his paper. "Austin, I've told you no games at the table."

"Fine!" Austin placed the phone on the table next to his spoon.

His father began to raise the paper again, but hesitated. "I expect you to come to the campaign rally this morning. Just so you know."

"Dad, come on! Why? I've heard your speech like a kazillion times. And it's not like a reporter from *Slate* magazine is going to ask my opinion on foreign policy."

"You know why, Austin. Because we're a family. That's what America wants to see."

"Mom's not going."

"She had a previous commitment."

"Her tennis lesson? Oh, come on. If she's really taking tennis lessons, why isn't she getting any better? She sucks."

"Watch yourself! You're on thin ice."

Austin scowled, but held his tongue.

"You're going," his father said. "That's that."

"Fine, I'll go, but I'm going to hang out with my friends. If you want photo ops, you better tell the cameras to get shots of me doing what other *normal* kids do."

His father drained his coffee cup and stood. "It'll have to do. But this conversation isn't over. We're going to talk about what's going on with you, young man."

Austin rolled his eyes. "Yeah, whatever."

His father glared at him and started to open his mouth, then looked at his watch and reconsidered. He hooked his coat off the back of the chair with a finger, shrugged it on, shot his cuffs and straightened his tie.

"I'll see you there," his father said on his way out.

Fuming, Austin could barely contain himself. The second his father was out of sight, he picked up his phone and booted up the game. Wolfsbane, his avatar, was at a critical junction in the game, about to meet the man rumored to be Wolfsbane's father. It was a trap! Wolfsbane's father had been turned into one of the undead and lay in ambush for Wolfsbane with a horde of zombies. Wolfsbane dispatched two of the grotesque creatures with shotgun blasts, cleanly sliced the head off a third with a single stroke of his broadsword, and rolled an incendiary bomb into the crowd, knocking several zombies over like bowling pins before the device exploded sending blood and body parts in all directions. When the screen cleared, Wolfsbane and his father were the only two left standing. They circled each other warily.

Just as Wolfsbane readied himself to attack, a vampire swooped in on his blind side, mouth open, dripping fangs about to sink into his neck. Austin's fingers moving at lightning speed across the controls on the screen. Wolfsbane whipped out a wooden stake and slashed the vampire open from groin to sternum. Screaming, the vampire stepped back, and Wolfsbane finished it off by plunging the stake into its black heart. Seeing an opening, the zombie moved in, arms stretched toward Wolfsbane's throat. Wolfsbane felt the bony, slimy fingers wrapping around his throat. With a snarl, he brought one arm up and over the zombie's and twisted his body, bringing his elbow down hard on the zombie's forearms. They snapped like brittle twigs. Wolfsbane immediately followed up with a backhanded punch to the zombie's face, nearly knocking his head off with the force of the blow. He reached in with his clawed fingers, ripped out the zombie's throat and watched the lifeless body drop to the ground.

Austin let out a cry of triumph, and looked around hurriedly to see if anyone had heard. The staff was too busy getting his father ready for departure to pay Austin any notice. Austin realized that this was his chance. He slipped upstairs and down the hall to his parents' bedroom, though he was pretty sure that his father slept on the couch in his study these days. His father had installed a safe in the master bedroom closet. Austin had found the combination in a file on his father's computer that also listed all his passwords, the first thing they taught you not to do when you learned to go online. Austin spun the dial with sure fingers, and within moments the locked clicked and the safe opened. Inside he found the aluminum case containing his father's gun. He pulled it out and opened it. Nestled in a foam cutout lay a black Sig Sauer P229 and two magazines. His father had chosen it because it was the same service weapon that his Secret service details carried. The magazines were fully loaded. Austin slipped them into his jeans. He tucked the semiautomatic into his waistband at the small of his back and pulled his shirt over it. It felt heavy and cold against his skin.

Now he was ready to go to the rally.

37

Tess listened intently as the others around the table wrapped up the strategy session. She could hardly believe they were in the nation's capital. The past few days had flown by in a blur, and she found it difficult to remember how it all had started. What was she doing here? What were any of them doing here? Chasing a possibility. Trying to find one kid in a sea of thousands of people on the chance that he'd been affected by a video game that might cause players to become overly aggressive. Austin Dunn might not even go to his father's campaign rally. The game app might not have affected him the way it seemed to have affected Matt.

She—they—were assuming a lot based on Derek's evaluation of how his software code had been altered and what Matt had done in the school cafeteria. But what if there was no cause and effect? What if Matt had gone loony tunes for some other reason? What if Derek was wrong about what the code changes were doing to the game? They could be running a fool's errand, the result of which would be looking like exactly that—fools. The board of directors would have Travis's head on a pike. He could lose his job. The family could lose control of the company her father had worked so hard to build.

But if there was even a chance that Derek was right and his altered game app might drive Austin to do something horrible, she had to try to help him. She couldn't let what happened to Matt happen to anyone else. Not because the fallout might damage the company, or her family's name, but because it was the right thing to do. She had to find a way to prove Derek's contention and keep the game from being released worldwide. And with the help of Derek, Oliver and Travis she had to find the people behind the conspiracy and Travis's kidnapping.

Besides, something told her she was right. She'd been the first to notice the correlation between the game and the change in Matt's behavior. She'd been the one to notice the connection between Marcus's absences and the change in his scent. And with a little help from Oliver, she'd been the one to pinpoint the place where they'd imprisoned Travis. Call it intuition or whatever you want, this blind instinct of hers had been right all along, and maybe she needed to trust herself a little more.

"Okay, bear with me here," Oliver said, breaking into her thoughts. I'm going to help you rig this comm system. I'm going to hand you this earpiece. It's attached to a throat mic that goes around your neck. If you drop the wire down your shirt and un-tuck your shirt, you can reconnect it to the transmitter and put that in your jeans pocket."

She put the earpiece in her ear and wound the mic around her throat like a necklace. Oliver's fingers fumbled with her shirt collar as she dropped the wire down her shirt. She blushed and pushed his hands away. Pushing her chair back, she stood at the table.

"I can follow directions," she murmured. "Just let me know if I got it right."

In seconds, she threaded the wire, plugged it into the transmitter and put the device in her pocket. She pulled the hem of her shirt down over her jeans.

"Look okay?" she said.

"It's fine," Oliver said.

"All set?" Travis said. "Let's move out."

Tess reached behind her for the jacket hanging on the back of her chair. The weather report had promised a sunny day with a high temperature in the mid-60s, but the day hadn't warmed up that much yet. Oliver plucked it out of her hand.

"Here, let me," he said.

"I can do it," she said. "I'm not completely helpless."

She held out her hand until he gave the jacket back.

"I wasn't suggesting that," Oliver said, frustration in his voice. "I just... It's just the way I was brought up. Where I come from it's called manners."

"Problems you two?" Travis said.

"No problem," Tess said between gritted teeth, shrugging the jacket on. Trust Oliver to make her feel stupid and petty. So much for intuition. She was giving him a hard time for trying to help her with the easy stuff, and here he was just trying to be nice.

"Then let's go," Travis said.

They filed out of the restaurant, Tess reluctantly hanging on to Oliver's shoulder. In the SUV, Oliver volunteered to get in back, leaving the middle row to Tess and Hanson, which was fine with her.

On the way into the center of the capital, Travis made them all test their communications gear. Unlike cell phones, the equipment enabled all of them to hear and talk to each other at the same time.

"Third and Fourth Streets are closed in front of the Capitol," Bergstrom told them. "The closest I can get you, I think, is the corner of Independence and Seventh."

"That's fine," Travis said. "That'll give us a chance to work the crowds on the south side of the mall. We can work our way across and up toward the Capitol from there."

"We're coming up on the intersection in about two minutes," Bergstrom said. "Get ready to jump. Security won't let me sit there for long. Miss Barrett, the mall will be on our right, so your door will be at the curb."

"Oliver," Travis said loudly from the front, "are you sure you want to go in unarmed?"

"Damn it, Barrett!" Hanson interjected. "We talked about this. You're licensed to carry. The kid isn't. If he's caught with a weapon, he's in deep doo-doo. If he discharges the thing and doesn't kill someone, he'll spend what's left of his youth as some con's plaything. Lord help us, if he did kill someone we'd all go to jail as accomplices to felony murder."

"All right, all right," Travis said. "I'm just worried about Tess and Oliver being out there with no way to protect themselves."

"It's okay," Oliver said. "It's just one kid. It's not like we're going up against an army."

Bergstrom interrupted the conversation. "Get ready to bail in ten, nine, eight..."

Tess felt the SUV swerve and come to a sudden stop. She yanked on the door handle and tumbled out, waiting by the open door until Oliver could guide her away. A moment later the doors slammed and the engine revved and faded away as Bergstrom pulled the SUV back into traffic. The air hummed with the conversation of hundreds of people all around, and from a distance, Tess heard the amplified echo of a man's voice over a PA system.

"The warm-up act," Hanson said gruffly. "Should give us time to find this kid before his daddy takes the stage."

"We'll work our way across the mall and then up toward the Capitol," Travis said. "Why don't you two take this side?"

"Let's go," Oliver murmured in her ear.

She put her hand on his shoulder and followed him into the crowd. The presence of so many people pressing in around her felt almost claustrophobic, and the drone of voices from all sides distracted her. She focused her thoughts on other things—the heat of the sun on her face, the soft tread of the grass under her feet, the scent of cherry blossoms. Despite the day's warmth, she shuddered involuntarily.

"Are you okay?" Oliver said.

"Don't lose me in this crowd," she murmured.

"Just hang on to me. You'll be fine." After a pause, he said, "Don't like crowds?"

"Not anymore. Too unpredictable."

"This isn't bad. Not like being at a concert or something, packed in like sardines. It isn't shoulder-to-shoulder until you get a lot closer to the stage."

"Whatever. Just don't lose me."

"I won't. You know we're never going to find him with all these people here."

She thought about it for a moment. "Yes, we will." She got her phone out, pulled the earpiece out of her ear, and said, "Call Derek."

"It's your dime," Derek answered.

"You're tracking Austin, right?" Tess said.

"I'm getting a lot of background noise. I can barely hear you. But, yeah, I'm watching his location.

Tess spoke up. "Can you track my phone, too?"

"Yeah, I can do that." Derek spoke faster as excitement gripped him. "And tell you where you are relative to his position."

"Exactly," Tess said with relief. "Do it. I'll keep the line open."

"You got it, Tess."

Derek put her on hold for what seemed like an eternity as Oliver continued to lead her through the throngs of people. Then he came back on the line.

"Okay, I've got you. You're about two hundred yards west and a little south of the kid. He got there about five, ten minutes ago. Moved around some at first, but hasn't moved much in the past few minutes."

Tess told him to hold on and relayed the information to Oliver, tugging on his shirt to get him to stop. "Don't tell Uncle Travis yet. We need to get to Austin first. If he does have a gun, and he see armed men coming after him, there's no telling what he'll do."

"Okay, I'll buy that."

"Tess?" Derek's voice said in her ear. "This program has a GPS refresh rate of about once every five seconds. I'm going to try to bump that to once a second or faster to give you guys more accurate info on Austin's location."

"Thanks, Derek," she said. "We're on our way. Tell me when we're getting close."

Oliver started moving again. Tess slid her fingers down his arm, took his hand and squeezed it hard. He gave hers a reassuring squeeze back, but didn't let go.

"Scared?" he said as they pushed through the knots of people milling about listening to the echoing voice from down the mall.

"Nervous," she said. "I hope we're doing the right thing."

38

Senator Jeremy Latham sat deep in thought at his desk in the Senate Office building, elbows resting on the leather arms of his desk chair, steepled fingers touched to his pursed lips. He'd come into the office early from his row house in Georgetown. Though most congressmen of his tenure and stature did not put in appearances at the office on a Sunday, it wasn't uncommon. Normally, he wouldn't be there—he had a golf game with one of the joint chiefs at the Congressional Country Club later in the day—but his office was his fortress, his command post, and today was unlike most Sundays. This Sunday, history would be changed, one way or another.

He would have come into the office on this particular in any event, but the disturbing phone call he'd received late the night before demanded his attention. Travis Barrett had escaped not only the confines of a makeshift prison cell deep inside an abandoned Montana copper mine, but had somehow managed to elude his pursuers and vanish from the state altogether. Latham had been furious at the level of incompetence displayed by those responsible for letting Barrett slip away. He had no concerns that Barrett's capture and imprisonment would be traced back to him. The guest ranch's ownership was so convoluted that his name could never be connected to it. And even if someone could link him to the ranch in some way, he could plausibly deny any involvement. After all, anyone could have trespassed on the ranch land and thrown Barrett into the mine. But he wanted Barrett found and neutralized.

Leaning forward, he opened a drawer and took out the untraceable cell phone he kept there. He pushed one of the speed-dial codes and sat back with the phone held to his ear.

"Report," he barked when the phone was answered.

"I have nothing beyond what I told you last night, sir," came the quiet reply.

"What the hell do I pay you for?" Latham fumed.

"Look, we know that one of the family's jet aircraft flew into and out of Libby, Montana, yesterday. It's possible he was on it when it left Libby."

"Four men and two vehicles left in a trail of destruction on the highway leading into town? And you only think it's *possible* he was on that plane?" Latham could feel his blood pressure rising and did his best to stay calm. "I want to know where that plane is at this very moment."

"It didn't file a flight plan. We put out feelers all over the country to see if anyone has spotted it, but so far we have nothing. It definitely didn't return to Seattle."

"Find it!" Latham growled. "Find Barrett! And put extra men on the ground at the event now! I don't want him interfering!"

"It's a madhouse there already! They'll never find him in that crowd."

"Just do it! And take Barrett alive. We need him."

"Yes, sir."

Latham slammed the phone down on the desk, picked up a remote control unit, and pointed it at a credenza against the wall. A flat screen television silently rose from the back of it, slowly flickering to life. Already tuned to Fox News Channel, the television screen showed live images of events happening literally outside his window. The cameras had a better view than he did, however, and their zoom lenses zeroed in on the action better and faster than he could have even with binoculars. Besides, from his vantage point, he would only be able to see his nemesis from the back. He wanted to see the man's face when he died. Though the sound was muted, he could tell from the way the director cut from camera to camera, with more shots of the crowds than the speaker, that the main event had not yet started. Even so, Latham was impressed—and disgusted—by the size of the mob of people on the mall. He picked up the phone again and speed-dialed another number, gaze still riveted on the television screen.

"Yes?" a voice answered.

"I'm watching right now," Latham said. "Is he there?"

"Yes, but he's not that close. Maybe five hundred feet away."

Latham waved dismissively even though the man on the other end couldn't see him. "I'm not worried about that. He can get as close as he wants and no one will stop him."

"You know there are no guarantees."

"You assured me he was ready," Latham said, his voice a knife's edge.

"He is ready. He's as primed as anyone could be. But there's always the human factor. And chance."

"Chance shouldn't have anything to do with this."

"We can't foresee every possibility, every permutation," the man protested.

Latham's vision narrowed. "Your job is to control the subject and limit the possibilities. But I'll concede that perfection may be difficult on a project like this. As you say, people can be unpredictable. I haven't found that to be the case often. It's a matter of knowing which buttons to push and when."

Latham paused and chuckled. "My inside source says the subject got into a fight this morning with his father. Apparently, he was mad enough to chew nails and spit rivets. And, according to my source, he has a weapon."

"Then let's hope he's mad enough to kill."

"Yes, you had better hope so. If he fails it could reflect poorly on you."

"I've done everything I can."

"We'll see." Latham disconnected before the man could offer up any more excuses.

He tossed the phone into the drawer and slammed the drawer shut. His eyes were drawn to the television again. The sheer number of people filling the screen was incomprehensible to him. The only time he'd seen as many was at the president's inauguration. Before that one would have to go back to previous inaugurations or as far back as the Civil Rights movement. And that was almost anathema to him. The only rights he believed in were his own inalienable rights to life, liberty and his pursuit of happiness. And while "happiness" was a foreign concept to him, he took it to mean the two things that gave him the greatest satisfaction in life—money and power.

And yet, all these people, these paeans, had turned out to hear a man who would upset the status quo, who would upend tradition. The man was running against an incumbent president, for god's sake. Not only that, but to add insult to injury, he was turning on the very man who had handed him the vice presidency on a silver platter. Ungrateful bastard! It was as close to treason as anyone could come. No, it *was* treason. To speak against your own President, to discount his legacy while acting as his right-hand man, was unpatriotic and traitorous beyond words. No doubt about it, Josiah Dunn deserved to die.

Latham turned up the volume on the television and leaned forward to watch.

39

"You buy this crap these kids are feeding you?" Hanson said as they briskly walked across the mall, eyes scanning the faces in the crowd.

Travis's mouth curved down in annoyance. "Are you with us or not, Hanson?"

"Oh, I'm with you. The kind of money you're offering? I'm your new best friend. But I find it hard to believe you're swallowing this story."

Travis grabbed the man's arm above the elbow and swung him around. He dug his thumb into a nerve and watched the man's face turn ashen with pain. But when Hanson saw the expression on Travis's face, he didn't complain or resist. Travis eased his grip.

His jaw clenched, Travis said, "You get this straight. I just spent the past three days in a hole in Montana because somebody with more pull than the president wants to keep me quiet and away from my family's company. I take whatever my niece says very seriously, most of it as gospel. And the guy who says this video game can brainwash people is the best software coder since my brother, and he was the best there is. Those 'kids' found me in an abandoned copper mine in the middle of Montana when the best security team I know of hadn't the slightest clue where I was. And that means either my team is stupid, which they're not, or there's a mole. It also means that my niece and her assistant are pretty damned smart.

"I consider Josiah Dunn a friend. If a game my company put out has messed up his son's head, I'm responsible. I wouldn't have flown all night to get here if I didn't believe Tess and Oliver. If you're with me, then you better believe every word they tell you, too, and you'd better be prepared to die for those kids because that's what it may come to today. You got it?"

Hanson nodded silently. Travis let him go with a last look of disgust and stalked off. He heard Hanson's hurried footsteps catch up to him.

"Hey, look, man," Hanson said. "I'm sorry. I didn't know."

"There's a lot you don't know," Travis said. "Like, three weeks ago those two got caught in the middle of a firefight when an assault team tried to take them out. An *assault* team! A dozen men with automatic weapons—H&K MP5s with silencers. Yeah, that's right, the same weapon you used to carry when you were a SEAL. Against a blind unarmed teenager and a college kid. And they survived. You hear what I'm saying? Not only did they survive, but they did a pretty decent job of outsmarting the bastards and holding them at bay until the cavalry arrived. So don't go telling me what I should and shouldn't believe."

"Yes, sir," Hanson said softly.

Travis glanced at him and saw the soldier he'd been, not the cocky mercenary he'd become.

"Tom spoke highly of you. I hope he was right. Let's do this."

"You got my attention, sir."

"Okay. I suggest we split up and cover more territory. I'll work my way toward Madison and head up that side of the mall. Why don't you take the center?"

"Yes, sir."

"If you can, try to keep Tess and Oliver in sight. I don't want us to be so far away we can't help out if they need us. Let's move out."

Travis watched Hanson get swallowed in the crowd, only the top of his head visible as he bobbed and weaved through the throngs. Setting out for the far side of the grassy park, Travis focused his concentration not only on faces, but also on noticing every detail. Metro D.C. police directed traffic out on the streets on either side of the mall. On the mall itself, Travis saw a few uniformed officers on foot patrol wearing the pale blue shirts and distinctively striped black trousers of the U.S. Park Police. Mounted USPP officers in their blue helmets sitting astride their horses above the heads of all the people were even more visible. He crossed 4th Street heading east. Through gaps in the crowd, Travis could see the stage set up on the other side of 3rd Street in front of the Capitol Reflecting Pool. Barricades where security was even tighter had been set up at least a hundred feet away from 3rd Street. Personnel in uniforms he thought were those of the TSA manned checkpoints, screening purses and bags of people who wanted a closer look at the candidate. And even from this distance, Travis noted the suited Secret Service agents standing at the edges of the stage, their gazes, like Travis's, scanning the crowd.

Holding a mental image of the general location of the security he'd spotted, Travis turned his focus back to picking Austin's face out of the sea of humanity. He moved quickly through the throng, excusing himself as he brushed past one group after another, turning briefly to consider and dismiss faces on those whose backs had been turned as he moved past. His pulse rate increased and his senses went on alert, feeding his brain even more input—snippets of conversation, a strange scent, an odd expression that seemed out of place. He absorbed it all, processed it and discarded anything that wasn't useful, constantly moving, turning, eyes searching in a grid pattern so that he wouldn't miss anything.

Sudden pressure in his kidney took him by complete surprise. He instinctively started to turn to see who had jostled him, but a hand on his shoulder stopped him.

"Don't turn around!" a voice whispered hoarsely in his ear. "Keep moving, Captain Barrett. Head over to the tree line."

Travis had never considered he might be hunted, too, and he mentally kicked himself for it. Whoever had known about his escape had figured he would come here to stop Austin, and had sent men to find him. With a gun pressed in his back, he had little choice but to follow the man's instructions and wait for an opening. No way he was going down without a fight.

The man behind him kept the gun pressed into his kidney and his other hand on Travis's upper arm, staying so close that no one around them had any idea Travis was being held at gunpoint. The man pushed Travis ahead of him through the crowd until it thinned out at the edge of the grassy mall near the trees. Several yards under he leafy branches, the man pulled on Travis's arm, signaling him to stop.

"What now?" Travis said, keeping his face forward.

"Someone wants to talk to you," the man said.

He let go of Travis's arm, and Travis heard him fishing in his pocket, followed by the beeping tones of a phone dialing a number. Travis felt sudden relief from the pressure on his kidney as the man jerked away from him. Travis whirled around, ready to face another foe. Hanson had Travis's captor in a headlock and was applying pressure to the man's carotid artery with his forearm. The man's eyelids fluttered and he went limp as the lack of oxygen to his brain rendered him unconscious. Hanson dragged him backward to the base of a tree and gently set him down, propping him against the trunk.

He gave Travis a big grin. "He'll only be out for ten or fifteen. We don't have a lot of time."

Travis regarded him with admiration. "I'm impressed."

"The game just got a lot more interesting," Hanson said. "Looks like we have a spoiler to worry about, too."

"I didn't think they'd be onto us this quickly. Thanks for watching my back."

"That's why you're paying me the big bucks, boss. We better keep moving."

"Good idea."

They hurried out from under the trees and blended back into the crowd, Hanson quickly making his way to the center of the mall and continuing his search. Travis worked his way up the side of the mall, this time paying more attention to the faces behind him as well as in front.

Movement on the periphery of his vision made him pause. He stood in one spot and did a slow turn to his left to pinpoint the distraction. *There!* A mounted USPP officer thirty yards away had stiffened and now stood up in his saddle, one hand holding the mic of his walkie-talkie close to his mouth. Something was up. Travis quickly turned away before the cop caught him staring and pushed through a knot of people. A commotion erupted in the other direction, and Travis glanced over to see two USPP uniforms on foot pushing through the crowd in his direction. Travis ducked into another large group of people and knelt down as though tying his shoe.

He thumbed his throat mic. "I think I've been made. Whatever you do, stay on target."

"Roger that," Hanson said.

There was no response from Tess or Oliver. Travis didn't have time to consider what that might mean. He took a ball cap that he'd purchased at the restaurant from his jacket pocket and put it on, pulling the brim down low over his eyes. Then he stripped off his windbreaker, taking his shoulder holster off at the same time. In the same motion he quickly turned the windbreaker inside out, wrapping it around the holster and gun. He stuck one hand inside the bundle and grasped the pistol grip. He placed his other hand on top of the jacket to hold it in place. Hoping the cursory disguise would throw off his pursuers, he stood and casually continued making his way up the mall through the crowd.

Judging from the sounds behind him, the two foot patrolmen had converged on the spot where he'd been. As others around him

craned their necks to see what the commotion was about, Travis
knew that if he didn't do the same his behavior might be suspect.
So he risked a backward glance to see the mounted cop part the
sea of people with his horse and converge on the other two cops.
They would quickly discover their quarry had disappeared and
start looking elsewhere so Travis picked up his pace, trying not to
tick anybody off as he pushed his way through what was
becoming a solid mass of bodies. Through a break in the mob, he
glimpsed a group of teenagers off to the side under some trees.
And on the edge of the group, wearing a baggy winter coat with
his hands in his pockets, stood Austin Dunn.

"I have the target in sight!" Travis murmured excitedly into
his comm unit. "North side of the mall. Fifty yards this side of the
barricade."

"Got it," Hanson replied. "On my way."

Travis angled for the open area between the edge of the crowd
and the trees where the teens hung out. The fact that Austin was
near them, but not part of the group, seemed further confirmation
he had something on his mind. Definitely an outsider. Travis
broke into the clear.

"Uh-oh," Hanson said. "You've got company. And it looks like
they're calling in reinforcements."

Travis looked around and saw the mounted cop and the two
patrolmen pushing their way toward him. Two more mounted
cops were headed his way from the opposite side of the mall. And
a pair of Secret Service agents leaped from the stage across the
street and the crowd magically parted like the Red Sea to allow
them passage.

When he turned back in Austin's direction, his opening had
vanished, filled by the milling crowd. He jumped up for a quick
view over the top of the crowd. Austin was on the move. More
determined than ever, Travis shouldered his way through the
mass of bodies, quietly exclaiming, "Excuse me, coming through!
Police emergency!"

When anyone threw him a doubtful look, he threw his thumb
over his shoulder at the mounted cops fifty yards behind him. He
made slow progress, praying he wasn't too late. When he looked
up again an instant later, his pulse raced and his heart sank. Tess
and Oliver had gotten there first.

He was already too late.

40

"**I** still don't see how we're going to find him," I grumbled.

Our roles reversed, Tess now guided me through an undulating tide of bodies that jostled and moved us here and there like so much flotsam and jetsam on the waves. She relayed instructions from Derek as our position changed and we grew ever closer to some magic spot where Austin's phone, if not Austin himself, would appear. But the GPS could only get us so close.

"He'll try to blend in," Tess said. "He'll hang with a group his own age. But unless he finds some of his friends, he won't be *in* the group. Know what I mean?"

Travis's voice came through my earpiece. "I think I've been made."

"Keep moving!" Tess said. "If they catch Travis, it's up to us. We've got to find Austin!"

"I'm moving, I'm moving!"

Someone bumped into me hard, and I lost my grip on Tess's hand. As if sucked into a vacuum, two people filled the sudden hole created between us and I got pushed farther away.

"Oliver!" Tess cried, her voice quavering.

I shouldered my way into an opening, shoved my hand through a gap of daylight, and grabbed her hand.

"Got you!" I hooted. "Let's go."

Tugging her between two pudgy middle-aged matrons who gave me the evil eye, I put my arm around her shoulder and pulled her close.

"Told you I wouldn't lose you," I murmured into her ear.

"Seemed awfully close," she said, her mouth a grim line.

Sometimes there's no pleasing people. I gripped her hand tightly and fought my way through the throngs. The noise, with the amplified speech reverberating down the mall and the hum of the crowd, blanked out all thought.

The next time someone jostled me, I turned with a smart comment on my lips. Before I could let loose, a short stocky man with thinning hair and buck teeth grabbed my arm in a vise-like grip. He took Tess's in his other hand, fingers completely encircling her slender arm.

"Well, well," he said in a high, squeaky voice. "What have we here? Blind girl, young guy. You wouldn't happen to be Tess and Oliver, now would you?"

He laughed at his own joke. But came out more of a cackle. He wore a windbreaker zipped halfway over his voluminous belly, and even though it was large enough to serve as a kid's tent, it wasn't big enough to hide the bulge of a pistol under one arm.

"Oliver?" Tess said, nervousness in her voice. "What's going on?"

"Pickpocket!" I shouted. "Thief!"

Heads turned toward us, and the fat man's smile faded. Tess stomped down hard, her shoe landing on his instep. He let go of us with a howl as he reached down and hopped on one foot.

"He took my wallet!" I hollered. "Pickpocket!"

A burly bearded guy in a short-sleeved plaid shirt stepped away from his wife and two small kids and pushed me aside to stand toe-to-toe with the fat guy.

"He's lying," the fat man said.

"Give it back!" our rescuer said.

"I don't have his wallet!" Fat Man insisted.

Burly Guy thrust his bearded chin at Fat Man. "Why'd you grab them up like that?"

"Hey, my watch is gone!" someone shouted.

More people pressed past me to confront Fat Man. I took Tess's hand and pulled her back into the crowd with me.

"Come on," I murmured in her ear. "Let's go, let's go!"

I put my arm around her shoulder, ducked down and we weaved through several groups of people who had turned to see what the ruckus was behind us.

"What was that all about?" Tess said breathlessly. "Did he really take your wallet?"

"Somebody's on to us," I said. "They know we're here to find Austin."

"The wallet thing was a diversion?"

"It worked, didn't it?"

When we were well away from the spot I took Tess's hand again and straightened up to get my bearings as we walked.

"That was close," I said.

"What?" Tess said loudly.

"I said that was close!" I called over my shoulder. I caught a glimpse of her holding the phone to her ear.

She leaned into me as I pulled her along. "Derek says Austin's not far away!"

I stopped and stood on tiptoe, scanning over the heads of those around me. Past a swath of empty grass at the edge of the mall, a group of kids horsed around under the trees. Near them, but not taking part, stood a kid in a bulky coat, looking miserable.

"I think I see him!" I said. I hesitated.

Tess stretched my arm as she strained forward. "Well, come on!"

"Wait! Just wait a second." I tried to put my thoughts in order. "I did a lot of thinking on the plane. Why would these people go to the trouble of developing an AI capability and sabotaging Derek's game app with it just to try to discredit the vice president? I mean, Austin's just a kid, right? If he misbehaves, his father's campaign staff can spin it and contain the damage."

Tess opened her mouth to interrupt, but her expression turned thoughtful.

I plowed ahead. "This is a beta test. They already did field experimentation—we saw an example of it with Matt. Think about it, Tess. Dunn is a sitting vice president challenging an incumbent president. These people want to make a point, and they want it to be dramatic."

"What are you thinking?" Tess said.

"I think they want Austin to assassinate his father. Why else would they be so intent on stopping us?"

She gulped and said, "All the more reason to get to him before anyone else does."

"But if I'm right, he's not going to like it if we interfere. He probably has a gun."

"He won't use it. I'm blind. He won't shoot a blind person."

"Okay. It's your funeral."

But I knew she was right. The kid wouldn't shoot a blind girl. It was my funeral we were talking about, not hers. I took her hand and once again plowed through the endless multitude, aiming for the relatively vacant strip of grass near the tree line. When we finally reached it, Austin was no longer where he'd been. I quickly scanned the tree line in both directions. Another thirty yards east, Austin trudged slowly in the direction of the stage as if reluctantly accepting his fate. I changed direction, towing Tess behind me. She stumbled, and I turned to grab her other arm and lift her back onto her feet.

"Take it easy!" she said.

"He's right over there!" I said. Like she could see. "Headed for the stage. Come on!"

The barricade stood another hundred feet or so beyond Austin. He could get through security and we couldn't. If he reached the barricade first, we'd fail. It made me wonder where his Secret Service detail was. He was supposed to have protection. I glanced around. Through the trees I finally spotted two agents taking a parallel path a discreet distance away on the sidewalk next to the street.

Travis's voice rang in my ear. "I have the target in sight! North side of the mall. Fifty yards this side of the barricade."

I glanced over my shoulder and could tell that Tess had heard it, too. We'd run out of time.

"Austin!" I yelled.

He looked around wildly, wondering who'd called his name.

I waved at him. "Wait up!"

He paused and peered at us suspiciously, but I could tell he was curious. The agents, paused, too, on alert, but Austin had given them no sign yet that he was in danger. Tess and I drew to within ten yards or so.

"Who are you?" he said.

"We're friends," Tess said. "We just want to talk to you."

"I don't know you. Hey, you, over here. Wait, are you blind or something?"

Tess gave a nervous laugh. "Yeah, 'or something.'"

"What do you want?" The suspicion was back in his eyes. "I have to be somewhere."

"You don't want to do this," Tess said.

"Do what? What are you talking about?"

"We know what you're planning to do. You've got a gun, right? And you want to use it to kill your father."

"What the hell?" His jaw dropped open and panic filled his eyes. He looked around as if expecting a horde of cops to rush out from among the trees and arrest him.

I let go of Tess's hand and did imaginary push-ups in the air. "Whoa, settle down! It's just the two of us, and we just want to talk."

He edged a few feet away face pale with fright. "Don't come any closer. How do you know me?"

"It's partly my fault," Tess said. "Well, my family's fault. Look, we don't have time for this. My uncle and another commando type are right behind us, and they're going to come in with guns blazing. You have to believe us! You don't want to go through with this."

"How do you know?" Austin snarled. His lip curled in defiance now. "Maybe this is exactly what I want to do."

"He's playing a character in the game!" another voice said, so faint it barely registered above the buzz of the crowd.

Startled, Austin said in a more normal voice, "Who's that?"

Tess raised the hand with her phone in it. "Derek? I forgot you were still on the line."

"He's slipping back and forth between himself and his avatar," Derek said.

"We want to talk to Austin," Tess said. "Austin, let me explain. The guy on the phone, Derek, he's the one who invented *Never Bitten*, the game you play on your smart phone. Only somebody changed it, made it brainwash people somehow."

"Oh, that's a load," Austin said. "Video games don't brainwash kids. There's tons of experts who say that's a bunch of crap."

"This one does," Derek shouted through the phone. "I know. I wrote the program. Whoever screwed with it is tracking you now with a GPS program. How do you think these guys found you?"

"Tracking me?" A bewildered look crossed Austin's face. "Why...?"

"To make sure you finish the job," Tess said. "They want to see you kill your father."

He looked more confused and frightened than ever. I took Tess's hand and edged a few feet closer to him.

"I don't understand," he said. "How did you know I was going to...?"

"It doesn't matter how," Tess said. "We just don't want you to go through with it. It will ruin your life."

"My father's already ruined my life!" Austin shouted. "Don't you get it?"

Tess pulled away from me, put her arms out and walked toward him. "Please, Austin, trust me. I lost my father—both my parents—a year ago. We had a fight right before they died. The last thing I told them was how much I hated them. Now I'd give anything to have them back. If you do this, he'll be gone forever. And you'll regret it. I know you will. You know it, too."

His hands clenched and balled into fists, and he fought back tears of frustration. "He just doesn't understand how hard it is to be the kid of somebody famous. He doesn't know what it's like to

228

be the biggest joke in school, to always get picked on and made fun of. This game? *Never Bitten?* This is the first time in, like, forever that I've felt strong, like I could take on anyone and win. *Nobody* messes with me in the game, or they die!"

"But it's just a game, Austin," Tess said quietly. "It isn't supposed too make you kill people in real life. We'll help you. I promise. Just come with us."

He squeezed his eyes shut tight and a tear rolled down one cheek. He swiped at it with the back of his hand. He nodded, put his hand in a coat pocket and slowly pulled out a gun.

Sudden movement in a corner of my vision caught my attention. The Secret Service agents had jerked to attention and now ran toward us at full tilt. Footsteps pounded on the grass behind me and hulking figures pulled up on either side of me.

"Freeze!" Travis shouted, semi-automatic pistol in a two-handed grip at the end of his extended arms.

41

"**D**rop the weapon, Austin!" Hanson yelled.

Oliver shouted a warning. "Tess, watch out!"

Tess stifled a scream as someone grabbed her roughly and pulled her into a chokehold. Cold steel pressed into her neck, freezing her with fear. No, not fear. Caution.

"You promised!" Austin shouted, his voice in her ear almost deafening. "You said everything would be okay! I never should have listened to you! Wolfsbane would have just killed you and gone on with his mission! You ruined everything!"

"It *is* okay, Austin," Tess said calmly, trying not to let her voice catch. "We can help you."

"No, you can't! Look what you've done!"

Ignoring him, she called out, "Uncle Travis! You need to put down your weapons. Austin's not going to hurt me."

"Can't do that, Tess," Travis said. "Not while he's got a gun to your head."

In a softer voice she said, "You're not going to hurt me, are you, Austin? You don't want to kill me. It's the game that's done this. The same thing happened to a friend of mine."

"I don't believe you!"

"It did," Oliver called. "I was there. He shot up a school lunchroom."

A bit of an exaggeration, but if it helped make the point that was okay with Tess.

Shouting erupted on two sides of her, and Austin's grip on her tightened, making it difficult to breathe.

"Police!" a new voice said. " Lay down your weapons! Now! "

"Get back!" Austin screamed, dragging her backwards.

She grabbed onto his forearm to keep from being choked to the point of blacking out. She heard a voice close by barking commands.

"...I repeat, we have a hostage situation! Secure Lone Eagle! Secure Lone Eagle!"

"I swear I'll kill her!" Austin screamed. "Get back!"

"Uncle Travis!" Tess shouted. With Austin's forearm still wrapped around her throat it came out a strangled cry. "Get them to back off! See, I'm trying to help you, Austin. You have to believe me."

"They're not *listening* to you!" he yowled. "I'm not telling you again, people! Get back, all of you! Take one step closer and I *will* kill her!"

"Take it easy son," someone called out. "No one has to get hurt here."

Austin sobbed, and Tess knew he was close to losing it. He was wiry and strong, but Tess could tell that under the bulky coat he was a skinny kid who didn't weigh much. She heard Yoshi's calm voice in her mind and felt her confidence grow. Obviously, the police and Secret Service had joined the party and they'd reached a stalemate. If she didn't take command of this situation quickly, Austin might spiral out of control and bullets would start flying. She shivered then took as deep a breath as she could manage and centered herself.

"Of course someone has to get hurt," Austin cried. "Someone always gets hurt! None of you get it! You don't know what it's like."

"Austin," Travis called, "listen to Tess. She's my niece, and she *does* know what it's like. She's been through hell, but she's still the smartest, bravest person I know. Trust her, Austin. She won't steer you wrong."

Tess was so startled by her uncle's words that for a moment she forgot herself, forgot where she was, forgot the danger. Austin pressed the gun's cold steel harder into her neck, bringing her back to the present. Again, she focused inward and found her center.

"I don't know who you are, sir," the other voice said, "but you need to put down your weapon, now! Let us handle this."

"I'm Travis Barrett, president of MondoHard. Josiah Dunn's a personal friend. I have security clearance! Check it out!"

Tess felt Austin tense and get agitated again. She steeled herself for what she needed to do.

"I! SAID! GET! BACK!" Austin screamed, his voice deafening her.

Suddenly, the barrel of the gun no longer dug into her flesh. *Now!* She gripped his forearm even more tightly, stepped to one side and flipped Austin over her shoulder. She heard the big huff of breath as the air left his lungs when he hit the ground. She pounced on him, knees landing on his chest and forcing the rest of the air out of his lungs. She straddled him, hands quickly feeling for his arm and traveling up to the hand holding the gun. Finding his thumb, she wrenched his hand back, heard a small snap, and the gun fell to the ground. His chest heaved as he sucked in a breath and screamed with pain then went limp beneath her, sobbing.

Shouts and footsteps converged on her, a heavy shoe kicked the gun away from her, and strong hands grabbed her arms and tried to pull her off Austin.

"Back off!" she snarled.

"Stop!" Travis shouted, "Leave her alone!"

"Tess, are you okay?" Oliver said breathlessly from a few feet away. His voice held a note of something other than just friendly concern. Did he...? She couldn't think about it now.

"I'm fine! Everybody, just back off and give us room! It's all over! Austin's okay now!"

She wasn't sure how she knew, but she was certain of it. He was going to be okay.

As if reading her thoughts Austin whimpered, "What did you do that for? That really hurts."

She could tell he was crying. "Sorry, Austin. I didn't mean to break your wrist. I just wanted you to let go of the gun."

"Gun? What gun? Who are you, anyway?"

Tess smiled down at the source of his voice. "A friend, Austin. Just a friend."

42

"**I**'m telling you, Jack," Travis said into his phone, "I've never seen anything quite like it. She flipped the kid, pretty as you please, and then just sat on him. The kid calmed right down. Acted as if he didn't know what happened. Maybe he didn't. Could be like some form of hypnosis, and the blow when he landed after Tess flipped him woke him up. We'll know a lot more when Derek has a chance to deconstruct the software code in that video game."

Travis stood apart from the crowd of government suits and uniformed cops that had gathered on the spot where the dramatic standoff had taken place a short time before. Mounted police had herded the crowd back so a few of the USPP officers could string crime scene tape around an area about half the size of a football field. When the initial commotion had died down and the facts of why the Secret Service had suddenly whisked the vice president away gradually came to light, event organizers had finally thought to make it clear that he wouldn't be giving a campaign speech after all. After that the crowd had thinned considerably.

Travis leaned against a tree and surveyed the enormous bureaucratic machine that had taken over as he listened to the general on the other end of the phone conversation.

"...ranch ownership is a dead end," Jack was saying. "Too many shell corporations. Evans, the manager, has been in an interrogation room at the county sheriff's office since early this morning. Says he thought you were a vagrant stealing food, which is why he sent his men after you. And he claims he had no idea the ranch hands he hired were being paid by someone else to hold you prisoner. He said that until a young couple asked him about copper mines in the area he had no clue anyone had been out at old mine on the ranch."

"Figures," Travis said. He sighed. "I know the problem is on my end, Jack. I still don't want to believe it's Marcus. His record's always been above reproach. Every other man on my team has a blemish on his service record, something to be ashamed of, which is why I gave each a second chance. In my heart I know they're good men. Marcus has always been best of the best."

"Don't move on him then until you have an ironclad case. He'll never forgive you if you're wrong. But in the meantime, you better stick eyes in the back of your head, son."

"That's about all I can do."

Silence hung on the line between them for a moment.

"Tess is okay?" the general asked.

"Better than okay, I think," Travis said. "This past year has been hard on her. I really think she lost her will to live during her recovery, and who could blame her? Losing Jimmy and Sally like that? I can't say it hasn't weighed heavily on me, too. But the past few weeks? She's a fighter again, Jack. You should have seen her. You'd have been proud."

"I *am* proud. Of both of you."

Travis suddenly flushed with embarrassment. "Yeah, well, I had nothing to do with the warrior princess she's becoming."

General Turnbull chuckled. "Sure you did. You've been a good uncle to her, a good parent. I know what you're going to say, No, you're not her father, but you're doing a good job, Travis."

"Yoshi's the one who's taught her to fight, not me."

"It takes a village, Travis. She's learning plenty from you. Don't worry. Speaking of which, you two have a board meeting to attend in the morning back in Seattle."

Travis's eyes glittered and his mouth hardened into a grim line. "I can't wait. I want to see who's the most surprised to see me."

"You want me to arrange a transport out of Andrews?"

"No, but thanks. Tom Foley, our pilot, went straight to a buddy's to rack out and get some sleep. He should be good to go by the time we wrap up here. We'll have to make a stop on the way home to refuel, but the little jet is fine. I think we're all so tired we could sleep anywhere."

"Have a good trip then. I'll see you at the meeting tomorrow."

"Thanks, Jack. Oh, and thanks again for verifying my bonafides with the Treasury guys. Man, talking to those Secret Service types is like conversing with a brick wall."

Travis heard the general chuckle softly again before hanging up. As he walked out from under the trees to rejoin Tess and Oliver he saw Hanson at the edge of the group surrounded by uniformed cops who pored over his credentials—private investigator's license, gun permit, carry-concealed permit, etc. Travis had let them grill Hanson longer than necessary as a little extra punishment for not taking Tess more seriously earlier. A twinge of guilt pricked him, and he changed direction.

"Give the man a break, fellas," Travis said as he approached them. "He's legit."

One of the cops looked up in surprise. "He's with you?"

"That's what I've been trying to tell you for the last twenty minutes," Hanson said.

"I hired him," Travis told the cop.

The cop pushed his cap off his forehead and scratched his scalp. "Well, I suppose that puts things in a different light, seeing as how you have security clearance and all, Mr. Barrett."

They handed Hanson's papers and gun back to him and turned to look for something else to do. Hanson holstered the gun and stuffed the papers in a jacket pocket.

He glanced at Travis. "Thanks."

"No problem."

Hanson looked at his shoes for a moment then lifted his chin. "No, I mean thanks for everything. I'd serve with you anytime, captain."

"It's Travis. And you're welcome. I was glad to have the back-up."

Hanson stuck out his hand, and after Travis matched his grip, he turned and walked away. Travis watched him until he melted into the groups of tourists that stood and gawked at the Capitol dome at the end of the mall. Hanson might come in handy again some day.

Travis wandered over to the spot where Tess had bravely taken on not only a crazed kid with a gun, but law enforcement of every stripe. He wondered if her inability to see the force arrayed in front of her while Austin had her in his grasp had given her greater courage, or at least lessened her fear. She and Oliver stood silently near the spot, attention on an ambulance that had pulled up onto the grass beyond them. As Travis joined them, paramedics prepared to load a gurney carrying Austin into the ambulance.

"Oh, hey, Travis," Oliver said, glancing at him briefly before turning back to the scene unfolding in front of them.

Vice President Dunn stood next to the gurney, speaking to his son. Austin nodded and Josiah gave a signal to the paramedics. They slid the gurney into the back of the ambulance, and a Secret Service agent and a uniformed officer got in behind it. The EMTs closed the doors, and Josiah stepped forward and placed his hand on it. As the ambulance pulled away, Josiah glanced in their direction and nodded once before he was swept away with his retinue.

"What do you think they'll do to him?" Tess said.

Her awareness startled Travis. At times, he was convinced she could still see.

"I don't know," Travis said.

A man approaching them from the side answered. "He'll be treated for the broken wrist. And they'll keep him under psychiatric observation for a day or two to get a sense of why he did this." He held out his hand toward Travis. "Special Agent Ed Stafford."

Travis shook his hand and introduced him to Tess and Oliver.

"That was a brave thing you did out there today, young lady," Stafford said with a smile. "You should get a medal."

"I think so, too," Travis said.

Stafford held up his hand, the smile gone. "I was about to say except for the fact that we understand your uncle's company may have been partly responsible for what happened."

"It's actually my company, Mr. Stafford," Tess said.

"Special Agent Stafford," he said quickly.

Tess shrugged. "The company had nothing to do with what happened. Someone sabotaged a videogame that our company developed. As soon as we discovered it we did everything possible to prevent a tragedy that *might* have been caused by that sabotage."

"But it—"

Tess cut him off. "I haven't finished, Special Agent. It's true that a software product MondoHard was close to releasing was hacked. The company will do a thorough investigation of how this happened and correct any problems with our security to make sure it doesn't happen again. And we'll do everything in our power to find the people responsible. But the fact remains that the game on Austin's phone was a beta version, not a finished product, and it may even have been hacked after he loaded it onto his phone."

Stafford's jaw clenched as he turned to Travis. "That was still a stupid stunt you all pulled today. With all the security it's a wonder that your actions didn't start a firefight and get innocent bystanders killed. You should have told us what was going on."

"Would you have believed me?" Travis said.

Stafford's forehead wrinkled. "Probably not."

"In which case Austin may have actually gone through with his plan, and somebody—the vice president, Austin or even one of your people—would be dead right now. What we did, what my niece did, may not seem smart to you, but from our perspective it was the only option available. Frankly, you *should* give Tess a medal. Oliver, too. If it hadn't been for these two, you'd have egg all over your face and probably blood on your hands. But I know how these things work. You'll spin it somehow, and you guys will take credit for saving the day. That's okay. You and I know better. And so does Josiah Dunn."

Stafford stiffened and clenched his fists. His jaw worked, but he swallowed whatever he wanted to say and spun on his heel.

Travis watched his retreating back. "I don't think he's going to give you a medal, Tess."

She shrugged again. "That's okay. We did the right thing, Uncle Travis."

Travis stepped between the two of them and draped his arms around their shoulders. "Yeah, we did. Now we've got a plane to catch. We have to get home."

Tess groaned. "That's right. Tomorrow's Monday."

"True," Travis said. "But you're not going to school. You have a board meeting to attend with me."

"Really?" she said, unseeing eyes widening just the same.

"Of course. I need you. The company needs you."

43

Tess gratefully sank into her seat on the plane, exhausted. What a whirlwind rollercoaster ride the past few days had been. She couldn't believe that she'd actually helped stop an assassination attempt! Well, maybe. Who knew if Austin really would have gone through with it? But he'd gone as far as taking his father's gun to the campaign rally, and if not for her and Oliver the day might have ended in tragedy. Excitement coursed through her along with the exhaustion. And now she was on her way back home to help Uncle Travis make sure that *Never Bitten* wasn't released to the public until all the bugs had been worked out and the hacked beta copies tracked down and destroyed.

Oliver had recovered her phone back at the National Mall, and she'd called Derek back to let him know she was okay and tell him what had happened. He had already started working on a way to turn off the AI function in the bad copies of the game just incase they couldn't track them all down. Assuming he could do it, and she was confident he could, he'd make his fixes part of an auto update that would download to a player's device as soon as they logged onto the game. All in all, she'd accomplished a lot in less than a week. So much that it surprised her.

Someone placed a hand on her knee, startling her out of her musings.

"I want to thank you, Tess," her uncle said. "For everything. Of course, now I have to ground you forever."

"Uncle Travis!"

"Just kidding. Seriously, though, I have to find a better way to keep you safe. It's my job."

"Get rid of Marcus," she said quickly. "The rest of the guys are fine."

"I can't do it, Tess."

"He tried to kill me! He kidnapped you and held you prisoner! What do you mean you can't get rid of him?"

"I can't prove it. Neither can you. I know how you tracked me to Montana—it's not proof. I can't just fire him, Tess. If he's as bad as you think he is, then firing him will just free him to do whatever he wants to us. With proof I can send him to jail. Until then, I'd rather he was someplace I can keep an eye on him. You know what they say about enemies."

"No, what?"

"Keep your friends close," Oliver chimed in next to her, "and keep your enemies closer."

She thought about it, and nodded. "If we have to. Just keep him away from me."

"I'll do my best," Uncle Travis promised. "Anyway, you proved to me that you can handle yourself just fine without me or any of the team. That doesn't mean you'll be safe in all situations. I still have to do everything in my power to take care of you. I promised your mom and dad that I would. I'm not going to go back on that promise now."

"Okay, fine." Tess slouched in her seat and crossed her arms.

After a moment, her uncle spoke again, this time so softly she strained to hear.

"You proved something else, Tess. You proved me wrong about you. I should trust you more."

She wasn't sure she could believe her ears. Uncle Travis admitting he was wrong?

He went on. "In fact, I've decided that I was wrong about letting you go to the spring dance. What did you call it? Tolo?"

Tess felt her chest tighten. She bit her lip, but despite how hard she tried to stop all her emotions from overwhelming her she burst into tears.

"What?" her uncle said, sounding bewildered. "What did I say?"

"Um, she asked someone to go to the dance with her a few days ago." Oliver told him.

She was sobbing so hard she couldn't stop him.

"What happened?" Uncle Travis asked.

"He said no. Someone else had already asked him."

"Oh, god, Tess, I'm so sorry," Uncle Travis said. "I didn't mean to... I didn't know."

She waved her hand and took a deep breath, trying to get her tears under control.

"I'm not crying about that!" she said. "I'm crying because *now* you decide to tell me you trust me, after everything I've been through!"

"Gosh, Tess, I... I don't know what to say."

Silence hung in the air like wet laundry for a moment.

"I'll take you," Oliver said quietly. "I mean I know the girl is supposed to ask and all, but in this case... If that's all right with you, of course, Mr. Barrett. Oh, and you, Tess. I mean, after all, you... Oh, I better shut up now."

Her sniffles stopped almost immediately. Did she just hear what she thought she heard? Was Oliver really asking her to tolo?

"I'm not a charity case," she sniffed. "It's not part of your job, Oliver, so you don't have to ask."

"I want to," he said firmly. "I mean you wouldn't have to pay me or anything. I'd really like to go with you, Tess. That is if it's okay. I missed a lot of this stuff in high school because I graduated so young."

"So what's the problem?" Uncle Travis asked. "I don't have any problem with the idea."

"You're kidding," she said. "You'll let me go with Oliver? But he's, like, a graduate student."

"Yes, and even old enough to drink legally," her uncle said. "But you won't, will you?"

"Heck no," Oliver said hastily. "Don't touch the stuff, actually, sir."

"Good. BTW, I'm not old enough to be called 'sir.' Call me Travis. Anyway, Tess, remember what Oliver just said about keeping your enemies closer?"

Since the accident, Tess had found it hard to trust anyone or anything, but after what had happened in the past few weeks she knew that she should have a little more faith in Travis and Oliver. And blind or not, she needed to trust her own instincts.

She smiled. "I'll do it. I'll go."

# # # #

Before you go, tell us what you think.
To rate this book, go to
http://www.michaelwsherer.com/feedback

Turn the page for an exciting preview
of the third Tess Barrett thriller,
BLIND TRUST

BLIND TRUST

1

The soldier crouched motionless in the dark, blackened face and woodland camo uniform making him virtually invisible. Rainwater dripped from the bill of his cap onto his nose, but he ignored it as it rolled to the tip and dropped soundlessly onto the forest floor. The small wooded area, a narrow strip of trees and dense brush between the parking lot in front of him and houses behind, was practically the only area of concealment on the whole block that surrounded the target. It had been enough to hide his approach, and enough, he hoped, to mask his intent until it was too late to stop him.

Who would suspect him anyway? He wasn't one of those sad, messed up kids who would be remembered after the fact as a loner, an oddball, someone whose social media account they'd find out later, was filled with angry rants and screeds about being misunderstood, bullied as a kid. Boo-hoo. No, he didn't even belong here, wasn't from here. No one would suspect because no one knew him here.

Soldier. He still thought of himself that way, even though it had been years since he'd served his country both at home and on foreign soil. He called himself that because he'd never been anything else. He'd joined the army right out of high school, had gone through boot camp and specialist training to qualify for every job in both the mounted and dismounted elements of a Stryker Brigade Combat Team (SBCT), from radio telecommunications operator (RTO) to operation of the remote weapons system (RWS) mounted on top of the eight-wheeled, armored infantry carrier vehicle (ICV). He knew how to drive it, too. The army had been interested in cross-training him on only a few positions, but he'd been a quick study. And his wide-ranging skills set had earned him two tours in Kandahar Province, Afghanistan.

The second tour had ended abruptly with his dishonorable discharge for striking a superior officer. The facts and the truth were entirely different.

Fact: yes, he had cold-cocked his platoon leader, a lieutenant whose name he'd rather forget.

Truth: Some bad HUMINT—human intelligence—had resulted in a disastrous mission. While out on patrol and despite the best efforts of their forward observer that day, one of the ICVs in the platoon hit an IED powerful enough to roll it over, taking out its weapons systems and most of the crew. The other ICVs had pulled into a defensive formation, and the men had dismounted from the vehicles and walked right into an ambush.

With both the rifle squad and weapons squad under heavy fire from terrorists, both the fire team leader and the platoon sergeant had taken direct hits and had been dragged back to an ICV by a couple of combat medics, putting the platoon leader directly, rather than indirectly, in charge of the firefight. Pinned down by the hail of bullets and watching men all around get hit, the lieutenant had suddenly lost his nerve and had started blubbering like a baby.

As the weapons squad leader, the soldier had been next in command after the platoon sergeant, So, he'd smacked the lieutenant. Hard. While the lieutenant lay in the dust in a daze, rubbing his sore chin, the soldier had shouted orders to the other men, gotten most of them behind cover, and rallied the weapons squad. Both the automatic rifleman on the ground and the RWS operator in one of the ICVs had laid down some withering return fire, giving the rest of them a chance to take up better positions and knock out the terrorist fighters one by one.

The platoon had lost more than a dozen men that day to horrendous injuries, but not one had died. But he and his squad and the rifle squad had dispatched nine enemy fighters. The squad's fire team leader had recommended the soldier for a medal for his actions, but the lieutenant he'd clocked had filed a formal complaint. Rather than press for a full court martial, the dickwad had settled for the soldier's dishonorable discharge.

The soldier's name was Sam. But he carried nothing on his person that gave any indication of who he was. When he'd returned home after his discharge he'd realized that the only thing the army had really taught him was how to kill. There were no Stryker M1126 ICVs driving around on the streets of Seattle, so he couldn't open up a repair shop. And there was little call for guys who were experts at handling an M289 SAW, a Javelin close-combat missile or shoulder-launched rocket munitions. He'd tried his hand as an Uber driver for a while, but mostly had hung out with the mostly Latino group of day laborers outside big home improvement warehouse stores to get odd jobs.

So when he'd gotten an anonymous call from someone willing to pay him to be a soldier again, he'd leaped at the chance. The caller had promised him half a million dollars. Sam had scoffed, of course, sure it was a prank call. Sam asked why he'd been picked. The caller had described Sam's army training and service in detail and said that Sam's experience was exactly what the job called for. Sam had still hesitated. The man on the other end of the line had been insistent, telling him he'd wire half the money into an offshore account as a show of good faith, and pay the other quarter million upon completion of the job. When Sam had asked what the job was, the man had simply said, "Kill someone." Sam had received an account number via e-mail, and when he'd checked the account, someone had deposited $250,000.

Now, here he was, not in the mountains of Afghanistan or Iraq, but the suburbs of Seattle, hiding in a grove of trees with only a parking lot separating him from his target. The misty rain had stopped for the moment, which was both good and bad. His visibility was much better, and he would stay a little drier, not that it mattered. But the rain would have helped camouflage his approach. He had some time still. The weather could easily change.

The large, sprawling building on the other side of the parking lot stood ablaze with lights. Muffled rhythmic thumping came from inside the building. For the past half hour, a steady procession of stretch limousines had pulled up in front and spilled their occupants—men and women dressed in black-tie formal wear—onto the wet sidewalk. Those with the foresight to bring umbrellas had gathered close together on the sidewalk under their cover and walked to the building, a procession of giant mushrooms bobbing up and down to the front door. The few who had forgotten scrambled out of the cars to madly dash for the door, the ladies hiking up their skirts or dresses and tottering as fast as they could on high heels. Now, he stiffened like a hound on point as a limo pulled up to let its occupants out.

After the money had been deposited, he'd been briefed on the target and what to expect. The limo arriving that night, he'd learned, wouldn't be a standard issue or stretch, but would look like an off-the-shelf black Range Rover. This particular vehicle, though, was a supercharged model on a long wheelbase tricked out with armor plating, bulletproof glass, and puncture-resistant run-flat tires. He'd been told that a detail of at least two bodyguards and a chaperone would accompany his target. Armed with that knowledge, he'd spent nearly two weeks observing the target's movements, schedule, and bodyguard contingents to discern patterns, assess both strengths and weaknesses in security, and figure out the best way to accomplish his mission.

The same Range Rover he'd observed and followed now disgorged two large men, one from each side, who scanned the parking lot before one of them opened the rear door closest to the building. A shorter, slender man in semi-formal attire emerged, followed by his target, a young woman in a simple but elegant black silk cocktail dress with spaghetti straps. Her long black hair, normally worn straight or in a ponytail, was swept up into a loosely braided bun, a few strands framing her face. Her escort snapped open an umbrella to hold over her head, and they walked slowly to the door with the bodyguards a few steps behind, heads in constant motion as they surveilled the surroundings. Behind them, the Range Rover pulled away from the curb. The driver would park and come back to stand watch outside. The soldier had to make his move now.

Party time.

He reached for the satchel on the ground behind him, unzipped a pocket, took out a pack of wet naps and used them to wipe the black greasepaint off his face. Slowly and carefully, so as not to get mud or dirt on himself, he stripped off the camo gear, revealing semi-formal attire beneath it. He traded his boots for a pair of black dress shoes, and finally pulled a suit jacket from the satchel and donned it over the special shoulder holster he wore. Under one arm a short-barrel, pump-action shotgun nestled in the holster. It had one shell in the chamber. He had a 10-shell magazine in his pocket. The holster under his other arm held a modified H&K MP7A1 personal defense weapon that could fire its entire 20-shot magazine in about one-and-a-quarter seconds. He also carried several small M84 flash-bang stun grenades modified to detonate via RF signal.

Patting down his pockets to make sure everything he needed was in place, he nodded to himself and stepped out of the woods onto the asphalt parking lot. His heart hammered in his chest, and he took deep breaths and rolled his head on his shoulders to relax and get his pulse under control. The guns and ammunition he carried weighed him down, but he barely felt it with all the adrenaline coursing through his system. He ran his fingers through his hair again, hoping he looked presentable enough. The suit was custom-tailored to hold everything without bulging or sagging.

As he approached the brightly lit front door of the building across the lot, he slipped two fingers into the breast pocket and drew out a fake plastic student ID and the slim piece of card stock waiting there. His ticket. The thumping sound became a visceral blast of hip-hop dance music that reverberated in his gut as he opened the door. The dull roar of hundreds of voices trying to talk over the music assaulted his ears. He blinked against the bright light. Red velvet ropes on brass stanchions guided him to a reception table. He handed his ticket to a fresh-faced girl of around seventeen sitting behind it, and flashed the student ID. His facial features, though hardened and more chiseled by both age and what he'd seen and done, were still youthful. He had one of those faces that still made store clerks and bartenders check his ID when he bought an occasional beer. The girl mouthed some words that he couldn't hear over the din. He turned and cocked an ear, and she leaned over the table toward him.

"I need to stamp you," she shouted.

He nodded and held out a hand, palm down. She inked the back with the stamp, and he moved aside as a group of half a dozen formally attired teenagers crowded through the door behind him, laughing and talking loudly. Round tables covered in white linen with seating for ten or twelve dotted the large room. Candles on the tables lit flower centerpieces with a gold "Oscar" statuette standing in the center. Spotlights hung from lighting bars high on the walls highlighted special areas around the room—a photo booth, a palm reader, and others he couldn't quite see. A red carpet led from the reception table to another room, the source of the throbbing music.

He took in the scene carefully but casually. Other than the detail assigned to the target, security was practically nonexistent. People thought they were safe here in the suburbs. There were no metal detectors at the entrance. Civilians manned the other exit doors to prevent unauthorized entry by uninvited guests. He spotted only a handful of facility employees, only two of whom were actively making rounds with watchful eyes. He didn't see the target, but wouldn't go searching until he was ready. When the layout and the key players were imprinted in his memory, he nodded and moved, his plan in place.

His first task: plant some diversions. He walked purposefully to the nearest men's restroom, and entered to find it empty. He locked himself in the nearest stall, and hiked up his trousers legs. He'd secured all four flash-bangs to his legs with gaffer's tape over fabric so they could be removed easily and still leave enough adhesive on the tape to mount them. He taped one charge low on the wall behind the toilet and leaned back against the stall door to look at the toilet from different angles. Satisfied that it wouldn't be seen, he removed another flash-bang from his leg and put it in his jacket pocket. He left the two others in place above each ankle and shook his pants legs down over them. As he unlocked the stall door, he heard the men's room door open. He froze.

Soundlessly, he turned the lock the other way, and backed up until his legs straddled the toilet, then opened his mouth to breathe silently. He didn't want people to remember him. A chance encounter in a men's room minutes before the place exploded might prompt someone's memory later. The sound of liquid hissing down a smooth surface slowly turned to the plashing of water on water as the newcomer relived himself at a urinal. Sam tipped his head back and stifled a yawn. Not enough sleep in the past two weeks. He shook his head. He had to stay sharp. He hoped this guy would hurry.

The lights flickered, and suddenly he was as alert as if he'd downed four double espressos. He heard muttering on the other side of the stall door, but it quickly faded away, and once again he found himself wishing this guy would just finish his business and get out. Impatiently, he reached for the lock, and the room went pitch dark. He froze again.

"What the actual fuck!" The shout echoed off the walls. "Dylan, if that's you, it's not funny! Turn on the damn lights!" The voice quieted to muttering again. "Jesus, I'm gonna pee all over my pants if someone doesn't turn on the lights."

Just as suddenly, the lights came back on, and the soldier breathed a silent sigh of relief. He listened to the urinal flush, then a soft zip, and footsteps to the door. Shaking his head in disgust that the kid hadn't even washed his hands, Sam changed his mind and pulled his hand away from the stall door, leaving it locked. He didn't want to take a chance on someone finding the explosive he'd left behind the toilet. Quickly lowering himself to the floor, he lay on his back and shoved himself into the next stall over, jumped up and pushed the lever on the toilet before exiting.

The soldier washed his hands thoroughly at the sink, staring at the worried face in the mirror. He needed to finish this tonight. A power outage would send everyone home, and he would have to start over. But the longer he stayed and watched for another opportunity, the greater the chance that the target's security force would detect

247

and neutralize him. He needed to do it now. He quickly dried his hands and left.

He sauntered over to a vacant banquet table, avoiding the scattered few where couples already sat and talked, and eased into a chair. Leaning forward as if to tie a shoe, he reached down and removed another flash-bang from around his ankle and taped it to the underside of the table. His eyes scanned the room all the while, checking to see if he had attracted anyone's notice. When he'd pressed the tape in place, he leaned back in the chair and casually gazed around the room. His pulse raced, but he felt an inward calm that came from intense focus on his work. Moving quickly, he rose and placed another charge on the wall behind him, a corner dim enough it wouldn't be spotted.

Through the doors, the room with music and dancing was dimmer, and swirled with couples and colored spotlights that moved in time to the music. The volume of both music and shouted conversations might have deafened him, but he had already pressed foam earplugs into his ear canals, muffling the noise.

He found another dark corner and taped a charge to the wall. The first two would get everyone's attention, but the last two would have maximum effect of an extremely loud bang and intensely bright flash that should disorient at least some people in each room within twenty-five feet. People any farther away in these big rooms would be little more than startled, but the combination of explosions would likely cause people to panic. He counted on it. Hundreds of people screaming and running for the exits would give him cover to get away when he finished the job. That was the plan, anyway.

Without pause, he walked the perimeter of the cavernous space, gaze directed toward the couples in the middle of the floor, eyes searching out his target. A low set of telescoping bleachers folded into a wall presented a natural shelf for another stun grenade. A glance over his shoulder several paces later confirmed his supposition that it would go unnoticed. He'd gone nearly halfway around the room when he spotted the target, her escort, and two of the bodyguards. Concern set in when he didn't spot the third bodyguard. He searched the crowded room, breathing growing shallower as concern almost turned to panic until he remembered the driver had probably stayed outside. He shook his head slightly at his own folly, and breathed deeply, relaxing his shoulders. This was no time to screw up.

Like all plans, though, his looked like it was going to change yet again when the few lights burning around the perimeter of the gymnasium flickered once more, went out for a second that felt like an hour, and blinked back on. He held his breath, but they burned steadily now. He glanced toward his target. Her two bodyguards had their eyes directed toward the crowd as he did, and didn't notice him. He ambled closer to the target, putting his hand in his pocket. His fingers found the remote RF detonator, and he thumbed the switch on its side to turn it on. He mentally accounted for each weapon he had and the muscle memory it would take to retrieve it.

Steeling his resolve, he touched the button on top of the detonator in his pocket. The remote was designed to change radio frequencies each time he pressed the button, so each flash-bang would detonate in turn. He watched the target as her escort leaned in close, as if to say something, their lips nearly brushing, and he pressed the button once.

After a half-second delay, the boom from the men's room stall, even at this distance, sounded like a cannon, jerking people's heads up. The bodyguards scanned the room warily but didn't move. He waited nearly ten seconds until the fear that had frozen the crowd started to dissipate like a slowly thinning fog. Couples began milling around on the floor, and the murmur of voices grew louder. He pushed the button again.

The second explosion was louder, followed immediately by screams from the other room. The music stopped, leaving the room in silence. The crowd in front of him froze again, then undulated as fear once again took hold. The target stood unmoving, but had covered her ears and was talking excitedly to her escort, brows creased with concern. He saw the two guards exchange a look, and one headed toward the other room. He pushed the button once more, and another explosion ripped through the other room, followed by more screaming and the sounds of obvious panic. The noise rippled through the clusters of couples on the dance floor, spreading fear like an airborne plague. Shrill voices urged everyone to run, to get out, and dozens broke for the exits, jamming doorways in their haste to get out.

He squeezed his eyes shut tight and pressed the button twice in quick succession, and the flash-bangs in the corner and on the bleachers concussed the air and threw off bursts of light so intense they seared his retinas even with his eyes closed. When he opened them, one of the bodyguards had disappeared into the other room, and the other swiped at his eyes as he looked toward the target and her escort.

"Get her out of here." the bodyguard shouted. He turned and staggered half-blindly in the direction of the bleachers, the source of the last explosion.

The diversions had worked. The soldier slowly approached the target, reaching inside his jacket to withdraw the personal defense weapon. He'd done it. He'd figured out a way to get through her phalanx of security and get close enough to complete his mission. He could have killed her on any of a dozen occasions in the time he'd scouted her security. He could have easily put her down with a sniper's rifle and a good scope. But whoever had hired him wanted him to get up close and personal, to send a message.

As he drew closer, though, he realized that the only thing he hadn't counted on was the girl. She appeared younger than he'd originally thought. She was beautiful despite the long, jagged scar that ran the length of her face, though he knew that already from photos and the long-range surveillance he'd done. But there was one piece of information whoever hired him had left out.

He stared at her now in the dim light, from not more than six feet away, noting the way she looked intently in his direction but not quite at him. She didn't paw at her eyes the way those affected by the flash did.

"You're blind," he said.

"Who's that?" her escort said, screwing his knuckles into his eyes. "Who's there? What the hell is going on? Tess, are you okay?"

The soldier ignored him, still mesmerized by the girl. No one had told him he would be killing a blind girl. His surprise, and the ethical debate that suddenly raged in his brain, caused him to hesitate. It couldn't have been more than a second or two, but that was enough.

"Tess!" someone shouted behind him. "Gun!"

Before the soldier could react, the girl moved. Not away, as he expected, but toward him, hiking her dress up as she dropped into a crouch and spun. Before he could bring the machine gun to bear on the blurred figure, her leg sweep caught his ankle and started to up-end him. And as he thought once more that he hadn't counted on the girl, he felt bullets rip into his chest with the force of sledgehammers before he heard the loud, sharp reports of gunfire. The world tilted on its axis and rotated as he fell. He didn't feel the hard floor crash against his cheek, but he saw the girl's face turned sideways as she crouched next to him, hands up, ready to fight.

He knew he was already dead, but the neurons in his brain kept firing, giving him an instant of regret, a feeling that he should have done it all differently. He felt ashamed that he'd taken money to assassinate a blind girl, and that his life had gotten so screwed up that he couldn't even accomplish that. And finally, he felt relief that at least his failure meant he hadn't killed her. With brilliant clarity, he suddenly knew what he had to do, to make it right, to redeem his entire fucked-up life.

He coughed, his mouth filling with blood, and with a last desperate gasp before everything went dark, he said, "S...Sam. Tell...them...Sam sent you."

About the Author

Michael W. Sherer is the author of the Tess Barrett new/young adult thriller series, including *Blind Rage* and *Blind Instinct*, as well as the adult thrillers *Mistaken Identity*, *Stolen Identity*, and four books in the Seattle-based Blake Sanders series, including *Night Strike* and *Night Blind*, which was nominated for an ITW Thriller Award in 2013. His other books include the award-winning Emerson Ward mystery series, and the stand-alone suspense novel, *Island Life*. He and his family live in the Seattle area.

Please visit him at michaelwsherer.com, or follow him on Facebook at www.facebook.com/thrillerauthor, @thrillerauthor on Instagram and TikTok, or @MysteryNovelist on Twitter.

Photo: Valarie Kaye-Sherer